Elai...

There's

away from

The Healing Tent

Hope the foot is
feeling better soon
& look forward to
having you back
in the mad house
All the best

James.

Also by James Kaye

A Shadow and a Sigh
iUniverse March 2003
ISBN: 0-595-27126-X

The Healing Tent

James Kaye

The Healing Tent

Spiderwize
Mews Cottage
The Causeway, Kennoway
Kingdom of Fife
KY8 5JU
Scotland UK

www.spiderwize.com

This is a work of fiction. Names, characters and incidents are products of the author's imagination. Any resemblance to persons living or dead is entirely coincidental.

ISBN: 978-0-9562392-0-4

Dedicated to my own wonderful family—Sarah, Sebastian and Rowland.

My love & eternal thanks for putting up with me

Chapter 1

The clocks didn't stop. The world failed to grind to a standstill on its axis, darkness did not immediately cover the land with its bleak, black shroud, and for some unknown reason my heart continued to beat. To my shocked, numbed mind all these things should have come to pass and so much more; but instead, the world and all its mundane machinations continued without faltering. People's muted voices filled my ears, their disconnected bodies rushing around my peripheral vision and through the window high above the bustling, rushing streets of London, silent, white clouds continued to languish indolently in blue skies. All around, life had not missed a single beat. No time warp, no blurring before the eyes as if one had slipped into a parallel and equally real dimension, or fallen headlong through waking moments to the land of dreams with its infinitesimal options and equational mixtures of fact and fiction.

Things were just as they had been a minute before; no pause or stop options for life's scenes unravelling before my eyes.

"I'm sorry, Mr Meredith, she's gone."

Such words I knew, deep in my heart, would come one day, yet had run from and refused to acknowledge them; a naïve attempt to protect my soul from such pain and impossible anguish. Yet these words now echoing around my mind so flat, so emotionless, almost impersonal had now been spoken out loud. The nightmare had become reality, fiction had become fact—no longer hidden in the depths of my mind to bring out every now and then to check like a litmus test on the sensitivity of my soul and whether it would one day be able to cope with such reality.

"Mr Meredith?" a voice penetrated the defences. "I said I'm sorry she's gone." This time a sugar coating of warmth and sincere empathy surrounding the bitter pill of truth.

"But I only went out to get a cup of coffee from down the hall," I mumbled, waving the cup of dark, hot liquid at the white coat standing beside the bed. Perhaps a deep subconscious attempt to justify that it was not only impossible for her to die whilst I had gone for a cup of coffee, but also to justify the guilty feeling starting to wash over my body from tip to toe.

"How could she die whilst I was buying a crappy cup of coffee, for God's sake?"

I had spent the last eighteen months with her, side by side, every step, doctor's appointment, scan, test and treatment. Every flinch and twinge of pain shared, from the darkest hours of cold winter's nights, to warm sun blessed days such as today, I had held her hand and tried, in vain, to love away her pain and our torturous sorrows.

Laura was dead and in her final moment I had failed her. What if she had woken and with her own pale, emaciated hand tried to reach out for my own. To say a final word, to let pass with her morphine dulled, yet still loving eyes, a message that was for my eyes only, to be present, to reassure in her ultimate moment of need.

"I should have been here—what if she had needed me?" I lamented to the white coat, wringing my hands in demonstration of my guilt and self-loathing. "After all we've been through together, at the final moment I have failed her. She died alone."

The man who filled the white coat, Dr Peter Fellowes, a sympathetic, professional friend these past six months, placed a protective arm around my shoulders as he led me towards the bed. "Laura didn't wake, Mr Meredith, she slipped peacefully away and I assure you she would not have known that you weren't there."

I didn't respond immediately as I gazed down at Laura. To a stranger chancing to enter the room she could so easily have been mistaken for being asleep, but I knew so differently. Her kind, beautiful face shouted out that she was at peace at last. The furrows and frown lines that had told me she was in such pain when her brave, protective words said otherwise, had miraculously been massaged away to leave features as smooth and serene as marble, though still warm to touch. The intrusion of wires and tubes had been removed, dignity and personal intimacy had finally returned.

I leant over and kissed her for the last time, squeezed her delicate hand and tried to savour every last contour and endearment of her features into my mind. Such precious memories would now have to last a lifetime.

"What do I do now?" I asked, helpless and uncertain. "What happens next? What happens to Laura? Do you need to move her? Where will you take her?" A hundred panic-struck questions driven by the uncertainty of immediacy. The funeral, the insurance, the paperwork had all been discussed during long, practical and yet tremendously touching moments in these clinically impersonal yet now familiar surroundings.

And oh, how these moments allowed Laura's humour, strength of character and practical nature to shine brightly in those dark mental corridors as we laughed, cried, debated and laughed some more during these moments alone, discussing these short term topics, but of such importance for Laura. She was not going to leave her boys stranded and helpless, she would do all within her power to protect and care for us long after she no longer felt the sun kiss her lips and a warm breeze caress her skin. "To put the Meredith boys on the right, bright road for a new future." She would attempt to justify such discussions that I found so hard and distressing to enter with any degree of enthusiasm or vigour. Such debates lasted well into the night and with just the light of the corridor nightlights outside her door we would reach out and, holding hands as if transferring our strength from one to the other, we arranged the order of service and our children's future. Night brought time alone, time to think. Bloody time. Bloody, wasted time. Time to scream in anger at the unfairness of it all, the helplessness to cure, to offer myself up to God as an alternative sacrifice, to rewrite the inevitability of future history. The discussions helped, or at least I told myself that they did.

"The boys. I need to tell the boys. They need to know, and Laura's sister, they're all coming in to visit later this afternoon, I should stop them." The brain latched on to one of many different things running through my mind.

"Come with me Mr Meredith, Laura will be fine here; we've got plenty of time. Let's go and find somewhere to sit and talk this through." I was aware of the warm, comforting embrace of the doctor as he turned me from the bed and led me gently from the room.

Cancer, tumour, malignant. Words to strike fear into any mind and set the heart thumping and skipping. I do not recall the exact conversation. Such words play tricks on the human brain and exact memories are quickly erased. Words we had heard eighteen months previously in a private hospital, from an eminent, sombre faced specialist. To make further point, along with a wealth of medical doublespeak, he had added brain, non-operable and terminal.

What had started out as a blinding headache, feelings of nausea and that Laura had gathered a wealth of bruises and bumps where she had misjudged, not seen or failed to navigate obstacles had driven her to our local GP; where we thought some minor ailment affecting the balance had befallen her. A worryingly quick referral and within two weeks we knew life was never going to be the same again as these savage, uncivilised words came crashing towards us over a sea of mahogany and axminster.

Life had not been precious before; it had been taken for granted. It was a God-given right and as such our plans in the past had only ever extended as far as inviting friends for dinner, arranging weekends away and if we were really on top of it all, the next family holiday. But no further and I doubted that we were alone in such thinking, or lack of. And now I recalled the large, thick brown manila envelope tucked away in the bureau at home. On the front, in Laura's expansive and artistic looping handwriting, just the one word—Meredith. To open only in the case of emergency, Laura and I had joked only days ago. The plan to be put into action upon her passing. A detailed, step by step set of action points, remember to's.., and the very specific order of service. I would need to go home and put the wheels in motion, soon, but not just yet; after all, there was no hurry—it wouldn't bring her back.

"Daddy?" I hadn't heard the door to the family room open and as my eyes flicked to the sound, I also noticed from the hands on the clock that I had lost two more hours.

"Daddy, where's mummy?" Tom, our youngest, asked innocently. Both he and his older brother Freddie entered the room still in their grey school uniforms, so grown up, yet still so young. Jo, my sister-in-law, stood behind them, a hand on each shoulder, a knowing yet disbelieving look in her beautiful green eyes. So much like her sister, my beloved Laura—

emotion caught in the back of my throat and I could not immediately answer.

"Daddy, where's mummy? We went to her room, but she's not there; has she gone for a walk?" Tom's innocent questioning persisted, Freddie still silent, apprehensive, almost reluctant to receive the answer.

"Come and sit down here." I patted the chairs either side of me and attempted a smile.

"She's dead, isn't she." Freddie finally spoke. Clear and to the point. No question, a simple statement and I could imagine his brain had been at work from the moment he saw the empty bed, working out the alternatives, the options and their probabilities. So Freddie, so much his mother's son.

"Yes. Yes, she's gone." And then the tears and soul destroying pain as I watched my beautiful boys' hearts break. Somewhere in the midst I surfaced from the boys embrace to see Jo still standing by the door, her hand to her mouth, silent tears running down her face. Tears shed for the passing of her younger sister; as well, I am sure, for the pain she was watching. I beckoned her with arms extended and she joined us in our mourning embrace.

Much later, I took the boys down to say their goodbyes. She looked so beautiful, so peaceful and with an almost religious serenity about her, the boys at first were hesitant and uncertain. Brave Tom, as always, took the lead and simply laid his head upon her, his arms embracing as much of his mother as he could envelop with his small hands. Freddie walked around the far side, as solemn and dignified as an undertaker, and looked down with his wide and adoring eyes, then slowly, gently reached out to touch her face.

"She's so cold." He snatched his hand back, bewildered and afraid at what he had just done.

"It's okay, Freddie." I soothed and placed a protective arm about him. "Look, mummy's not in any pain anymore."

"But why is she so cold?" Typical Freddie, his thirst for knowledge overcoming his natural fear as he reached out once more and stroked her face and neck.

"I'll tell you later." I smiled down at him. The hour's car journey back home later would not be a quiet and introspective time. No bad thing, I mused.

"Is mummy in heaven now?" Tom wanted to know, not moving from his position at her side.

"Yes Tom, she's in heaven now," I answered, though my one sided discussions with God were yet to reconcile my belief in his existence. How could such a travesty be allowed to take place in his dominion?

"Will she be an angel?"

"Yes Tom, a guardian angel, watching out and protecting us."

"So I can talk to her all the time now?" He looked up hopefully, the sheet where his head had been now damp from his sorrow.

"Of course you can Tom, anytime you like." What did one say to a child when his mother had just died? Was this the right thing to be saying; was there any right or wrong at such a time?

He smiled briefly, returned his head to lie beside Laura and shortly I could hear quiet whispering.

Jo was waiting for us outside the chapel, time for her now to say goodbye.

"I'm going to take the boys home now, Jo; will you be alright?" I whispered as though such a place deserved such biblical treatment.

"I'll be fine, Meredith." She smiled back bravely through red, tear-filled eyes. "I'll give you a call when I get home. And if there's anything I can do to…" Jo left the sentence hanging, unfinished, as if thinking about the funeral, the house, the boys, the future; wanting to say something, but not certain quite what.

We hugged and then standing in front of the door Jo took a deep breath, dabbed a small, plain handkerchief to the corner of each eye, raised her chin in defiance at her sorrow, then entered the room closing the door quietly behind her.

Chapter 2

Though it had only just turned six o'clock when we reached the house, February's cold, clear skies had already succumbed to the dark of winter's last throws before Spring's colour, light and new life won through the inevitable battle of the seasons. The house was of course empty, Mrs Fry the housekeeper had long since left for the day and the only sign of welcome came from the outside approach light and the constant and impersonal beeping of the house alarm as I opened the door. Habit fortunately kicked in, lights were turned on, coats hung up, school bags dumped and feet naturally made their way downstairs to the kitchen cum family room, the heart of the house. Mrs Fry had been a star and the smell of lasagne warming in the oven filled every corner of the warm, spacious room. At the flick of a switch a dozen ceiling spotlights lit the clean, white room. Twin, worn sofas casually dressed with brightly coloured throws from India and a Persian carpet runner added to the illusion of the warmth, whilst beautiful individual charcoal portraits of Freddie and Tom, aged five and three respectively that we had commissioned for our wedding anniversary four years previously, hung either side of the wall-mounted flat-screen television.

"Who's for garlic bread with their lasagne?" I called out from the kitchen, though already pulling a pre-prepared stick from the deep freeze. Garlic bread always went with lasagne; it was as much a habit as sausage and chips, as familiar as roast beef and Yorkshire pudding.

The only response was the dull ping of the television coming to life and the sound of two bodies sinking into deep, enveloping sofas. Channels were surfed and indistinct muttering as to which programme to watch was debated.

"Anyone for garlic bread?" I raised my voice to compete with the goggle box.

"If you like."

"Don't mind," came the responses. Automatic, not thinking; just a reply to an annoying distraction.

I poured myself a whisky, then laid out the trays in preparation for the next electronic ping, this time from the oven to warn that it had fulfilled its duty and that whatever had been inserted had run its course and was now ready to be extracted. I did not want to join the boys, to force uneasy conversation upon them and break the bond of silence that they had formed in such a short space of time. Their simple decision, not to discuss Laura's death, not to consider what future lay beyond, unless a specific question came to mind. Just to be.

So, like the guilty and unwanted, I lingered quietly in the kitchen; occasionally opening random drawers and cupboards to peer inside, not with any conscious intent or interest, merely a mental distraction that prevented me from thinking about what needed to be undertaken next, what this meant for us as a family and just what to talk about with the boys. One couldn't just not talk, so was it right to talk about school, what they had done that day? Their mother had just died, for God's sake. How petty and insignificant were school lessons compared to the death of Laura? What an insult to her, but perhaps that was what the boys wanted, how they were dealing with it, in their own way?

Unable to escape from the inevitability of time, the oven pinged and after a hot facial blast and a nasal assault, food was placed on plates, which were placed on trays and like trains shunting in the yard, they were collected in silence and ferried back to the sofas.

I sat alone at the pine kitchen table and nursed a second glass of whisky, closing my eyes to savour the warm massage as the brown liquid slipped down my throat.

"Just like Jesus in velvet trousers," I heard Laura's familiar saying from deep in the recesses of my mind and smiled to myself. Then the stabbing reminder that she was dead. She had died that afternoon, whilst I was buying a crappy cup of instant coffee. I was not going back to the hospital to visit again. Even when we knew that she was dying, slowly slipping away from us, we had a routine that offered false comfort, perhaps false hope. Certainly it suspended the need to think beyond what would happen once the routine needed to change and the reason behind it. But today was different—the reassuring habit, the routine had been broken forever.

Our world now teetered on the brink of chaos; a new routine needed to be established, a new order to bring law into an otherwise lawless and anarchic state. It was a cocktail of two powerful forces. The heart mourned for the loss of a soul mate and of a future that would never be realised. The sense of bereavement and of loss. The head did not mourn, but it feared. Ice-cold fear gripped the brain in a vice-like grip, squeezing the organ until it could no longer think properly. Like a scratched CD jumping back to repeat the same line of a song, my mind was stuck on a looped message. What happens now, what do we do tomorrow, next year? How will the children grow up without maternal succour, who will help me make life's decisions for the future? What will the future hold?

It suddenly became very hot in the room, beads of sweat broke out on my forehead, my vision swam and my mind started to spin slowly at first then faster and faster, a pulse in my head drumming a quickening beat until there was just a constant and incessant white noise. The smell of the hot mince and garlic overpowering other senses, until I could feel a lurching heave in the pit of my stomach and the distant taste of acrid bile in the back of my throat. I rushed to the kitchen bin just in time, and like the cramps, the convulsions bent me double and, powerless to control my body, I retched. Hot, gushing liquid forced its way back up from the stomach, burning my throat, though not touching the insides of my cheeks as it liberally hosed the inside of the bin. Breathless, raw and with eyes flooded with tears, I waited patiently for the heaving to subside.

"No carrots," I thought to myself and spent a few minutes trying to determine what had already been in the bin versus what I had added. After a couple of dry retches I felt that the smell now emanating from the bin was just as likely to make me vomit again. And with sight and mind now back in control on both the vertical and horizontal axis, I felt it safe to take my head out of the bin.

I quickly scraped the offending lasagne from my plate into the bin and then ran the dish under the hot tap to remove all evidence before putting the plate in the dishwasher to fully exorcise the sensory demons.

The bin bag containing the evidence was spirited guiltily out of the back door and jammed deep into the waiting jaws of the all-consuming, black wheelie bin. A quick whisky mouthwash to anaesthetise the caustic burn and blunt the taste buds and then I sat back down at the table and started to convince the mind that all that had just been was just an illusion.

When my mind finally returned, I realised I had left the boys in the family room, and from a quick glance at the kitchen clock I had lost yet more time in a dark void.

"Boys, do you want anything else?" I called out.

Silence resounded.

"Boys, do you want anything else?" I repeated, though the silence suggested that I was alone.

The family room was, as the silence had warned, empty. The television had been switched off and the two trays dumped carelessly on the floor before the sofas suggested the boys, at best, had only played with their food; one plate was completely untouched.

Without bothering to turn on any lights I made my way quietly up the three flights of stairs to the boys' floor where the light on the landing offered a narrow corridor into the darkened bedrooms beyond. I tiptoed into little Tom's room first. How many times had Laura and I, hand in hand, secretly snuck into their rooms and stood in silence, in wonder, so in awe of what we had created; our hearts so full of love and compassion at the bundles that lay before us, so angelic, so innocent and so much in need of our protection.

But there was no mop of mousy brown hair protruding from the duvet, no shape, no form beneath. The bed was still made, untouched, though an array of clothes lay strewn about the bedroom floor. My heart lurched and my hand fumbled for the main light switch. The bed was empty. In the silence my heart beat loudly and quicker as it echoed off the four walls and the palms of my hand were bathed in sweat as I pushed open Freddie's door.

Relax, there they were. Side by side, separated by their individual dreams, but brothers together, contra mundum.

Freddie's bedside reading light still burned brightly and though he had removed his glasses, a book lay open, precariously held in place by the folds of the duvet.

Not a line, not a crease befell their features. Perfect in their creation. Thick dark brown hair, uncontrollable and with a mind of it's own that continued to writhe and weave long after a hairbrush had swept through like a military division; green eyes passionately defended by dark lashes and small chests rising and falling in sync with one another.

And oh, how my heart and love reached out to them both. I wanted to pick them up to smother them to my chest, to let them feel the depth of love that I was unable to articulate adequately. My heart beat, fast and strong, fear now replaced by love and desire. Desire to protect, to defend; to the death if necessary. My hand had no companion and I reached out for Laura's. The warmth of her grip, the gentle squeeze that said so much, that we were feeling the same, sharing the same thoughts of love. A physical embrace, where words had yet to be invented that could do justice to such powerful and all-consuming emotions. My hand fumbled the air momentarily, for something that I knew was not, nor ever again would be there. I was now sole caretaker of such precious memories.

I placed the bookmark at the open page and laid the book gently on the floor before turning off the bedside light and retracing my steps to the doorway.

"I love you," I whispered to the sleeping forms. "And I love you too." My eyes turned upwards to the ceiling, as if seeking beyond the physical barriers to the heavens above. "Oh, and how I miss you so much already."

I slipped back downstairs and trying to delay the inevitable went to check for any messages on my business phone in the study. A groan of disappointment escaped my lips to see the red digital '0' blinking in the darkness. I went through into the sitting room and with leaden feet, approached the George Third mahogany bureau. I turned on the delicate table lamp that rested on top of the bureau, its light reflecting in the well-polished mahogany surface, though leaving the remainder of the room in welcome darkness. I drew out the bureau arms, the sound of wood sliding against wood delivering a pleasing honest sound, unusual in this modern world of metals, aluminium and chipboard, turned the brass key in its escutcheon lock and rested the fall front on its arms. From left to right I opened and shut each of the secretaire drawers, not registering their contents before my hand came to rest upon the secret drawer. Taking a deep breath, I slid the cover back and revealed the brown, manila envelope lying in the bottom of the drawer.

I twirled the envelope between my fingertips, spinning it around time and time again, I raised it to my nose: it smelt of antique wood, slightly musty, but not of Laura. At last, sitting down in front of the bureau in the matching mahogany elbow chair, I slipped the cavalry sword-shaped paperknife under the seal and slit the envelope from side to side. An awful and ugly sound at the best of times, but none more so than now.

I laid the envelope carefully on the desk and noticed there were four main parts forming the contents.

On top, the requirements for the order of service. Laura and I had discussed this in minutia detail during numerous hospital visits and I had taken the rough draft home and printed the final requirement off on the computer before returning for her final approval and entry into the envelope. Beneath this came an index of things I needed to know. Which company we used for each utility, when the various bills were due and which account they were paid from. Also where I could find important documents and items around the house. Again I had typed this up for Laura, though the two sheets of this section had several revisions and one addition as things had obviously sprung to mind.

Thirdly was the "to do" list. This was detailed, extensive and prioritised in order of importance. Claim Life Assurance, clear mortgage; photocopy death certificate to forward as proof to get various policies and documents put into one name. These were straightforward, clinical actions that in her mind needed to be undertaken, to enable the transition, to allow closure, before moving forward into the next phase of life, whatever that may hold.

Still numb from today, I couldn't even accept that she was gone, never mind contemplate closure and flicked over to the second page and scanned the lines.

The last and most painful action points were what to do with her clothes, her personal belongings such as her perfumes, her make-up, books. Clothes and books to a charity shop, underwear and all cosmetics straight to the bin. Her helpful aside, written in a shaky hand, though I could still recognise the writing as Laura's was that this should be undertaken within two weeks of her passing away. The conscious immediately rebelled at the thought of throwing away such close, personal, visible and tactile links. It was almost too much to bear and these latter points would take a great deal of mental struggle to accept and implement.

The ultimate document was a surprise, a smaller, plain blue envelope, again with the single word "Meredith" written across the face. I knew nothing about this and like Pandora's Box, I was not sure that I could cope with exposing myself to its contents. I laid the other documents reverently on the desk and put the envelope in my jacket pocket, promising myself to open it later. Not too much trauma at any one time, so lessen the pain by spreading it out. Not a convincing argument by any standards, but one that I could live with for that evening. Hopefully.

Returning downstairs to the family room, I had just refilled my glass when the phone rang.

"Meredith?" I almost failed to recognise Jo's voice. Usually so strong, so vibrant.

"Jo, hi. How are you?" I added inanely, not sure what to say, or how to react.

"Oh you know, a couple of bottles of wine and... Meredith, I can't believe she's gone, it's just not real." She started to sob down the phone.

I could picture her face, expensive eyeliner still immaculate despite the flood of tears; a single string pearl necklace surrounding her graceful neck, set against the backdrop of a black, cashmere poloneck, all hiding the uncontrollable restriction on her chest as she fought to speak.

"Oh bugger," her voice came back stronger, "and I promised myself that I wouldn't cry. I'm sorry Meredith, I'm just a stupid, stupid woman and it's you that we need to be strong for."

"Don't you worry Jo, you're not being stupid in the least," I tried to soothe. "Even though we all knew it was coming, it's still been one hell of a shock, so…so unexpected."

"Yes, you're right, that's exactly how I feel. Such a terrible shock. How are we going to cope without her, Meredith?"

The sixty million dollar question, I mused to myself. One will because one has to. We will remember to breathe in and out, to get up in the morning, to go to work, to eat, to exist until it's time to go to bed again.

"I don't know Jo, I really don't know. But I know that for the children's sake I have to." The moment my thoughts turned to the boys lying asleep upstairs, emotion caught me unawares and choked me. I sipped at my glass and caught my breath.

"How are the boys? Can I do anything to help?" Jo sounded stronger now. Perhaps someone weaker needing her strength raised her resolve.

"They're asleep now, but it's been one hell of a strange evening. They don't seem to want to talk about it and I'm not sure that's altogether too healthy. It's also bloody difficult because it's all I can think about and want to talk about. Christ Jo, I even spent some of this evening hiding in the kitchen so I didn't have to talk to them. Running away when they need me most—what kind of a father am I?" I confessed, taking another large swig of the whisky.

"Meredith, don't you dare beat yourself up. You're a great father; even Richard is jealous of the great relationship you have with Freddie and Tom." I heard whispering down the other end of the phone. "He sends his condolences and will catch up with you soon," she added hurriedly.

"Tell him thanks, it's appreciated." I nodded my head at no one in particular.

"Meredith, this has been an awful day. The worst ever and it's going to take time for us to get back to any degree of normality. I would just let Freddie and Tom run for the time being, I'm sure it will all sort itself out given time."

"Thanks Jo, I'm sure you're right. It's just all such a bloody mess and Laura has left me this list as long as your arm and some of the things on it are just so... oh, I don't know." I dropped into one of the sofas. My eyes stung and suddenly felt so very tired. "Not to worry. Forget it Jo, I'm just having a winge, all a bit tired and all that."

"I'll come around in the morning and perhaps we can have a bash at this list and see what we can do to help out." Jo's voice had returned to its usual firm and assured timbre. Jo, as beautiful as her sister, and so much like her sister, needed to be in control and at the epi-centre of all things.

"Oh, not to worry, Jo, I'm sure I can get it sorted." I half tried to talk her out of it, but it all sounded rather weak and pathetic, an anchor bed for Jo to hook into.

"Nonsense, Meredith. Laura was my sister and I love you and the boys very much as well. I'm sure there are heaps of things needing to be done, never mind arranging the funeral and so on. This is the time you need your friends around you. I'll be there about eleven; have the kettle on."

"Thanks Jo, see tomorrow," I said and hung up. I hoped my voice sounded sincere, as I really wasn't sure whether I wanted to see anyone, never mind face up to the practical side of what now needed to be done.

The whisky slipped down so smoothly and swinging my feet up to hang over the arm of the sofa, I laid my head back into the embracing cushions and closed my eyes to savour the temporary port in the storm.

I woke to the clatter of noise in the kitchen, daylight streaming through the windows and an all too cheerful television presenter blurting out the morning news. Whilst momentarily disorientated, from the clues I picked up, namely the taste in my mouth and thick tongue, the pounding in my head and the empty bottle of scotch on the table beside me, I was quickly able to deduce how I came to be asleep on the sofa; stiff and still wearing the previous day's clothes.

As soon as the eyes had become tolerant of the light and were able to focus, I swung myself into a sitting position and immediately wished I hadn't moved quite so quickly. Holding my head in my hands helped and after a minute I was able to make a reasonably dignified entrance into the kitchen.

"Morning Mr Meredith, lovely day." Joan Fry's cheerful voice rang in my ears like a peal of bells at a church wedding. Whilst not the biggest woman I had ever met, Joan Fry somehow always managed to make a room seem small. This probably had something to do with her constant chitchat, often to no one in particular, and an inability to stand still for more than a minute. Bright and to my mind garish, dresses that seemed to jut straight out from the neck and flow down to below her knees in one continuous undulating cliff face. Always bustling from one place to another, often with no rhyme or reason, just on the move. This had always generated much debate and humour within the family as we sought reasons for this behaviour. Tom was convinced she was a land shark, air being forced into her lungs through hidden gills and that she would die if she stopped moving. Freddie, serious as ever, believed that she had Attention Deficit disorder and had promptly undertaken a full investigation of the condition on the Internet. Laura's inherent personality would not stretch to the unkind and stated that she just had a sunny disposition, though when pushed did go so far as to suggest ants in her pants. My suggestion that she was a frustrated actress, playing all the parts in a play, saying her lines, then running from one part of the stage to another to reply received short shrift from Laura, though much applause from the boys. I would of course always take things a stage too far and attempt to mimic our inimitable housekeeper and the topic of conversation would soon move on to equally engaging topics.

However, to her credit and our eternal good fortune, Joan Fry was also a truly genuine and generous woman. Generous, with both her money, always buying little presents for the boys, as well as with her time. She arrived early, stayed till the job was done and over the past five years we had come to regard her as a part of our extended family.

"Good morning Joan, I can smell coffee, but am damned if I can see it," I whispered hoarsely, eyes still screwed protectively against the sunlight streaming into the kitchen.

"Jus' you sit down, Mr Meredith, I'll have it with you in a jiffy," she declared brightly, kindly overlooking my dilapidated state.

"Thanks, much appreciated." The aroma coming from the caffitiere I could now see sitting on the work surface promised rejuvenation and a cure to the dry mouth and skull pounding. The morning paper and letters, neatly stacked, were already placed before the chair where I would usually conduct the first chores of the day.

"You must have had a late 'un last night, even the boys ain't surfaced yet. Did you stay late at the 'ospital? How's Mrs Meredith? I've brought some flowers for you to take for her, so make sure you give her my best when you see her later." Not a breath taken, a monologue that despite more than half her life spent in London, still rang out a Dorset upbringing.

Memories of the day before came flooding back. Not in any particular order, but the outcome was still the same.

"Joan, come and sit down. I need to tell you something." My voice little more than a whisper.

"I'll be there right now, jus' finishin' the coffee for you." Her voice still so cheerful and unaware.

I allowed her the luxury of a minute more of blissful ignorance, then a coaster swiftly followed by a steaming mug of coffee lay before me on the table.

The coffee scalded, but immediately the benefits started to coarse through the veins to all the organs.

"Joan, over the years you have become such a part of our lives and I especially can't thank you enough for what you have done for us all, to help us through these past six months. You have kept us afloat." I was unable to come straight to the point.

"Now don't you go fussin' about me." Mrs Fry laughed gaily, placing a motherly hand upon my forearm and she started to rise from her seat.

"No, wait a moment, there's something I need to say." A firmer voice, though whether it was that or the faint echo of a plea that checked her I couldn't be sure, but she sat back down again in a swirl of red, orange and yellow.

With my gaze firmly upon her still smiling eyes I fumbled my lines. "I'm not sure how to say this and I don't think any words can make it any easier to say, but Laura died yesterday."

"Oh no, Mr Meredith! No, no, not our Mrs Meredith!" Her hands flew to cover her mouth, her bright blue eyes filled with tears and the lines of her face contorted with pain. "I'm so sorry, Mr Meredith," she sobbed "Oh, and those poor darling boys upstairs, what they must be goin' through."

With her ample bosom heaving she pulled herself to her feet and like a chicken pecking for feed she grabbed the nearest dishcloth and started to rub away at real or imaginary marks on the kitchen work surfaces.

Quickly I went to her and turning her around I gave her a hug. Her strong forearms gripped about my back and we stood in the middle of the kitchen for what seemed like an age until her sobs subsided and her heaving chest stopped punching into my midriff.

"I'm so sorry, I don't know what came over me and lor' what I must look like." A small handkerchief appeared from her sleeve to dab inadequately at her red nose and eyes.

"It's okay Joan." I smiled down at her with tight lips. "She went very peacefully and at long last she's not in any pain."

"I jus' can't believe it." She wiped away the tears still falling down her cheeks.

"Me too." I nodded in agreement. There was nothing left to be said and we both sat back down at the table, whilst I, grateful for the silence finished my coffee.

The silence did not however last long. Footsteps in the family room announced the arrival of one of the boys and I felt a cold hand of fear at the back of my neck as I braced myself to greet my youngest son.

"Morning daddy, morning Mrs Fry." Little Tom padded into the kitchen still in his pyjamas; his face still creased with sleep though his angelic smile radiated across the room.

"Morning Tom, sleep well?" I asked, pushing a smile on to my face as I ruffled his already tousled hair.

"I'm starving, can I have some toast?" he replied as he made his way over to the bread bin, his crocodile slippers making no noise across the slated kitchen floor.

"Of course you can, what would you like on it?" Mrs Fry immediately sprang into action, relieved at having something to do.

"Jam please, but…"

"Yes, I know, but no butter," Mrs Fry interjected as she reached for a plate and the strawberry jam at the same time.

"Is Freddie awake yet?" I asked

"Yup, he's been awake for hours. We've been playing games on the Internet, but I got hungry so came down for something to eat." Tom's matter-of-fact response and innocent face showed this was the simple truth of the moment and that there did not appear to be anything out of the ordinary playing on his mind.

"I'd better go and ask him if he wants anything to eat?" I scraped back the chair and left Tom in Joan's capable hands.

Like a starving child over a bowl of food, Freddie's nine-year-old frame was hunched up over the desk, hungry and thirsty for facts and figures on the topics that took his current interest.

Freddie was not what you would call either a sporty or team orientated lad. Football, rugby, cricket held no interest for him whatsoever, and whilst I had reluctantly agreed to sign him off these afternoon school games, this was only subject to his agreement to take up an alternative physical recreation in their place. This *quid pro quo* agreement worked in Freddie's favour, taking up shooting, fencing and swimming as suitable alternatives. It also spoke volumes about his character. A bit of a loner, more than happy in his own company, precision, bordering on an obsessional desire for detailed perfection, self reliant rather than trusting in others.

These sports provided two further benefits not recognised at the time. Firstly Freddie was a compulsive reader. He devoured books and whilst factual and especially historical books were a favourite, the bookcase in his bedroom overflowed and bowed under the weight of boys' fictional adventure. Explorers, adventurers and soldiers of fortune across all periods of time filled the shelves and these new sporting activities allowed him to truly bring the books to life. This in turn fuelled his enthusiasm for the sports and much to his surprised parents' pride and joy, he was turning out to be extremely good and had a natural aptitude for these sports.

The second advantage was that he did not then have to compete with Tom. Whilst Tom was a full two years junior to Freddie, Tom was everything that Freddie was not. Tom was not unintelligent, but just wasn't interested in learning. He couldn't sit still for a moment, became easily bored and thus distracted, and whilst this tended to make him one of the more popular boys in his class, it inevitably led him into trouble with his schoolteachers. His day only really started the moment he ran onto a pitch, entered a court or sporting arena. Tom threw himself into every sport he could fit into his hectic day, size of ball irrelevant, stick, bat or racket required also irrelevant. Whilst also highly competitive to win, it was just to be able to play that fuelled his passion. And boy, when he was playing, he held nothing back! No sense of pacing himself, it was full on right until the final whistle.

"Freddie, do you want to come down and have some breakfast?" I asked, smiling at his concentrated form.

"Dad, you scared me!" Freddie jumped at the intrusion to his world. He swung round in his chair angry at what the shock had caused him to feel. "No, I'm not hungry," he added before swinging back to concentrate on the screen in front of him.

"What's that you're looking at?" I went over to the desk and peered at the screen, laying a paternal hand upon his shoulder, feeling the child's frame beneath me.

"I'm studying the American Indians, their culture that sort of thing really." He relaxed as his initial anger faded quickly.

"Interesting?" I enquired, trying to draw him out a little.

"Oh yes," Freddie said eagerly. "They were the most amazing people. They were so clever and made all sorts of amazing things like traps and clothes from the animals they caught. They could tell an animal from its footprints and follow it for days and they used the stars to guide them because they didn't have maps. They're really cool."

"Sounds pretty interesting to me, Freddie, is this for school?" I asked.

"No, just I was watching a film on T.V. the other day and it made me curious. Mr Phillips, our history teacher, said he wants us to do a project on something from history for the summer holidays, so I may do it on the Indians."

"Excellent, and you'll have to let me read it afterwards so I can find out more about them as well?" I could feel Freddie's chest puff with pride at my interest in what he was doing and an opportunity to teach me something I didn't know.

Now that I had him talking, relaxed and in his comfort zone, it seemed a good idea to bring history up to date and talk about more recent events in our lives.

"Now, Freddie, whilst I've got you on your own for a minute, I just wanted to have a quick chat about…about yesterday," I started awkwardly to broach the subject.

"Dad, you know, I think I am a bit hungry. Can I go and get some cereal?" Freddie slid out of his chair and before I could say more, he had hotfooted it out of his room and had nipped down the stairs.

"Of course," I said to no one in particular. "I just wanted to talk to you about your mother," I muttered to the empty room.

A quick stop off in my bedroom for a shower, shave and change of clothes and I felt a good deal more awake and ready to face the day when I reappeared in the kitchen. The boys were still at the table joking with Mrs Fry, though the conversation immediately came to a close when they heard my footsteps coming across the family room.

Joan turned her back on the scene and bustled around the work surfaces again and minutes later a fresh cup of coffee was steaming away in my hands.

"Mr Meredith, Tom wanted to know if he and Freddie were meant to be goin' to school today and…and I said I'd ask you?" she stammered, clearly embarrassed by sailing so close to the wind with such a question.

Neither of the boys would look at me, instead taking a great deal of interest in their empty bowls and plates in front of them.

I had completely forgotten the day of the week, never mind what time it was.

"Well, given everything that has happened, I think the school would fully understand it if you were to stay at home for the next few days. Give us the time to talk and sort some things out. How about that?" I smiled paternally at each of the boys in turn and finished my cup of coffee in one gulp, noting as I put it back on the coaster, Joan's eyes dart to the now empty cup and didn't rate its chances of staying there for more than a minute.

"Oh no, Daddy, please can I go to school today, we've got a football match this afternoon, please, please?" Tom bemoaned, immediately wiping the kind, considerate fatherly smile from my face in an instant.

"Me too, I've got biology and we're going to dissect a frog. Please can we go to school?" Freddie joined in the mutiny.

"Well, I'm blowed," I heard Joan say under her breath, before clamping a hand to her mouth and grabbing my coffee mug. "Sorry, Mr Meredith." She quickly apologised, then scurried to the sink.

"Bloody hell," I blurted out loud as I ran my hands through my still drying hair. My first and most immediate reaction was to say of course you can't bloody go to school. Remember your mother? The one who died yesterday? Have some respect and be as miserable as the rest of us about it. Fortunately, despite the poor start to the day, my brain and mouth were still co-operating with one another and though I had misgivings, I consented—no, I conceded—to their requests.

"Okay, but I am going to have a word with Mr Rogers and let him know what the situation is and that if either of you want to come home, you go and see him and he'll give me a call and I'll come straight round. Deal?"

"Deal," they both yelled enthusiastically. The smiles on their faces came readily and showed real relief at being allowed to go to school. In turn, I forced the smile on to my face and gave each in turn a hug and a kiss as they raced out of the kitchen to get changed into their uniforms for the great day that lay ahead of them.

"I'm sorry Mr Meredith, I was out of turn. I shouldn't have said anything, my mouth jus' ran away with it." Joan turned back to me, a fresh brew of coffee as a peace offering in her hands and I noticed she had been crying again.

"Joan," I laughed out loud for the first time in days, "you only said what I was thinking. How odd's that then? How many parents want their kids to stay at home and how many children can't wait to get to school? I think I must have slipped into some parallel universe." I shook my head with a mixture of wonder and concern. It was going to be a long day. Perhaps a lifetime of long days.

By arriving late to drop the boys off at school, I managed to avoid the rat run where the parents congregated to chatter and discuss the many inane topics that so filled the lives of those who did not work and had nothing better to do with their time. And though Jo had succumbed and become one of the so-called inner circle, neither Laura nor myself had the time, or inclination to become the playground gossips. Mr Rogers, as formal and stately a headmaster as ever I had known, offered his condolences, though the words seemed to trip off the tongue like some well rehearsed patter. And though he thought it a trifle odd, unnatural even, for the boys to return to school the day after their mother's death, he agreed that it was a sensible solution to call me should events unfold to the contrary.

I returned home fighting the eternal traffic congestion that every Londoner so hated, such a waste of one's life. After a call to Jonny Pearce, my business partner to break the news and let him know that I would be taking at least a week's compassionate leave, I spent the next hour tidying up lose ends in my study cum office. A document signed here, an email to a client there and batching up a number of contracts to post, that Jonny had readily agreed to oversee in my absence.

A knock at the door an hour later brought me back from my work life and forced me to change into home mode, ever the tussle with those who had an office at home. It was Joan.

"Mr Meredith, I've cleaned the drawing room and the dining room, an' I'll do the bedrooms tomorrow, an' I was jus' on my way out when Mrs Waugh arrived. I've left 'er in the Drawing room with a fresh pot of coffee for the both of you. I hope that's alright?"

"That's great." I groaned suddenly remembering the conversation from last night. "You get yourself off, Joan, and many thanks for this morning."

I was not prepared for the image that greeted me when I entered the Drawing room. Standing and looking out of the large bay window with her features in profile, detail obscured by the bright daylight from behind, she could have been Laura.

"Christ almighty," I swore out loud, stopping dead in my tracks in the doorway.

Jo turned, startled. "Well, hello to you too."

"Jo, sorry. I just thought for a second… never mind." We kissed on both cheeks, then sat in the sofa nearest the butler's tray where the coffee and a small plate of assorted biscuits lay in wait.

"Did you think I was Laura?" Jo blurted out once coffee had been poured and she had settled back into the deep sofa.

I nodded, still in shock.

"It's odd, but I had never seen a likeness between us, until yesterday. When I got home I opened a bottle of wine and pulled out the old photo albums. Strange, really, as I had never really noticed it before."

"You both have the same build and overall shape, but it's only when you get up close that you really notice it. It's in the eyes," I stated simply, then felt the usual twinge and visible flush of embarrassment when discussing a woman's features or paying her a compliment.

"Mmm, I agree," Jo replied whilst sipping her coffee, ignoring any sign of embarrassment she may have noticed. Though holding her gaze for a moment I realised that despite an excellent make-up job, she had spent a good deal of time crying since we had last met, all that time ago in the hospital.

"So how's it going?" she enquired.

"Oh, so-so. Got a bit pissed last night, which seemed to help for about five minutes and felt bloody awful this morning. Thankfully good old Joan came to the rescue and resuscitated me with a litre of caffeine."

"Me too. Richard had to carry me to bed; I must have been a terrible nuisance for him. I also seem to recall being sick, not a very ladylike thing to do." Jo smiled for the first time that day, though it looked more like a thin, pale scar below her nose, rather than her usual full-lipped affair that had smitten many a suitor in her time.

In her time? God, she was…what? Only thirty-seven or eight, and still beautiful. Beautiful to look at, beautifully dressed, an appealing mind and a beautiful personality. So like her beautiful sister.

We smiled again at one another in the shared conspiracy of our drunken states and settled into a moment's comfortable silence, just appreciating the quiet and brief cessation of the high-speed merry-go-round. Nothing needed to be said, we had both suffered the same extreme sense of loss and recognised that the shared silence was of mutual understanding and mourning.

It couldn't last, of course; we had work to undertake, but the moment had been precious.

The first task had initially been a painful one, but one eventually became numb to the experience after the first half dozen or so. Phoning friends and relatives to break the news. Jo, God bless her, had already spoken to her parents and the relatives on her side of the family, so we divided up the remaining list and with me on the office phone and Jo on the home line, it was a relief to be able to tick off the first item an hour later.

We were able to tackle a few more tasks before breaking for a quick bite to eat. I hadn't realised I hadn't eaten for twenty-four hours and feeling delighted that I had faced up to the challenge and constant reminders of Laura, none more so than her penned corrections and addendums, I was famished.

After lunch we returned to the drawing room and with Jo sitting on the floor, her shapely legs tucked elegantly beneath her, reminding me of an exquisite plain, un-fired china figurine

Jo had bought for our fifth wedding anniversary, we put aside the task list whilst I reread the funeral tasks and order of service.

"It's beautiful and so very Laura." Jo cried uncontrollably once I had finished reading. "She would have loved it."

"Yes, she did," I agreed, recalling the smiles and sense of satisfaction and perhaps even peace, when Laura lay back exhausted on her pillows, the final draft completed by the light from the bedside lamp reflected in the window enhanced by the darkness that lay beyond.

"It won't be too much for everyone, do you think? I couldn't bear to have too much howling and beating of chests?" I asked Jo, wanting to offer her the chance to approve, to be involved in the decisions, to show that I recognised the support and love for her sister that welled within her.

"Sod them!" she exclaimed bravely from the floor, her head bowed, allowing the dark cascade of her hair to fall over her tear-stained face like a magician's handkerchief protecting the trick from the audience.

"That's exactly what Laura said," I laughed, clapping my hands on my knees in momentary delight. "Word for word."

"Did she really? Yes, she would have done, and how right she was as well." Jo lifted her face up to me and her eyes shone brightly through her tears.

For such a proud and strong woman, it was such a personal gesture; in that single moment to show me her suffering and pain, that perhaps nobody, not even Richard would ever see.

"And now sod it, look at the time, I'm going to be late picking the boys up from school." Jo leapt to her feet, slipped into her loafers and started to help me gather up the paperwork we had spread about us.

"I'll give you a lift Jo. The monster's back from the garage, so we can all squeeze in." The monster I referred to was a bright red, long wheelbase Landrover with a capacity to seat twelve. Not the most intelligent vehicle for London traffic, and a far more practical Japanese hatchback filled our daily needs, but as an architect, it suited me well when needing to visit the various building and construction sites our partnership was managing, or for carrying models, perfectly built to scale to a prospective client.

That evening, after listening to the stories of heroic goal scoring and the pros and cons of vivisection, I put two contented boys to bed, then settled down in the Drawing room nursing a very pale scotch and water. With the added luxury of Bob Dylan playing quietly on the CD player, I looked out at our sadly neglected back garden and in the fading daylight let the mind reflect upon a life lived to date.

An only child, born on the 5th November 1969 to Frederick and Elizabeth Meredith at St Mary's hospital, London. Christened shortly afterwards Tristan, Frederick, Maynard Meredith, I was a somewhat podgy child with a shock of unruly mouse brown hair and somewhere beneath the locks lay a pair of dark brown inquisitive eyes. Strangely the reflection that now stared back at me each morning from the mirror when shaving showed pale green eyes, though still equally inquisitive and not without a glimmer of humour. They were also now being besieged by the first signs of crows' feet and low-lying trenches across a high forehead. Well, perhaps not a high forehead—realistically I had fallen foul of the family trait of a receding hairline, but what's the difference amongst friends?

I cannot put my finger on the day I was just called Meredith. I am sure that Tristan is a fine name, though I seem to recall that self-survival techniques quickly learnt during my early days at preparatory school necessitated a degree of subterfuge.

Was it a Percival or a Peregrine, I can't recall, though I do recall the poor chap being debagged and pushed out into the school playground during break time.

"That's not for me!" I decided promptly and set about the creation of a suitable nickname. Clearly I was not a creative individual, fear perhaps cloying the mind, so Meredith it became. Variations appeared over the years as I progressed from prep school through public school and on to university; MM, Merry, Hobbit, Mirror-Mirror and even the less than friendly Merde, but fortunately no public debagging or other such humiliation.

To the constant amusement of my parents, I went through various adolescent phases, usually driven through music. At the age of about ten, I discovered that it was "cool" to play the guitar and with the benefit of being able to play by ear, I would strum or pluck away at the latest hits. Friends in my dormitory would soon add their voices to the well-known songs, someone would thump away on makeshift drums and a fun time was had by all. New Romantics led to women's blouses and eyeliner, a brief fling with the Goths, a more rebellious sixteen-year-old pogoed with the punks before I turned the corner and started to appreciate the likes of Bob Dylan and Eric Clapton.

Even after discussions with my parents we were not able to discern any insight from an ordinary childhood that suggested I would eventually find a career as an architect. I drew, but no more than any other child. And much to my father's amusement and my mother's annoyance, I, and often the surrounding walls and carpets would be as coloured as the picture I had drawn.

However, this desire led me to university in the West Country where, on my first day of lectures, I met a fellow student also at the time believing that a latent Lutyens lay beneath his worldly charm and relaxed nature. With nigh on twenty years now passed since that first day at university I could still call Philip Douglas my closest friend. Son of General Sir Alan Douglas, educated, though his school masters would debate that point, at Eton, Philip was a natural rogue and charmer who would not have been out of place in a Scott Fitzgerald novel. We shared digs for that first year and many a wild night of debauchery and drunkenness ensued. At the twinkle of an eye, the most beautiful girls would decorate his side for as long as they could hold his attention and with seemingly endless coffers, I enjoyed a life hitherto prohibited by a combination of a lack of self-confidence and financial limitation.

A year later however the future history of architecture breathed a sigh of relief when tutors decided, on Philip's behalf, that he and architecture were not a stable concoction and he was summarily despatched to the family estate in Wiltshire to reconsider which profession would most benefit from his attention. A month later his exasperated father gave him the gift of a year to reflect, wrapped around a return ticket to anywhere in the world, as long as it wasn't Wiltshire. So Philip packed a rucksack and laughed all the way to the airport. A year later a disgracefully tanned prodigal son returned to Wiltshire, announced that he was going to become a city trader and promptly left for London.

That was 1990 and two months later he held a belated going away, or coming back party. He had found an enormous flat in Clapham for which he paid an unnaturally low rent. Rumour had it that he had had his wicked way with the elderly landlady which, whilst a pretty disgusting thought, he did not refute this allegation, but neither could we elicit the truth. Still a poor, debt riddled student, I tucked a sleeping bag under one arm and an embarrassingly cheap bottle of plonk under the other and caught the London train. A tube ride later I hit Philip's doorbell at eight-thirty, though I had to repeat the exercise a number of times before the sound of an electric buzz announced that I was clear to enter—and was let into the flat by an unconcerned stranger. Five minutes after hiding my poor excuse for a bottle of wine amongst many finer bottles in the kitchen and dumping my sleeping bag in an empty bedroom, I walked into the main room scanning the crowd of black suits and little black dresses for Philip. From that moment onwards, life would never be the same again. Instead of finding Philip, my eyes, followed quickly by my heart, were caught by the most beautiful girl in the world. I was transfixed. She was standing over by the window, dark hair with natural blonde highlights falling forever around her shoulders, full lips lightly glossed and a very bored expression on her face. The man she was talking to, or rather was listening to, was already half cut, an unhealthy, sweaty sheen upon his face, and was clearly finding the conversation far more interesting and humorous than she did, as he leaned and swayed ever closer. Her eyes briefly caught mine, smiled momentarily, then reverted back to their glazed state as the man finished a sentence then roared with laughter, before starting his one-man spitting contest once more.

Pouring myself a large glass of wine I swallowed half in one gulp, then quickly refilled it. I had to meet her, I had to talk to her, even if it meant making a complete fool of myself. I was love struck and must have floated over to the far side of the room, for I certainly don't remember walking there.

"Hello," I smiled, showing far more confidence than I felt. "You don't happen to have seen a damsel in distress around here somewhere do you?"

"I might have, why?" she smiled back, animated and alive at last.

"Well, someone in the kitchen asked me to come in and grab a girl, but I've forgotten her name. Tell me yours, it may just jog my memory."

"Now listen here, I don't know who you are, but why don't you piss off." The swaying suit splattered me with a blend of spit and alcohol, his flushed face screwed up in a concentrated effort to focus on this threat.

"It's Laura," she rose to the challenge.

"*That's* the name—what a stroke of luck! Come on, let's get you back to the kitchen. Oh and," I turned to the suit, "thanks for looking after Laura."

Taking her gently by the elbow I steered her through the crowd to the hallway and freedom.

"Is he following us?" I asked with a degree of concern.

"No, he's still standing there." She giggled. "I'm not even sure he's noticed we've left."

It was quieter in the hallway and though voices still needed to be raised, we could at least have a conversation.

"Is this how you pick up all your girls?" she enquired, studying me closely over her glass, a light smudge of pale lipstick surrounded the rim distorting the lower half of her face, which only made me concentrate harder on those green peek-a-boo eyes.

"Limpid pools of perfection!" Philip would have called them and no doubt would have swept Laura off to his bedroom moments later.

"No, never," I laughed nervously, my mind flipping inside out as I started to think about how to impress, how to amuse and attract this gorgeous woman. "In fact, my legs are still shaking."

"Well, though it was pretty cheesy, it was rather fun and you really are my knight in shining armour. I thought I was going to keel over at any moment, either that or have that wretched man's hands all over me in the next five minutes." She laughed out loud and her hand reached out to touch my forearm. A cattle prod would have passed less voltage through my body.

And that, as they say, was that. We stood in that hallway for three hours, an overburdened coat rack on one side and a full-length mirror on the other, witnessing the start of a relationship that was cemented with our wedding in the summer of 1994. Philip was of course the best man and has claimed the credit for our meeting ever since, despite not actually having shown up to his own party. Something to do with a bear market he needed to discuss with a pretty trader from some bank or another.

Freddie was born in 1997 with Tom following up two years later. And somewhere amongst all of that I managed to pass my exams, find employment, get made redundant, find further employment, sign my life away with the mortgage from hell to buy our house in Clapham Old Town and start up my own business. My parents had died, mother whilst I was still at university and father five years ago, which, whilst permitting me to pay off a chunk of the mortgage, still threatened to financially choke us at any given moment.

And that brings me up to date. Now I was single again, a widower, a debt free homeowner with two children and a successful though still immature business. Not quite how I expected to be described several years before my fortieth birthday.

Surfacing, I found the eerie reflection of a man I did not care to recognise staring back in the window. I looked down into my lap and found that even in my dream state I had managed to polish off the contents of my glass.

Time to go to your bed, I thought, rising stiffly from the armchair. Your bed? Said so casually, so effortlessly, just slipping off the tongue without a thought or pause. What happened to Our bed, Our bedroom? Her perfume and make up still stood proudly on her dressing table, a silk dressing gown on a hanger over her wardrobe, its doors slightly ajar, as though she had only just popped out for the evening. Perhaps only props for a play, to deceive the mind. We knew that once Laura had gone into hospital, she was never coming home; yet I had left things as they were, to drift in false comfort until the inevitable ripped away the stage curtain and revealed the play of naked reality and demanded that the actors spring into action.

Not having been slept in for forty-eight hours, the bed felt cold and unwelcoming. And keeping as I always had, to my side of the bed, I flicked off the bedside lamp, pulled the rich, heavy duvet around me and nestled my head into the pillows, though it was a long time before sleep released me from my mental prison.

Chapter Three

The hands on clocks and days of the week on calendars continued to move about us, changing scenes quietly in the background, almost unnoticed by us actors in the play. A New Year began, February, became March which moved into April; the earth shrugging off its cold, hard blanket of frost, allowing life once more to stir and grow. The sun's rays seductively stroked the land, arousing lines and clumps of daffodils that heralded the season's change, and delicate apple blossom briefly turning our usually bland street into a breathtaking visual display of pinks and whites. The House Martins returned and the first butterflies flittered amongst the year's first colour adding small dashes of white to an Impressionist painting. Mankind responded in its way; up and down the street lawnmower engines coughed, then whined to inform me when Sunday afternoons were upon us.

In the grand scheme of life, a funeral had taken place, attended by a small group of people. A dry, clear day promised much, though a biting north wind made the occasion seem drab and colourless. It was a beautiful, personal, funny and touching service. And though handkerchiefs were much in evidence, dabbing eyes with occasionally discreet noseblowing, moments of laughter echoed high up amongst the vaulted ceiling and smiles bounced about the walls and pillars as memories were unlocked and tribute paid.

Despite having arranged and been through the service on numerous occasions, it still caught me by surprise and I spent much of the service staring fixedly ahead with blurred vision. The boys, one on either side, smartly dressed in their school uniforms, though tidy hair, even plastered down with gel was caught and whipped back into an unruly mess by the wind prior to entering the church. And Laura would not have wanted it any other way.

It was a wonderful distraction for the boys to see their grandparents again. Since Laura's parents had migrated to New Zealand five years before, they only came back once a year for a month's whistle stop tour to visit friends and family. I must admit that I was still concerned about the boys seeming lack of desire to talk about Laura. Throughout the ceremony they remained dry eyed, occasionally leaning past me to smile at one another, or turn their heads to wave at their cousins, Guy and Dominic, Jo and Richard's two boys, who they rushed off to play with the moment the ceremony was over.

I did not begrudge them their happiness, absolutely envied the apparent freedom that their state of mind allowed, though was still hugely concerned that they showed no sign of loss, no mourning, no sadness and no tears. Had the fact that Laura had spent so much time in hospital enabled them to already mourn her loss? Religiously they had visited three times a week, but she was not otherwise a part of their lives. All that time she was not a physical presence at home, an ethereal one perhaps, and had become a relative to visit. She no longer put them to bed and kissed them goodnight, put salve and plasters on cut knees and soothed away the fears of nightmares.

Laura's parents had flown back from New Zealand and were staying at Jo and Richard's house in Cavendish Walk. They could of course have stayed with us, but quietly I was pleased that they had opted for the former. Nonetheless we had an enjoyable dinner and once the four boys had been spirited away by the calling of some computer game or another, we, the grown ups had adjourned to the drawing room and spent a warm and memorable evening recalling our fondest memories and stories of Laura. It was an informal celebration of her life and though emotion tugged, we could see smiles through the tears and laughter helped soften the blows to the heart.

A school term ended and another one began. Somewhere in the middle the boys spent days at a time over at Jo and Richard's playing with their cousins. When at home, I could usually find them either glued to the television in the family room, or hear them thumping around on the top floor playing in their bedrooms. Even when they may have been quietly engrossed on the Internet, or watching some DVD, I knew, I could feel that they were in the house.

I returned to work and whilst this meant that I usually worked from home as often as three days a week, a couple of new contracts monopolised my attention. I still took the boys to school in the morning and picked them up again in the afternoon, though on several occasions having to pull the fat out of the fire at the last moment, by quickly calling Jo who was already at the school waiting to pick up her own boys and beg her to pick Freddie and Tom as well. Each time I castigated myself for being such a deficient father and promised myself it would never happen again; but it did. And each time the look on Jo's face, when I picked them up from their house, was less and less tolerant. Not angry that she was forced into undertaking an arduous task, more that she was concerned for me, the boys, our relationship and was this to be our routine from here on in.

By the end of May I managed to finish the last of the tasks on Laura's list. These last items were of course the most painful and ones perhaps I felt that I could overlook for a good deal longer. Jo, however, filled with her direct approach and bulldog tenacity, kept on at me and this, coupled with her patience and understanding, helped bring me round and make me see reason. And as the strong shoulder that I had so much come to rely upon to help pull us through, she spent a day with me helping to clear out Laura's drawers and wardrobe. Armed with a thick roll of black sacks, a few cardboard boxes and a pot of strong coffee, we set to work in the bedroom.

The dressing table was stripped of make-up, perfumes and other cosmetics, all heading for the bin. The contents of the wardrobe were neatly folded and placed into the bags to head to a well-intentioned charity shop. Belts, scarves, shoes, gloves, dresses, trouser suits, shirts and coats, all were reviewed, so many pulling back a distant memory and subsequent heartache as it was packed away for the last time.

In the end we could shut the doors to the wardrobe, leaving a last orchestral cacophony as metal and plastic coat hangers banged and crashed against each other and then silence; it was done. The dressing table stood void of any surface clutter, its drawers also empty and a dozen black sacks filled the back of the beast, whilst I also craved the dustmen's indulgence for a wheelie bin lid that could not be closed that week.

Now I could start to call the room mine, if I so wished or the subconscious allowed. Cathartic? I don't really know. Removing the physical does not stop the mind from thinking, but perhaps it lessened the chance of thinking about, being drawn back to the past, enabling the mind to start to build on a future.

With one problem over I could now breathe a sigh of relief, but as I did, so life's cruel game slipped another card into the deck. It was about this time that a new problem arose as cracks in the relationship between the boys and myself began to appear. Though the future may have looked uncertain, it now started to look loaded against us.

Forgetting to pick the boys up from school was the tip of the iceberg, though its cause was at the foundation of all that was driving us apart. Me.

I had thrown myself back into my work. The instincts of the hunter-gatherer dominating, the need to provide a safe and secure environment for my family. It was not a conscious decision, nor deliberately a selfish one; just how it was. With all that male testosterone and ego strutting around in my head, I had forgotten that the children now lacked the comfort, the nurturing; the careful balance of ying and yang. I was building a future without a heart; food that choked, air that suffocated.

Over supper one Friday night my head, still filled with the excitement of the deal and the scent of the hunt, I served up one of my toad in the hole specials, always a favourite with the boys and broke the next let down for the children.

"Boys, I've got some bad news about this weekend." They looked up from the kitchen table, concern etched on both their pale faces.

"I've got a really important contract that needs to be finished for Monday, so I'm going to have to work over the weekend and that means I don't think I'm going to be able to take you to the cinema." Bringing in the Frinton contract was a major coup for us and the first real sign of my business climbing up the first tentative rungs to compete with the slightly larger and more established firms. The pressure was on and though I could have entrusted a good deal of this work to the team, I was not prepared to lose this deal over someone else's mistake.

"Aw, dad, but you promised us and we really want to go to the cinema." Not surprisingly I received a duet of protest backed up by a visible remonstration at how unfair I was being.

"I'm sorry, but I just can't; but I promise to make it up to you. How about we go the following weekend and I'll take you out for a pizza afterwards?" I tried to pacify with a little extra, though knowing full well I would have taken them for pizza anyway.

"It's not fair, you never take us out," Freddie rebuked me, pushing his chair back to storm out of the kitchen.

"Hey, hey!" I called after his retreating form. "You know that's not true."

"Okay, so when was the last time you took us out?" he shouted back, his face red, fuming with frustration.

"Well, what about… what about that film with the kids who disappeared into the fantasy world and all the robots? And what's more, before that I took you two, Guy and Dominic bowling at the centre. Don't tell me you've forgotten that as well?" I sat back momentarily pleased with myself for thinking I was outsmarting a child, but his response sent a shock right through me.

"That was last year, when mum was alive. Remember? We went to the hospital first, then we had to go to your office and you made us sit in the car for over an hour waiting for you, then you took us to the cinema." Freddie had tears in his eyes, perhaps caused by the frustration, perhaps the memory of a time gone by.

"Mum always used to take us to the cinema," Tom joined the fray with a stake through the heart. It was a simple statement quietly spoken, no malice, no raised voice, just a fact.

I opened my mouth, but nothing was coming out. Was it really that long ago? Of course it would have been—Freddie would know, his head was filled with such detail.

"I'm sorry, boys," I started to apologise, perhaps even to back down, the mind already working on how I could get the contract finished, an early start on Monday, a late Sunday night.

"Oh, forget it dad, don't bother. Not to worry, Tom." Freddie looked at his crestfallen brother and put a protective arm about him. "We'll ask aunt Jo, I'm sure she'll take us if we ask her nicely."

They left me still standing in the kitchen, my hands half raised like an innocent man found guilty by a judge, their heads held high in defiance, food untouched.

The following morning, ensconced in my office, poring over the paper and drawings spread over every available work surface, the phone rang.

"Meredith, it's Jo." A distinctly cool voice this morning.

"Jo, hi. Look, I'm sorry to be a bore, but I'm a bit tied up at the moment, can I call you back later?" My eyes scanning over the detailed drawings before me.

"I know you're a bit tied up at the moment, the boys told me. That's why I'm calling," Jo replied frostily.

"Ah yes." The spell cast by my work was temporarily broken. "I've got a big deal on at the moment, Jo, and I can't afford to lose it. I know the boys were a bit upset last night but I said I'd make it up to them next weekend." I tried to pass it off as a nothing, a flash in the pan.

"Meredith, the boys were in tears on the phone to me last night. They told me this isn't the first time you've let them down at the last minute and what with you asking me to pick them up from school…What's going on?"

"Look, Jo." I pushed back against this intrusion of my family's private life. "I said I'd take them next weekend and I will."

"Well, I've already told them that I'll take them this afternoon. So unless you want to disappoint them again, I'll be over at two to pick them up." The voice was clear, firm and very much in charge and running true to form. I backed down.

"Okay, well thanks Jo, it's much appreciated." Like spitting out sawdust, the words were dry in my mouth.

"Look Meredith, I think we need to talk. Perhaps we can discuss when I drop the kids off when we get back."

"Oh okay Jo, see you later." I slammed the phone down in frustration. Frustration at my own weakness for not telling her to piss off and mind her own business. Frustrated that the boys had actually phoned her and not waited so I could take them. Frustrated that they were right and when I reflected upon how I had behaved over the past few months, I didn't like what I saw one little bit.

"You're a bastard," I said to my reflection in the window and, though my heart was no longer in it, I forced my attention to the mounds of paper on the desk in front of me to get through this as quickly as possible.

We secured the contract and though it at last set us firmly on the map as a player, it was a hollow feeling of victory and whilst it was right to celebrate this milestone, I left the party at the pub, deciding not to follow them onto the restaurant. The food would have made me choke.

I drove home tired but still on a high from the successful outcome of the day, the radio playing some unknown garbage with no apparent beat or rhythm, neon streetlights and shop signs illuminating their interiors and the familiar route home.

People busy going somewhere, heads bent against the evenings chill, perhaps also to avoid eye contact with the strangers about them and the beggars still calling out from doorways, holding out for the last coins of charity to drop their way. Car headlights like an interrogator's light causing the eyes to squint through the windscreen to keep an eye on the pavement and other such signs to keep the car safely on the road. My mind slipped away from the backslapping and feeling of jubilation around the office, to the quiet, introverted feelings at home. The boys' faces powered into focus, unhappy, quiet in the solitude that was home, depressed; turning to irritability, frustration, ending in stark anger and ugly confrontation. Jubilation was beaten back into its box, the lid secured once more, its victor a heavy and debilitated heart.

"Laura, what am I to do?" I whispered under my breath as though, embarrassed, I might be overheard. "As you no doubt have been seeing I've really been cocking things up. The boys are unhappy, I'm unhappy as buggery and I can't seem to find the balance to be all things to everyone and still be happy myself. What should I do?"

No response, except the garbling from the radio which I quickly turned off.

"I've been called into the school twice by Tom's teacher and once by Freddie's. Nothing new for Tom, but Freddie? He's not in any trouble, but they'd noticed his work slipping; not throwing himself into it with his usual enthusiasm and was everything alright at home? Had I noticed anything? What do you say to that? Well yes, his mother's been dead for less than six months, he doesn't appear to have missed her, just got on with things, whilst his dad seems to be ignoring him completely, too wrapped up in his work. Now sod off and mind your own business."

Without thinking, I switched on the windscreen wipers to clear the rain that was blurring my view and causing car lights to sparkle like a thousand diamonds; only to realise that it was still dry outside and it was the tears coursing down my cheeks that were to blame.

I found the first place to stop and pulled over, folding my arms over the steering wheel and burying my head in the warm, enveloping darkness and waited until the sobbing that wracked my body had subsided.

Shortly, back under control and mustering what dignity I could in front of the small group of people waiting for the next bus, I sat back in the seat, wiping my eyes on the sleeves of my shirt and after struggling for a moment I managed to release my handkerchief from a trouser pocket and blew my nose. Lights from the cars behind lit the rear view mirror and I caught a glimpse of a human wreck staring back at me. Someone on the edge of the pit of despair; not quite given up hope, but without a plan, reliant upon luck, good fortune to pull him through. And like a person suffering from vertigo, the ground was calling out to jump, it's warm in the pit and then everything will be all right.

"No bloody way, I'm not giving up, I just need to figure it all out. We're going to get through this and you're going to be proud of us." I snorted air deep into my lungs, nodding to myself in physical support and strangely a smile briefly caressed the corners of my mouth.

"Joan, many thanks, you are a star for staying on to look after the boys this evening. Everything all right?" I asked cheerfully, reaching for the whisky and a glass.

"Everything was fine. The boys were as good as gold, ate everything on their plates and are now upstairs doing something on the computer thing. I'm not sure what as these things are all over my 'ead, goodness knows what they'll invent next." Joan Fry's jowls wobbled into action, blurting out her words as though she had been storing them up for hours and now needed to spit them out, else explode with too much energy self-contained within.

"That's great and many thanks again, Joan," I repeated.

"Tis no bother Mr Meredith, a pleasure's what it was. Now I'd better be gettin' off, else my John is goin' to think I've run off with another man." She chuckled stretching her coat about her and donning a big knitted, red woolly hat. "Oh, and you had a call from Mrs Waugh. Said she'd be around about ten tomorrow. Said you know all about it anyway. It's my day off tomorrow, but would you like me to come in and prepare anything for you?"

"No, that's fine thanks, you get yourself home and give John my regards and my apologies for keeping you out so late." I ushered her towards the door, lest run the risk of being held at bay in the kitchen for another half an hour chatting.

Leaving the boys to their own devices, I put my glass of whisky and the bottle on a table beside one of the sofas in the family room, then nipped upstairs into my office and grabbed a pen and notepad.

"Right now then, if we need a plan, let's first jot down the problems, the causes and what else may be coming at us in the next couple of months. Then perhaps we can see the problems and find a way out of this god-awful mess." I gulped purposefully at the whisky, then put pen to paper.

Of course it wasn't too difficult at all to get to the root cause of it all and I should have seen it ages ago, no doubt everyone else had. Time was the commodity in short supply. Take one person out of the equation who had been the main support for the boys and replace it with someone who took them to school and probably only spent half an hour with them at and around supper time; it left a big gap in filling their needs. The answer certainly wasn't to rely upon Jo, Joan or anyone else for that matter to stand in for me at home as surrogate parents, so I could get on with making a success out of the company. It would merely highlight and confirm to the boys that they came second in my life and that was the very antithesis of what I was setting out to achieve. The trick in the first place was how to release time to spend with the boys and secondly then what to do during that time?

Before trying to find answers to these two devilish questions I turned to a fresh page, wrote, then underlined the title— Coming at us (up to the end of the year).

The list started well enough and I was pretty pleased that half a dozen events were soon consigned to print; birthdays, Christmas, that sort of thing. Events then began to dry up, though I had that nagging sensation in the back of my head that said you were missing something pretty fundamental and this led to a good deal of pen chewing and a fresh glass of whisky was poured, to help release the inspirational juices. One sip later and...

"Bugger!" I said out loud and like some nervous reaction I immediately reached again for the whisky and took a long gulp. "Summer holidays! Shit, damn and derision!" I exclaimed loudly to the four walls. "Two whole months at home. How the hell do I cope with that length of time, and even if I could, what the bloody hell can I do with them?"

The pen ripped the page as I repeatedly underscored the words "Summer Holidays." Another mouthful of whisky and an evil thought crossed my mind.

"I could send them to New Zealand to stay with their grandparents. They would love to see their grandchildren and the boys would love the chance to see another part of the world."

I almost persuaded myself that this was the ideal solution, before guilt washed through me at the thought of such a selfish act. I was still tempted to put it down, but because it did not resolve the issue of me spending more time with the children, there was no room for it on the otherwise empty "Resolution" page.

By midnight, hungry, half-pissed and stiff from lack of movement, the answer was clear; the only problem was that I didn't like it. Not one little bit. However, it was the only solution that met the desired outcome, leading to an ultimate resolution to the first part of the problem.

"I'm going to have to spend less time working, perhaps go part-time, get another partner in, sub-contract, worse case, sell the business." There really was no other option, though the devil in me had no qualms in providing a few helpful suggestions.

"The situation isn't as bad as you're making it out. This is overkill; you're over-reacting. Typical reaction to the nanny state we're living in. They'd be a damn sight more unhappy if you lost the business, the house and were living in a cardboard box for Christ's sake" And like a smoker trying to persuade himself that he can't live without cigarettes, I battled the demons inside.

The following morning, having had to stop off to buy some milk after the school run, I had only just got home and put the kettle on before the doorbell rang.

"Hello Meredith, how are you darling?" Jo's voice had regained its warm resonance, though I noticed I did not benefit from the customary kiss on both cheeks this morning. As ever she looked stunning. She had only been out to drop her boys off at school but she may just as well have stepped off the catwalk. Her dark hair shone with the sun picking out and rejoicing in the chic, but no doubt extremely expensive, highlights. A cool white, open necked shirt beneath a well cut, dark blue blazer that could have been tailor made as it hugged the contours of her svelte figure. A dark blue skirt rode above the knee, blue tights and matching penny loafers; simple and understated elegance. No doubt all with a designer label and price tag to match; though on Richard's salary he wouldn't even feel the pinch, but neither would he have noticed or remarked upon how beautiful she was.

"Jo, sorry I missed you at school this morning, had to have a chat with Mr Rogers. But may I say how simply stunning you look! You give reason to the word breathtaking." I applied the charm and added one of my boyish smiles, usually to good effect.

"Meredith, you're a complete sod. You always know the right things to say and here I am trying to be angry with you." She smacked my shoulder lightly, and returned my smile, anger deflated, friends once more.

"I'm just making some coffee and I thought we could sit outside; be a shame to waste such a fabulous day. Is that okay with you?" I said over my shoulder as we descended to the kitchen.

"Mmm, sounds a great idea. I feel like I've been stuck indoors for months and am about to get cabin fever."

Thankfully I had a cash-in-hand deal going with Jean's husband, John, each summer for the past three years. He had been helping out in the garden over the past few weeks and though still a long way to go to regain complete control, it left a certain cottage garden wild charm that I was thinking of keeping.

"How's Richard, haven't seen him for ages?" I asked, opting for one of the reclining garden chairs while Jo placed her coffee on the wooden table to settle in the roofless swing seat with as much decorum as her modesty would permit. Once on board, she rearranged cushions, then swung her legs up, her ankles resting on the arm at the other end.

"That feels simply wonderful." She closed her eyes and lifted her face up to bask in the sun. "Sorry, what did you say?"

"Just wondered how Richard was doing," I repeated. "Haven't seen him for ages."

"Oh, he's fine. Loving his work of course, as ever. Well, I assume he's enjoying it as he's always so busy, but it's not the sort of thing he talks about of course. All that secret squirrel, must protect England, we shall fight them on the beaches and all that."

"Still up at the crack and getting home late?"

"Oh yes, nothing changed there. I'm beginning to think that if it wasn't for the weekends the boys would think he was just a figment of my imagination." She laughed though there was a certain sadness that despite my own predicament, made me feel sorry for her. As I was just starting to find out, it was a lonely existence being a parent flying solo. Yes, it was fine whilst as a hunter-gatherer, I hunted and gathered, but it had not taken me long to see that the demands made of the person in charge of the nest and the fledglings could be a selfless, monotonous and claustrophobic one.

Like the frozen river starting to thaw and run once more, babbling and gushing unimpeded to its destination, in the embrace of the first warm rays of sun that year; so our own cold, pent up feelings and frustrations that had built up through the winter gave way to free, easygoing conversation and the gentle song of laughter. And as ever, Father Time continued his eternal march.

"Bloody hell, it's twelve o'clock! I've got to get home to sort things out around the house, then it'll be time for the school run. Just when I was starting to enjoy myself." Jo made to rise from her comfortable seat.

"I tell you what, stay for lunch. You lie back, relax and enjoy the sun and I'll rustle us up something to eat. Nothing special, though we can at least wash it down with a glass of a rather good white that I've recently discovered."

"I really should be going." Jo made a half-hearted attempt to rise from her comfortable position.

"Nonsense, I absolutely insist that you stay."

"I'd like that very much, thank you Meredith darling." She sank back into the deep cushions of the swing seat and stretched her arms above her head.

I returned ten minutes later with a tray piled high with an assortment of meats, cheeses and bread; all that could be reasonably scraped together from the fridge.

"I must have nodded off, what a luxury." Jo started at the sound of the cork being extracted from the chilled bottle of wine.

"Help yourself. Apologies it's not to the usual high standard of culinary skills of the Meredith household, but it should keep the wolf from the door." I poured two glasses of the light white wine.

"To a long hot and happy summer." We raised glasses in salutation to one another and drank, before grabbing plates to fill with various colours, smells and textures.

"So what are the plans for your summer holidays? Going somewhere hot and exotic?" I asked, noisily tapping a spoonful of pickle onto my plate to join the slab of cheddar cheese.

"No, not this year. Richard's got something on that means we won't be able to get away until October, which is a bloody nuisance."

"That's a shame." I agreed.

"Typical more like. He's going to miss the whole of the boys' summer hols. And if we want to go away as a family that means we won't get away until Christmas and that just isn't on. So I thought I might go down under and take the boys to stay with mummy and daddy, they're always saying how much they'd love us to go out and see them. Then I can leave Richard to do his thing; it's not as though he'll miss us and after all that's happened in the last six months, I think we deserve a bit of a break."

"I bet the kids would love that," I nodded in agreement, though smiling inwardly about my thoughts from the night before.

"I also noticed when they were over last, for the funeral, that they're getting on a bit, especially daddy; so it would be nice to spend some time with them."

Jo sipped quietly at her wine, seemingly unaware that she had shown me, albeit briefly, a part of her that she was usually protective of—the dutiful wife presenting a unified front to all.

It would have embarrassed both of us if I had chosen to ask whether everything was all right, or could I do anything to help. Jo would have clammed up, left within five minutes and berated herself all the way home and then been completely uptight the next time we met. And what could I have done anyway? Whilst I had not previously appreciated that Laura's death may have significantly affected anyone else, Jo would not thank me for offering sympathy.

"Well, I've got a little bit of news for you," I whispered in mock secrecy.

"Oh, do tell, I could do with cheering up." She swung her feet down and leaned forward, eager to hear what I was about to divulge.

"I haven't got a full plan yet, so bear with me as it's only a vague, rough outline, sketchy sort of a plan at the moment."

"Okay, Mr Detail, spit it out."

"You're not to tell the boys, okay? I've not said a word to them, because there's still a lot to sort out and one or two people are going to be a bit pissed off and I need to smooth all that out first."

"Come on, just get on with it, before I get pissed off as well."

"Alright, alright, I'm getting to it," I replied in mock exasperation. "Now if you're sitting comfortably, I shall begin?"

"Just a minute, it's hotter than I thought it was going to be so I put tights on. So excuse the strip show, but as I'm not going anywhere just yet, they need to come off so I can get some sun on these lily whites."

Slipping her hands under her waistband and shifting her weight from one side to the other she started to wiggle her hips.

"Feel free to look away and spare a damsel's modesty," she reprimanded in jest as she noticed my open stare.

"What, oh yes, of course, sorry." I felt the familiar rush of blood fill my cheeks.

"This is no bloody good. Look away, Meredith, this is going to be very tarty."

With that and before I could react, she quickly hoisted her skirt around her waist and whipped her tights down to her knees, providing me with a glimpse of delicately embroidered, white knickers. Decorum was regained shortly as she allowed her skirt to return to its usual position and she sat back into the swing seat, pulling the offending tights off with a beautifully pointed toe.

I took a long swig of my wine to hide my embarrassment, most of which went down the wrong way causing me to choke and cough the liquid down the front of my shirt.

"Serve you right, you pervert," Jo laughed, revealing perfect, white even teeth.

"Can't help it," I spluttered as I regained my breath. "It's not every day that a floozy flashes at me in my own back garden. You should come with a government health warning."

Once my breathing was back under control I continued where we had left off.

"Right—now then, before I was so rudely interrupted by this garden nymph, I was going to tell you what I had in mind for the summer. As you know, things haven't been going so well here between the boys and me. Ultimately there just aren't enough hours in the day for me to be both mum and dad; something's got to give. So after coming up with a number of non-starters I have come to the decision that the only way that I can make this work is to give up work, so to speak."

"Give up work? What, are you mad?" Jo shot back at me, frown lines appearing over her darkened sunglasses.

"Calm down and let me finish." I went to sit beside her on the swing seat, taking her hand as if to physically reassure her.

"It'll only be for the summer holidays, call it a sabbatical. It'll allow us to spend all the time we need together; rebuild whatever it is that we've lost in our relationship. Also, as you said earlier, it's been a very tough last six months or so and I could also do with recharging the batteries."

"What are you going to do?" she asked.

"That's the bit I haven't figured out yet. Get away from here. that's for sure. Do something different, something the boys will enjoy, but that will bring us together."

"Well, I think you're mad, but brilliant mad, marvellous mad." Jo laughed without restraint and wrapped her arms around my shoulders in a warm embrace. "I think it's just what the doctor ordered and in fact I'm really quite jealous."

"Jealous, I thought you were going to take the boys off to meet the Kiwis?" I breathed in light but celestial perfume.

"Mmm, but I sometimes wish..." The sentence trailed off unfinished and she snatched at her empty wineglass.

This was the second time she had opened the door to her more personal thoughts. Was this a subconscious cry for help? Did she want to talk?

"Wish what?" I gently pressed as I filled her glass and finished the bottle.

"Oh nothing."

"No, go on. You've been so good at listening to me over the past months, it's now high time that I started to listen back."

"Oh hell. I just sometimes wish that Richard would be a little bit more aware of us as a family and of me as an individual, a woman, not just a mother. I wish that he would do something a little bit mad, more spontaneous, more... more alive, like you've just done."

I cant's say exactly what caused it, how it happened, whether it was ordained in the stars, or whether we created a shift in our own destinies, but the next thing I knew was that Jo and I were kissing.

"We shouldn't be doing this." I broke off at last, scarcely able to hear myself over the noise of the blood haring around my body caused by my thumping heart.

"Why not? I want you now, Meredith," Jo whispered, her fingernails gently scratching down my spine, raising goosebumps all over my body despite the heat of the day.

"Think of Richard, the boys." I tried to fight nature's impulsive demands.

"I'm not talking about an affair or, God forbid, a divorce. I just want to have some fun, to remember what it's like to be a woman." She stared deep into my eyes and started to kiss me gently on the cheeks, eyes, neck and eventually the mouth.

What little resistance I had half-heartedly raised was quickly worn down and diminished completely when, without warning, Jo pushed me back into the swing seat and swung herself into my lap to face me. With her knees either side and her pale thighs pressing against me, her green eyes smiled down into mine as she seductively pulled her skirt up over her firm buttocks to sit around her waist, once more revealing those exquisite knickers and the promise of what lay beyond.

I would like to say that I felt assuaged by guilt; that I felt I had been unfaithful to the memory to Laura. And with the added sin of having made love to her sister, that I was to be cast into Dante's Inferno, charged with unnatural lust and doomed to run for all eternity. But I didn't. I was elated, satiated and for the first time in a long time, I felt both physically and emotionally relaxed, at peace with the world.

I would also like to have said that the first words to tumble from my mouth once the brain had regained control of the body and I could speak were: "We mustn't let this happen again." But they weren't.

With her shirt buttons still undone to the waist and the inner curve of her small, pale breasts exposed, I could not take my eyes away from her for a second. With the occasional lick of the gentle breeze catching underneath the light cotton, causing it to billow like a sail and tantalisingly reveal far more than a man should see of his sister-in-law, I was mesmerised.

Jo lay back against the cushions, her eyes closed, the angry red flush on her chest rising and falling as she too regained her breath; unashamed, proud even of her careless nudity.

"Now I wish I hadn't given up smoking," she murmured.

"Sorry it was all over so quickly, I'm a bit out of practice," I replied somewhat sheepishly.

"It was fantastic, sex for sex's sake. I haven't felt like this for so long." She reached a hand out to reassure.

"You are so beautiful, so fantastic, he's a very lucky man." I couldn't bring myself to use Richard's name, perhaps on account of a slight stab of guilt at having made love to his wife, or perhaps a feeling that it would have dirtied what had been a truly wonderful moment.

"He is," she smiled, "but he doesn't know it. It's nothing like this with him, when we do you know what."

"And for us, this is just today, a moment only?"

She said nothing. Words to confirm one way or another would have brought our temporary world crashing down around us, and it was too soon, the moment to be savoured to last as a memory forever.

"I shall wake tomorrow and believe it was all but a dream, but deep down I will know that it was real."

"Our very own Brief Encounter, but in a swing seat, not a train station." She giggled huskily.

We continued to sit in silence, basking in the warmth of the sun and our own feelings of warm, contented drowsiness that is only brought on by lovemaking.

"Stop staring at me, you'll go blind," Jo purred faintly, her eyes lazily flicking open for a moment before succumbing to the effort and closing once more.

"I can't help it. You are a beautiful woman, Jo. Intelligent, gorgeous, and incredibly sexy. I want to see you like this for all time. I am bewitched."

Jo smiled broadly and made no move to cover herself; in fact, I swear she pulled ever so slightly, an almost imperceptible movement, at her shirt to allow the cool breeze and kiss of the sun's rays greater access to her.

"I was thinking."

"Is that a good thing?" I emptied the contents of the second bottle of wine into my glass and savoured the gentle, though no longer chilled grape before allowing it to trickle down the back of my throat.

"Yes." She took the glass from my hands and took a sip, before returning it to the table, her hand coming to rest on my thigh. "I was thinking that if we were to make a couple of quick calls... I mean, it would be a shame to waste the rest of the afternoon, especially when today is going to have to last us a lifetime." In the bright glare of the sun, her eyes had taken on a light emerald hue and for all the years that I had known her, they held a twinkle I had never before noticed.

I will forever cherish the sight of Jo and myself running indoors as quickly as was humanly possible. Me, with the half-full bottle of wine in one hand, trying to keep my trousers up with the other. Jo, with wine glasses in one hand and various garments in the other; also trying in vain, to hold her shirt together whilst her breasts struggled and successfully evaded all attempts at being restrained.

I felt as though I was a teenager again, rejoicing in the freedom of not having a care in the world and the feeling that can only be enjoyed as a youth that one will live forever. To be immortal, that summers will last forever, that every sunset will be a perfect blood red and bring a perfect day on the morrow.

That night I lay in bed alone with Jo's delicate but still arousing perfume lingering fresh upon the pillows, mentally and physically exhausted from our lovemaking, my stomach muscles aching from the laughter and the irrepressible smile of a contented man upon my face.

Still caught up in the passion and euphoria of our lovemaking I wanted to pick up the phone, to rush into the street, to tell anyone and everyone what we had just done. I had already made a start as I recalled that I had certainly called out to God enough times during the afternoon to let him know what I was doing.

I was not so naïve as to realise that it had all been but a brief respite, a refuge, a sighting of St Elmo's fire, but it had rekindled a fire I had thought forever extinguished. Life could be enjoyed, not just endured. Excitement and personal fulfilment were not an illusion like gold at the end of the rainbow. I had loved Laura with all my heart and for as long as she was alive I had wished for no more; but this afternoon urged and assured me that life could go on, a life full of passion, emotion, physical love and achievement without reproach, remorse or guilt.

The fears of a barren and meaningless existence had been banished from my world and it was with a lighter heart, though not without a degree of trepidation that I fell into a deep and fitful slumber.

I woke to a new day, the curtains failing to hold back the glorious sunlight of a new day and ignoring the harsh sounds of cars accelerating and changing gear in the road outside, I leapt out of bed with a spring in my step and the joy of a plan to be unleashed in my mind.

Showered and dressed for a day in the office, I burst into the kitchen to be assailed by the heady aroma of freshly brewed coffee.

"Well you're looking mighty chirpy this morning Mr Meredith," Joan Fry greeted my arrival and proceeded to tell me all that had taken place in her life in the past twenty-four hours and with a smile still upon my face I allowed her to answer her own questions and for the chatter to sail unimpeded over my head.

"Good morning boys," I hailed with all due excitement and enthusiasm as they arrived at the table together, both looking at me suspiciously as cereal was poured into bowls.

"Don't look so worried, it's a beautiful new day and with a bit of luck by the time I come to pick you up this afternoon I'll have some exciting news to tell you."

"Why, what's going on?" Freddie's naturally suspicious mind sprung to the defence, leaving his spoon half-raised towards his open mouth.

"Ah, that'd be telling now, wouldn't it, and I wouldn't want to spoil the surprise." I wagged my finger at nobody in particular.

"Please tell us daddy!" Tom pleaded, but to no avail and with some light-hearted banter all the way to school, throughout which numerous guesses and ideas were hurled up for consideration, I refused to be drawn.

"I'll see you later, be good and if you're not I've forgiven you already!" I shouted as they wandered off into the playground where their respective friends were congregated. They were quickly swallowed up in a bland sea of blue blazers and grey trousers; the only colour being drawn from the mass of multicoloured rucksacks and bags swung indifferently over shoulders, or being dragged along the tarmac.

"Hello Meredith," an almost shy voice greeted me as I passed through the wrought iron entrance gates.

"Jo, hi, how are you?" I glanced nervously around to ensure the playground gossips weren't in earshot. "You look stunning," I added in a quiet conspiratorial tone.

"Don't, you'll make me blush," she warned in an equally low voice, eyeing the small group of mothers slowly making their way towards us. "How are you?"

"You'll need to pinch me, because unless I was dreaming yesterday, I was the luckiest man alive, because I made love, several times I hasten to add, to this simply gorgeous woman."

"Meredith!" she sounded shocked, but there was still very much a twinkle in her eyes and the upward curve of her mouth suggested it was a shock to revel in and be delighted by the delicious praise.

"I can't believe we did it," she whispered, her eyes occasionally catching and holding my own as she continued to scan over my shoulder.

"Did what?" I acted the innocent.

"You know! It!" she stamped a foot on the ground in frustration.

"What, you mean make love? All afternoon?"

"You know bloody well what I mean, you sod," she exclaimed, still talking in a hushed tone.

"Well, I feel wonderful. I've got a smile a mile wide and despite having had my wicked way with a married woman, I feel no guilt whatsoever, either." I smiled knowingly at her.

"Me too," she giggled, quickly bringing her hand to her mouth to restrain herself from further unseemly behaviour and casting a long, guilty glance all around.

"How are the boys?" I asked in a normal voice as the last group of parents passed through the gates and went their separate ways.

"Meredith, I know we shouldn't, but I want to see you again!" she continued to whisper even though we were now quite alone.

"But what about what we said yesterday? It can't go anywhere." My heart rate began to quicken.

"Damn it, I know that. But all last night, this morning, even whilst making breakfast for Richard and the boys, driving here, all I could think about was how simply wonderful I feel. I know it's not going to go anywhere and I wouldn't let it, but just for the moment, selfishly I know, but it's made me feel alive. I'm not just a housewife and a mother, underneath all that dutiful obedience to the rulebook, I'm still *me*. And me has needs, and that means you!" She lowered her eyes demurely and fingered the single row of pearls at her throat.

Jo didn't do embarrassment, blushing or retiring. She was too outgoing, vivacious and too much a dominant personality and they were simply not a part of her make up, but she did a very seductive line in shyness.

"What are you smiling at?" she demanded angrily, momentarily forgetting her surroundings.

"I was just remembering seeing you sitting in the swing-seat and that got me on to wondering what you're wearing today. You really are one very sexy lady, you know."

"Stop that." She slapped me playfully on the shoulder, but her smile spoke volumes. She was finally hearing words she had longed to hear, feared that she would perhaps never hear again. Words that allowed her to feel special, to feel herself free as an individual; not the self-paralysing, claustrophobic, strangulation that came with being a part of a job lot.

"Can we meet?" she asked once more, a greater sense of urgency in her voice this time.

"It'll have to be tomorrow, as I have to go into the office today. But straight after school, my place?" Our first tryst was agreed.

And so began our affair, though we did not see it in such terms. We saw ourselves as two friends, clinging together in difficult times of personal upheaval, providing one another with that which they needed most. The ultimate in friendship. Selfish? Beyond doubt. Egocentric, narcissistic, smug and full of mutual adulation? I couldn't refute, but was that so wrong? Rewarding? Absolutely. Responsible? There was more than enough of that going on in the other part of our lives.

Some could argue that we brought out the worst in each other; I would say that we brought out the best. We became alive and our joy and that irrepressible desire for life transcended across into our other lives to affect those closest to us.

With images of Jo still running through my mind and the delectable promise of things to come, I calmly fought my way through the rush hour traffic to the office.

I hadn't even made it half way down the corridor to my office when Jonny Pearce's warm embrace knocked the air from my lungs.

"So what do we owe the honour of your presence today?" Jonny's deep voice boomed around the glass ceilinged atrium causing four heads to peer over the first floor railings, then disappear quickly as though fearful of reprisals at being caught idling by the boss.

Jonny filled rooms with both his sheer size as well as his huge often over-bearing personality. Having turned forty last August, an occasion heralded throughout the land with an extremely enjoyable, but outrageously expensive party on the lawns of his back garden, his once powerful frame was now starting to show signs of running to fat. His belt and collar both struggled manfully to hold back the tide of good living and a sedentary occupation; but his sporting days were now well and truly consigned to history. A wealth of amusing anecdotes, one for every occasion, kept the memory alive and somewhere in the bowels of his house, a number of sealed boxes held an array of cricket, rugby, tennis and sailing trophies, medals and other sporting memorabilia.

Hunching my shoulders in preparation for the subsequent slap on the back, which could remove false teeth from the uninitiated, I then used the created momentum to propel myself through the door of my office and to my desk before further physical damage could be inflicted.

"Grab a seat Jonny and we can have a chat, unless you've got anything else on now?" I laughed inwardly, noticing that Jonny had already made himself quite at home in one of the comfortable sofas I used for informal meetings. He waved nonchalantly and was straight on the phone to Selina, our fiery, redheaded, but inordinately efficient personal administrator, to order coffee and a plate of his favourite chocolate biscuits.

Whilst waiting for the coffee to arrive I quickly sorted through the pile of post stacked neatly in the middle of my desk. All had been opened and Selina's fine handwriting filled the top right corner of each letter, advising on action taken or decisions required. I am sure we would have been quite lost without our Selina. Her hard work, running our defence against the boring, mundane administration of daily business life, so often unseen and subsequently unrewarded, allowed Jonny and myself to fill our time with the fun, creative work that had driven us to the business in the first place.

"Good morning Mr Meredith," Selina said briskly, despositing a tray with two cups of coffee and the habitual plate of biscuits on the low table in front of us.

Despite having worked for me for the past three years, I was never quite sure whether she actually liked me, or whether her business-like tone was just an extension to her efficient and professional manner.

"Good morning, Selina," I replied. "Jonny and I are going to be in a meeting for the next hour, so if you can ensure we're not disturbed I would be most grateful."

"Of course, Mr Meredith." A flick of her ponytail suggested I was stating the obvious and that a squadron of tanks would have to run over her body before being allowed to disturb us.

"Once we're finished, I need an hour or so of your time and then if he's available I'd like a half hour teleconference with David Locksmith at Frinton's, for say about one o'clockish?"

Jonny raised a quizzical eyebrow at the mention of the teleconference, but I ignored the gesture; explanations would come shortly.

"Of course Mr Meredith, I'll get on to it straight away." A quick darting glance at Jonny, and unless my eyes deceived me, the briefest of smiles, then she left, quietly closing the door behind her.

A couple of weeks previously, whilst hiding in one of the cubicles in the men's toilet, trying to clear my head of the white noise that was preventing me from any conscious or sustained thinking, I had overheard two of my office juniors debating the new office rumour that Jonny and Selina were, in their terms, having it away.

That briefest of conspiratorial smiles that had passed between them more than suggested recent developments in their manager-staff relationship and for a moment I was angry at them both for this breech of professional conduct and somehow a betrayal of my trust. It was irrational and, what's more, I knew it and my anger dissipated as quickly as it had flared. They were both mature adults, single and otherwise carefree. Jonny had been married, but had divorced his wife Helen ten years ago and they had had no children.

Good for them, it's none of my bloody business, I thought to myself as the recollection of my meeting with Jo earlier that morning flitted into my conscious mind.

The crunch of a biscuit brought me back to my surroundings and a quick glance at the plate suggested that Jonny did not see our friendship extended to an equal share of the chocolate biscuits.

I had underestimated the time we would need as we spent the first hour discussing the general state of the business, accounts on the books, and a quick flick through the financial figures. Thanks to the Frinton contract it promised to be a very good year for us and for the first time since founding the company we even enjoyed the luxury of muting the concept of a potential staff bonus at the end of our financial year, the following April.

It was an enjoyable meeting, both of us comfortable and relaxed in each other's company, as had always been the case since we had sat next to one another at a business networking dinner some eight years previously. At that time, though, I had very much felt overawed by this loud, over-friendly but extremely amusing older man. With his powerful physique still at its peak, he carried himself with natural confidence and his ability to turn his charm on and off at will was wondrous to behold—especially to one such as myself, still finding his place in life.

"Right, now the bullshit's out of the way, what did you really want to talk about?" Jonny cut to the chase.

"Never was any good at hiding anything from you." I threw my pen on the blank pad in front of me and sat back in my chair as if in a juvenile sulk.

"No, you're not cut out for it. Too bloody nice. It's that effin' public school hoity-toity upbringing. That's why we work so well together. You're too honest for your own bloody good and that's where I earn my money; making sure you don't get stiffed. Good cop, bad cop." We laughed easily at the humour, though had both recognised long ago that there was more than a degree of truth in the matter.

"Okay, okay." I surrendered as Jonny sat forward to give me his undivided attention, causing an avalanche of biscuit crumbs to slide down his blue and white striped shirt and free-fall into the carpet around his feet.

"Things haven't been going too well at home recently, well, since Laura's death really," I started, noticing the pain crease Jonny's features at the mention of her name. From the moment I had introduced him to Laura they had hit it off. She had given him no leeway with his charm or schoolboy cheek and he had placed her on a pedestal and worshipped the ground she walked upon. And when the time came both Laura and I agreed that Jonny would be a perfect Godfather to Tom. It was a role he filled admirably though not always to our own liking, buying him trumpets and drums, his first penknife when Tom was only four and taking him to watch his first football match which secured him hero status in Tom's youthful eyes. Jonny became an extended part of our family and I know he felt her death keenly.

"I'm sorry to hear that, Meredith." His large beetle brows came together in sympathy.

"Well, to cut the story short, I need to take some time off, to be with the boys and as a result I've decided to take the summer holidays off—call it a sabbatical if you like."

"Shit Meredith, I don't know what to say." He was clearly caught between our personal friendship and shared sense of tragic loss, but his no-bullshit, take no prisoners attitude towards the protection of the business and his personal interests ran deep. "You know how sorry I was about Laura, it was a shitty thing to happen and I know you've been to some pretty dark places in your head over the past few months. But holy crap, I mean we've just hit the motherload and the chance we've pissed blood for years to get this company onto a healthy footing—and now you want to bail out on us." Stunned, he shook his bear-like head.

I kept silent. Experience over the years told me to let him rant, wave his arms in the air, smash a few things—he'd come round in the end.

"I mean, you know I love you like a brother, for Christ's sake, but how do the rest of us keep it going with you off on a beach somewhere when we need all hands on deck?"

Now we were getting through to solution mode and time to add my tuppence worth. "Well, I've thought about that."

"Should bloody well hope so," he muttered but allowed me to continue.

"You remember Simon Ponsonby?"

"Yeah. Bent as a five bob note if I remember rightly. No doubt got more than most out of his bleedin' public school education. Wouldn't have lasted five minutes in my old school I can tell you," he growled. "The bugger did some work for us a while back on that family run hotel out near Stansted; didn't cock it up—at least we got paid for it."

Praise indeed, I thought to myself, though the battle was far from won.

"That's him. I gave him a call a couple of days ago. He's free and willing to come on board and cover for me for the two months whilst I'm off. We know his work, he knows how things work here, we can trust him. He's been around the block and you know you can rely on him to do a first rate job for us. I think he'd be a good stand-in."

"But he's a self employed contractor, he'll cost an effin' fortune, we can kiss a chunk of that staff bonus goodbye and you can kiss my arse if you think I'm happy about that." His ham fists banged down on the table in frustration, sending a cup spinning to the floor.

"No, he won't and though you're one of my closest friends, I've no intention of kissing your hairy, flatulent arse. He's not got anything on at the moment and I bent him round to agreeing that he'd rather have something trickling in than sweet F.A."

Jonny didn't do praise. Keeping your job was praise enough in his books; but the softening of his tone when I gave him the figures I had tentatively agreed with Simon implied that he would have been hard pushed to have done better himself.

"Of course, I also won't be drawing my salary either," I added my last card in the hand.

"Should bloody well think not, you'd have been taking the piss if you had." Jonny scowled, but the fire had gone out of his voice.

Jonny still wasn't ecstatic about the idea, but I'd dragged him back off the ceiling and grudgingly he admitted it wasn't a bad solution, as long as Simon kept his hands to himself.

He held the door open for Selina to come in, then left, his parting shot still ringing in my ears: "Don't you effin' well dare send me any 'I'm having a great time on this beach' bastard postcards, or I'll shove them up your arse when you get back."

I laughed, then noticing Selina's gaze and disapproving look, I sheepishly retrieved the fallen coffee cup and unsuccessfully tried to remove the small dark stain in the carpet with some spit and my handkerchief. Then it was back to business.

I picked the boys up on the way home, refusing to be drawn on my plans until supper time, I left them to get on with their homework whilst I prepared the food.

"Right then, boys, I promised I'd tell you what's going on, but I also warn you that I'm going to need your help and input on this as well, okay?" I smiled at each of them in turn, noticing their interest turn to concern at the mention of my need for their help.

"Okay," they both agreed, though not without hiding the reservation in their voices.

"Good. Now if I recall correctly the summer holidays are fast approaching, unless you wish to remain at school for the duration?" I attempted a feeble joke and it got the response it deserved.

"Yeah, very funny dad," Tom shook his head sadly.

"Yeah, come on, what's going on?" Freddie demanded, impatient as ever.

"Well, I've realised that we've not spent much time together since, since..., well, for some time now, and with my work keeping on getting in the way, I know it's not been fair on you. I've not taken you places and done things that we should have done."

No comment back, no interruption from the boys. I was stating the obvious, though looking at Freddie I could see he was holding his breath, waiting for the bombshell, Dad's great idea, the catch that would ruin their summer holidays.

"I've been talking to Uncle Jonny today and it's now all agreed. I'm going to take the whole summer off, so we can spend time together and I can do all that stuff with you. How about that?" I must admit I had expected a response of some kind, even if it was a "That's great dad, now can I have some ice cream?" But I hadn't expected silence.

"Now this is where I need your help," I continued, refusing to be phased by the lack of interest or warmth I was generating so far. "What are we going to do and where are we going to go? The only stipulation is that we go away from here, get out of London. We don't have to be away for the whole time. But I want us to get away for at least some of it." I could have bitten my own tongue off as the image of Jo slipped into my mind and the thought of what I was going to be missing. Still, this was for a noble cause.

"I don't want to go away," Freddie reacted. "We'll miss the summer with our friends and Guy, and Dominic said we could go over and stay with them." A crash and we hadn't even got off the ground.

"And they've just built a really cool tree house in the garden which they said we could play in," Tom chimed in his protest.

"And I've got to do my school project," Freddie rejoined the fray.

"We don't have to go away for all of the holiday, just for a bit, a couple of weeks. We could go to the South of France, Italy or Spain?" I fumbled to recover.

"Have you forgotten I get heat rash, besides which it'd be boring; there's nothing to do there." Freddie gave the youth perspective on Europe's current attractions.

"They don't play cricket there either." Tom's one-track mind put a nail in the coffin of a European trip.

"What about New Zealand? We could go and see Grandma and Grandpa? And they're rugby mad out there," I added for Tom's benefit.

"Yeah, but I don't want to miss the cricket season." A stubborn chin with tightly pursed lips, so like his mother.

"And I get airsick." Freddie's turn to close another option down.

"Okay, so we stay in Britain. Good, now we're getting somewhere," I added, trying to persuade myself, never mind the boys, and that this was progress. "Now Tom, you want to watch some cricket; Freddie, you want to do your project; what else do you want to do?"

"Stay here and see our friends."

"Play."

"Watch TV, go to the cinema."

"Stay up as late as we want."

"Go on the Internet."

"Stay with Guy and Dominic."

"Okay." I held my hands to quieten their sudden enthusiasm. "All of that we can and will do when we get back. What I want to do is figure out where we're going to go and what we do when we get there. Now shall I throw some ideas into the pot?"

"If you want." Shoulders were shrugged and interest waned once more.

"We could go to Somerset, or Devon, somewhere in the West Country. We could rent a cottage, take our bicycles and find some trails, go off bicycling for the whole day, take a picnic. We could go and watch a game of county cricket, live at the grounds. Go to the coast, swim, learn to surf. Freddie, we could even do a project together on smuggling. You've just finished reading Moonfleet. Cornwall, Dorset, they're full of history on smuggling—it would be really interesting." I was on a roll and could see that I had tickled Tom with the idea of cricket and lots of outdoors activity.

"But I'm going to do my project on the American Indians. I've already done lots of research on the Internet. Remember I told you before, ages ago." Freddie remained stuck to his guns, the attraction of home and all its comforts a strong magnet.

"Then we should buy a tent and make a camp and cook things on a real fire; then we could be just like the Indians—that'd be really cool," Tom said, excited at the idea that had sprung to mind.

"Yeuch, sleeping outside being bitten by mosquitoes, burnt food, no loo and no TV. That's just stupid, Tom," Freddie shot back, scornful of his younger brother and angry that their union had been breached.

My own immediate reaction had been to agree with Freddie for a change. I was too old to be a Boy Scout sleeping in tents, on uncomfortable beds, more often than not in the pouring rain where everything gets wet and nothing ever dries.

But the more I thought about the idea, being brought together in a close environment, sharing in excitement and adventure, fresh air, being at one with nature and to end the day with a good old sing song around the campfire, the more I liked it.

With Tom now on my side it took us another five minutes to batter down Freddie's defences and get him on board and included a solemn promise that we would return at the end of a fortnight. This was greatly enhanced by agreeing to let him find us the tent, and knowing Freddie it would not be your normal outdoor camping shop special; but it was a cheap price to pay for his interest in getting behind the idea.

A pen and paper were gathered from a drawer in the family room and a list of items required started whilst the boys' interest still held strong. Much to their displeasure, leading to threats of further mutiny, I had to draw the line at a portable TV and DVD player, though the list still ran into a second page at the end of our first attempt. And where our knowledge and experience of camping failed us, enthusiasm and a bookcase filled with boys' adventure stories more than made up for this cavernous hole. We all agreed however that it would be worth an outing to the nearest outdoor camping store that coming Saturday, to seek their advice.

"But where are we going to go? We're not going to one of those awful holiday parks, I want to be out in the wild, in the middle of nowhere," Freddie, logical as ever, reminded us of a further part of our grand design that needed investigation and a satisfactory solution.

"Leave that one to me. I've an idea that Uncle Philip may be able to solve that one for us." An idea had sprung to mind. "I'll give him a call later."

My call as ever went through to Philip's voicemail. Nowadays, when he wasn't busy making money, he was busy living life, in the present and to the full. I'm sure he had taken up the mantle of the fighter pilot lifestyle, living each moment to the utmost, sucking the very marrow from the bone of life. To those who didn't know him well, or were self-righteously unforgiving about social etiquette and boundaries, he could be seen as a selfish, thoughtless hellraiser, bent on self-destruction. It may take him a few days to get back to me, but call he would. One just needed to be patient and understanding of his lifestyle.

A noise brought me back from wherever my dreams had taken me. The telephone was ringing beside my bed. It was two o'clock in the morning. It could only be one person.

"Philip."

"How are you old boy?" he was shouting into the mouthpiece, threatening to be drowned out by deafening background noise.

"You'll have to speak up, I can hardly hear you, Philip!" I shouted back, for some unknown reason sticking a finger in my other ear.

"Taking...clients...on the town... night-club." Was all I could make out.

"How are you, Philip?" I ran my tongue around the inside of my mouth and teeth to try to create some moisture and dampen the tickle that was about to turn into an uncontrollable hacking cough.

"Yup, Great, fantastic, you?" his clipped tones hollered down the line.

"Yup, fine thanks, boys send their love."

"As the senior Godfather to Freddie, I deem it my duty to bring him to this place for his eighteenth. I have also taken it upon myself to ensure that he becomes well acquainted with the ways of the wonderful fairer sex. My God, Meredith, you should see this place! I thought I'd seen it all before, but oh my God, there's this blonde up on stage…"

"Philip," I cut in, "I'm taking the boys camping this summer and I wondered whether we may be able to stay in the grounds of your ancestral pile? It would only be for a couple of weeks."

"No problem, old boy. Place is so big, they wouldn't even know you're there. Tell you what, though, I'll give the old General a call, then call you straight back. Bye."

"Wait a moment, Philip!" I yelled back down the phone. "Not now—do it tomorrow."

"Carpe diem and all that old boy. Seize the day." He laughed.

"Philip, it's two o'clock in the morning." I eyed the digital numbers flashing away on the bedside table through heavy lids.

"Not to worry, the General will be on guard duty, manning the battlements, defending the realm. Speak to you later."

"I was thinking more about me," I spoke down the now dead line.

How the hell did he manage to survive off a couple of hours sleep, day in day out? I was now fully awake so decided to go downstairs, get a drink and await the return call from Philip.

Only bothering to turn on the lights once I reached the family room, I went on through to the kitchen and in the warm glow of the fridge light I poured myself a glass of milk and retired to the comfort of a sofa. Picking up the remote, I flicked on the TV and waded through multiple channels of mindless drivel and promptly turned it off again, wondering why I bothered to pay for a TV licence.

I reached out an arm to give the radio a chance to captivate my attention and as I did so, the neck of a long forgotten and neglected friend caught my eye.

"God I haven't played that in years." I stared fondly at my old guitar, perched up on top of a cupboard, placed there a good many years before to keep out of the reach of curious, sticky fingered little children. It was only a basic classical six string, bought for twenty pounds many years ago, but it had sentimental value.

Hell, how things had changed over the years. Twenty pounds had been a small fortune to a poor student and if it hadn't been for Philip's generosity, I probably wouldn't have eaten for a fortnight when I had bought her.

"I wonder?" And pulling the once much loved instrument down I turned it over in my hands, recalling the now familiar marks and nicks in the main body and the numerous cigarette burns in the headstock, where, back in my student days I had jammed cigarettes between the nut and strings.

"She gets everywhere," I laughed in wonder, realising that there was no dust on the guitar and that Joan Fry really was one in a million.

A quick tune, then settling into one of the chairs in the kitchen, the furthest room in the house from the boys' bedrooms, I worked my way through the chords.

"Bloody hell," I swore as fingers refused to do as asked.

"Bugger." A spasm of cramp gripped my right hand.

My love-hate relationship with music had been rekindled.

"Dad, I've found our tent," Freddie announced triumphantly at breakfast the following morning. "It's brilliant and there'll be room for all of us and all our things."

The Internet had struck gold and before we were allowed to head for school, Tom and I were willingly dragged up to Freddie's room to peer over his shoulders as he competently worked his way through search engines and web pages.

"There you go." He sat back proudly as a series of pictures of a tent, taken from various internal and external angles, downloaded.

"What the hell have you got there?" I blurted out, peering closely as he scrolled down pausing only briefly at each of the various pictures.

"It's called a Yurt."

"A what?" Tom laughed.

"A YURT." Freddie repeated each letter slowly. "It means dwelling place and they were originally used by the nomads in Central Asia—places like Mongolia and Kazakhstan."

"It looks like a cake with a door," Tom scoffed, unimpressed.

"I must admit Freddie, it's not quite what I was imagining and. bloody hell, look how much they cost! Look where the dot is." I balked at the list of prices.

"You said I could choose our tent and that's the one I want. Look at the inside—we can have a real fire and everything."

I must admit that as far as tents went it was very pretty and my architectural eye noted with pleasure the smooth, simple lines and use of space. It was of course completely excessive for what was going to be a two-week camping trip, which was unlikely to ever be repeated, but there was also something romantic about the white canvas and poles that pulled at the heartstrings. And, a promise was a promise and the tent wasn't even in the same league as the price of three tickets to New Zealand that I would have happily paid for without a qualm.

With some difficulty due to sore and stiff fingers, penance for having neglected the guitar for so long, I jotted down details to peruse the site later in greater detail, and then with thoughts turning to the delectable Jo, I impatiently hustled the boys back down the stairs and out into the car.

Chapter Four

"**R**ight, boys, next stop the Douglas Estate!" I shouted cheerily over my shoulder, as the beast's two and a half litre, turbo charged diesel engine kicked into life.

"Are we there yet?" Freddie's bored voice cheekily came back, eyes glued to the handheld computer game in his lap.

"Very funny, Freddie," I joined in with the sniggering laughter from the back. "Now, both of you wave to Mrs Fry."

"See you in two weeks!" I called to Joan Fry who was waving frantically from the top of the house steps, a handkerchief clenched tightly in her hand lest the emotion of the moment became too much. "You've got my mobile number if you need to reach me."

For once I was glad that the boys were engrossed in their electronic toys; for it was with a sense of mixed emotions that I threaded the Landrover through the busy streets to join the main exodus of traffic leaving London for the West. On the one hand euphoria—that sense of light-headedness and jubilation resulting from the release and subsequent freedom from the shackles of work and daily mundane machinations; but balancing those scales, a sense of loss. Over the past two months, like a couple of junkies, Jo and I had unwittingly become totally dependent upon one another. Every parting a soul-shattering wrench and every meeting a whirlwind of love, attention and emotion unleashed. We had stumbled across an adrenaline filled rollercoaster ride, we had screamed, shouted and with no rhyme nor reason we had laughed throughout, like lunatics and clung on to each other at every twisting turn. But every ride comes to an end and with it comes the bitter sense of deflation and disappointment. Hearts had raced and thumped in our chests, pumping hot, passionate blood throughout revitalised bodies letting us know we were alive and thriving in our new, self-made world.

The school term had ended the previous Wednesday and wild-eyed children swarmed through the school playground like locusts hungry for the fields of plenty. Jo and I had been standing next to each other, not talking, just happy to be in one another's shadow, recognising that the sands of time had almost run their course. The temptation to reach out and entwine my fingers in hers, to touch her smiling lips with my own, was almost unbearable. Then she was swept away by the rampaging froth of blue and grey. Helpless, she turned to give one last look over her shoulder, a brave smile with damp eyes; and then resigned to the inevitable, she turned and was gone.

It was a warm sunny morning in mid-July when we set out on our adventure, our exploration into the unknown; to find ourselves and a beacon that would light our way forward for the future.

For three hours the landrover slowly groaned its way down the motorways, the boot crammed to the ceiling with what were considered the basic essentials for our foray. Upon its roof the wind whistled over, through and underneath Freddie's pride and joy, causing knots in my stomach at every noise and creak and my eyes to peer in the rear view mirror, expecting to see an expensive white tent fly down the motorway behind us.

At last with a sigh of relief from the Landrover and all its occupants we turned off the main road, through a set of large, ornate wrought iron gates, and onto a narrow private drive leading to Woodholme Park, the Douglas family home.

A long tarmac drive lined on either side by towering beach trees and recently painted fencing with open parkland beyond filled our view. So used to the claustrophobic limitations of London streets and buildings hemming in the sky, it was an impressive sight.

"Cool!" Freddie shouted excitedly. "Look—deer, loads of them."

I stopped the Landrover. He was pointing at a small copse no more than three hundred yards away.

"Where? I can't see anything." My voice sounded unnaturally loud without the background noise of the diesel engine filling our ears.

"There. Hiding under the overhanging branches and in amongst the trees. Look, there's hundreds of them."

Raising a hand to shield my eyes I peered intently at the wooded area but still could see nothing. Suddenly a flick of movement, a change in the shadow formation and the scene became clear and focused. Beautifully camouflaged amongst the trees, nonchalantly watching us with calm intelligent eyes was a herd of some fifty deer.

"And there's a white one," Tom whispered in awe of its beautiful poise and almost magical aura as it stepped out of the shade, oblivious and uncaring of our presence.

"That must be the head stag: look at those antlers, they're massive!" Freddie unhooked his safety belt and stuck his head and shoulders out of the window for a better view.

"Wouldn't want to be chased by him." My voice was almost a whisper, caught up in the magic of the land we had just entered.

Still moved by such majesty and grace, but equally desirous to get to camp and put to bed my nagging fear of erecting the Yurt for the first time, I restarted the engine and continued down the drive. A few minutes later we rounded a corner and there, set with its back protected by a wooded hill, leaving its front aspect to look down over a valley of lush, rolling meadow, protected on either side by thick forest, lay, as Philip so irreverently called it, the ancestral pile.

"Wow," Tom whistled between his teeth.

"Wow exactly, Tom." The clever use of landscape, the winding drive, all led to the climax of a discovery, a hidden treasure, building the expectation and leaving the best to last.

I pulled up in front of the house and by the time we had climbed down from the Landrover, an elderly figure clad in a worn tweed suit had already opened the heavy front door and with the aide of a stout walking stick, was gingerly descending the worn stone steps to greet us.

"Hello, hello, you must be the family Meredith. How do you do? I'm Alan Douglas, Philip's longsuffering father." General Sir Alan Douglas shook hands with a surprisingly firm grip. "Not related to old Ginger Meredith, are you? Spent a year in a prisoner of war camp with him in Korea. Scotsman, had a place up near Moray, I think it was. Yes, that's it, Moray, excellent fishing I recall."

"No, not related as far as I know, General." And I introduced the two boys and myself.

"Well, don't just stand there, come on in. Cook's prepared us some lunch—hope you're hungry." And with that he turned about as smartly as if on parade and disappeared back into the house.

"He's scary," Freddie whispered, hanging back to follow in my footsteps.

"I wonder if he's ever killed anyone? I bet he has. Lots of them, I expect." The eagerness and enthusiasm in Tom's voice showed up one of his less attractive traits and I reached out and gave the back of his collar a quick yank to stop him from rushing after the old General to interrogate him in more depth.

We followed the General into the dark, unlit hallway and down a long high ceilinged corridor to the dining room. Two original eighteenth-century sashed windows allowed the bright daylight to stream through, reflecting upon the long table that ran down the centre of the room. In the glare of the invasive daylight fine particles of dust danced in the musty air and away in a corner, hidden in the shadows, the loud tick of a grandfather clock matched our footsteps on the worn wooden floorboards. A large fireplace dominated at one end, above which an equally large painting of a fierce looking cavalry officer sat astride a black horse looking down at us with indifference. Upon closer inspection the picture, along with many others in the room was ingrained with years of soot that had dulled the life originally breathed into it by the long dead painter.

"It smells funny," Tom blurted out before I could stop him.

"I am sorry General, how very embarrassing." I glared at Tom. "Apologise immediately."

"No, no, he's quite right," the old man laughed sadly and patted Tom affectionately on the shoulder. "It's a big house, far too much for one old man and wretchedly expensive to heat. So I only use a couple of rooms downstairs, the drawing room and the library I have converted into my study. I had a small table put in there as well so I can take my meals in a degree of comfort and warmth and the rest of the rooms are kept shut up.

Cook rules with an iron rod in the kitchen of course." He waved to us to take a seat and sank heavily into a sadly split and sagging, cane panelled walnut armchair at the head of the table.

"Now when I was a young lad," he continued, lancing a large piece of ham from the plate of meats in front of us, then waving his knife around in the air encouraging us to help ourselves. "Same age as you two boys, every room was used. House parties every weekend, summer parties, hunt balls, servants running to and fro. It was like a small village living under one roof. And then there were the stables. Every box filled with some of the best hunters in the land. Spent hours down there; nothing like it for a young lad. Now of course it hasn't seen so much as a horse's fart for twenty years. The roof collapsed—must be fifteen years ago—and as I'm too bloody old to go gallivanting around the countryside like a young blade it just sits there rotting away. Bloody shame really."

"It's still a magnificent house. Has your family lived here long?" I enquired between mouthfuls.

The General's mane of silver white hair shook in the negative and his thin moustache, so elegant and in vogue during the heyday of Douglas Fairbanks and Errol Flynn, wriggled and undulated like an epileptic caterpillar under his nose as his jaws furiously worked at the ham.

"My great, great grandfather, that rather pompous looking chap up there..." He pointed to the picture above the fireplace, "did rather well out in India, made a fortune, came home and bought the place. Must have been eighteen thirty, forty, well thereabouts, so about hundred and sixty years or so. Not long in comparison with some of these family estates that have been there for centuries, trace themselves back to the Doomsday Book, what."

The boys were clearly impressed and looked about them with a renewed sense of awe and respect.

"From the outside the house seems to be all original; no new wings added in more recent times?" I asked with professional curiosity. I had always thought that the late eighteenth century taste for Italianate country houses produced stunningly attractive, architecturally pure buildings. Clean lines, symmetrically sympathetic and always imposing upon a location, where any lesser building would have been dominated by the landscape. The wretched Victorians had a vile habit of remodelling, adding wings and extensions, vulgarising and demolishing the original balance of the building.

"No, all original, some odd buildings around the back of the house though." A small chunk of semi-chewed new potato escaped and settled on his lower lip and remained unnoticed until transferred to the lip of his wine glass, whereupon he ran his little finger around the rim and put it back into his mouth.

"No prisoners what!" he chortled and winked at Tom who had evidently developed a bad case of hero worship and with his mouth agape had been hanging off the General's every word, his food scarcely touched.

Noticing Freddie fix his gaze upon an arrangement of swords and spears, spread in a circle like a steel sun, their blades pointing to the core, the General pounced on a fresh topic. He was clearly relishing the opportunity to talk, and especially to such attentive listeners.

"Ah, you like that, do you? Did it myself. Kept tripping over the bloody things, all over the damned house."

Freddie nodded. "I do fencing at school."

"You do, do you? Well, good for you." An eyebrow raised, the General was evidently pleasantly surprised and the family Meredith was raised in his estimations.

"Go and get one down, have a play."

"Gosh, really? Daddy, can I, please?"

Freddie looked quickly from the General to me for permission, his large brown eyes beseeching, his face flushed with excitement.

Before I could give my consent, the General had taken command.

"Course you can my boy. Move those plates over there and climb on the sideboard. You, too, if you want to." He smiled at Tom.

The next half an hour was spent with the General, eyes blazing, recounting the history of how each of the weapons came into the Douglas family possession. Freddie and Tom pulled down each of the blades in turn and, gripping with both hands due to the weight and a mad incoherent yell in their throats, they sliced and stabbed their way through regiments of an imaginary enemy.

Crimean, Zulu, Assaye, Boer, Afghan, Napoleonic, Quebec, Yorktown. Generation after generation of the Douglas family had heard the sound of the drum and faithfully and bravely served their monarch and country in all corners of the world.

"My favourite is the Assegai." Tom danced around the dining room table imitating the stabbing thrusts and foot stamping that the General's father had witnessed first hand and the General himself had brought to life so vividly.

"This is mine." Freddie waved a particularly wicked looking curved sword around his head.

"Do you know, young man, that's my favourite as well. It's called a Tulwar. It's an Indian sword, far better than our British swords. Cut a man's head off without so much as a shiver, then still as sharp and the blood still running down the blade it could cut a silk handkerchief in half."

Freddie gazed in fascination and awe at the magnificent sword, stroking the dish-shaped pommel and cruciform guard in reverence; his mind already transported to the heat and dust of battle.

"I think you've found yourself two admirers, General," I said to the General, who was now beaming widely as noise and laughter once more filled his home.

"Stuff and nonsense," he muttered, squaring his shoulders in defence of the preposterous, though the pleasure was written all over his lined and dignified face.

"It was very kind of you to let us camp on the estate. Is there anywhere in particular you'd like us to pitch?" I noticed that the grandfather clock was about to strike two o'clock and I wanted us to be set up and ready for our first night, well before darkness found us wanting.

"Feel free to camp anywhere. Just about everything you can see from the house belongs to us, so help yourself." There was no boast in his voice, just a generous honesty to extend his hospitality and desire to bring some life back onto the land.

Thanking him for his hospitality and accepting his offer of baths and dinner the following week, I marched two protesting boys back to the Landrover, leaving the General in the hallway, muttering about rifles. I picked out a faint track overgrown with thick clumps of tall grass, that was heading in the general direction of the valley we had seen through the dining room window and decided it was as good a place to try as any. The rough track had been carved out of the hard ground by heavy vehicles over many years and with nature's resilience reclaiming large tracts, forcing the Landrover to pitch and yaw like a ship in high seas as we made our way slowly down the valley. With my eyes glued to the track ahead, Freddie and Tom had the task of scouring the landscape for a suitable place we could pitch our tent and call home for the next fortnight.

Half an hour later we had found our site. Even to an outdoor novice the site was perfectly situated. A hundred yards from the chosen spot, a small river undulated through the open field, disappearing into a small copse, ideal for wood for the fire.

"Well done Freddie, eyes of a hawk!" I called out as I pulled on the brake and switched off the engine.

Silence welcomed us. And if it had not been for the sound of tree tops caressing one another in the gentle breeze, grasshoppers sending out their warnings and the occasional shrill scream from a pheasant safely ensconced deep within the copse, I could have sworn that I had lost my hearing. An eerie sensation to city folk used to the hubbub and noise from inconsequential man in a city that never sleeps.

Doors behind me opened and were slammed again.

"Right, let's get this Yurt of ours erected, then we can unpack and make this a proper camp. Who's going to help me get it off the roof? Boys…? Boys...?"

They had already disappeared into the copse and though I could hear them hollering and whooping like Indians as they crashed through the trees, I was loathe to add my own voice to the noise that had suddenly erupted in this perfect location.

Despite the encouraging words from the Yurt company suggesting the self-supporting structure could easily be set up within an hour by one man, it was some two hours later by the time I finished struggling and swearing manfully with hazel, canvas and groundsheet. Standing back to admire the fruit of my labours, it was, I had to admit, an ingeniously clever construction—rigid, aerodynamic, watertight and adaptable to the changing seasons. I figured that if the Yurt had not been invented a thousand years ago, a modern architect could make a decent name for themselves today by designing such a practical, portable home of equal beauty.

Oh, and the joy to step beyond the sweet chestnut wooden doorframe and split screen door! Light airy, spacious. The golden texture and different shapes and lines of the natural wood set against the white canvas background. The blended and heady smells of canvas—natural wood and jute. Spacious, elegant, practical and romantic, the perfect home for the three of us to mend and heal.

Half an hour later and this time with the boys' assistance, we unpacked the contents of the Landrover. Camp beds were put together, sleeping bags unrolled and after a brief tussle with the instructions, a brand new gas cooker was removed from its box, hooked up to its bottle and a kettle was successfully on the boil.

"Well boys, what do you think? Our home for the next two weeks." With my hands draped fondly across their shoulders, I was finally starting to relax and look forward to the next two weeks.

"Cool dad, it's just as I imagined it would be. Now we're just missing a campfire and then it will be perfect." Freddie still wore his naturally serious look upon his face, but it was a positive start for someone who never wanted to come in the first place.

"Let's go and get some wood!" Tom yelled and promptly dragged Freddie off to gather a suitable stock for the evening.

Our first dinner however was not a great success. The sausages burst apart and stuck to the bottom of the frying pan, and whilst I was trying to salvage what I could, the peas boiled dry and also burnt themselves to the bottom of the saucepan.

Instead the boys opted for some bread that they stuck on the end of sticks and cooked over the campfire. Burnt, black and with a heavy taste of charcoal, they stuck the remnants of the sausages between the folded toast and thereafter swore it was the best meal they had ever had. Before joining the boys outside, I made myself a strong cup of coffee and with a flick of the wrist laced it with a healthy dose of scotch, smacked my lips together in appreciation and went out into the warm night air. Having part rolled and part dragged a large log out of the copse, the boys were still sitting beside the roaring fire, watching the swallows sweeping and diving through the half-light for their own evening meals. Drawn to the mesmerising light of the fiercely glowing embers, the insect nightlife was providing the swallows with a sumptuous feast and for us a spectacular aerial display.

As we sat outside our new home, our eyes turned to the heavens and we discovered that nature had provided us with one further unexpected joy—to watch a blood red sun slide slowly over the horizon without us so much as having to leave our grassy doorstep. I couldn't even remember the last time I had even seen the sun go down. Hell, the only time we sat outside after seven o'clock was when we used to lay on the occasional summer drinks party, or the famous annual Meredith barbecue with friends and family. Thinking about it, that was the most likely source of the boys' penchant for the taste of charcoal and burnt food.

"You know what they say? Red sky at night, shepherd's delight. It's going to be a beautiful day tomorrow," I promised like some wise sage who had spent his life studying the weather.

"Yeah, right dad," Freddie replied sleepily. "It'll probably rain now."

"Come on, let's test those beds out before you fall off your perch." I got to my feet, shivering as the evening breeze and with it the damp air that had unknowingly permeated our clothes chilled through to the bone.

"Very funny dad." Tom's equally sleepy voice came out of the darkness, but neither of the boys had the energy to protest and they went willingly to their beds.

Before following them inside, I turned once more to the setting sun and, like the deer we had seen that morning, I lifted my nose into the breeze and breathed in the scent, the very essence of nature. Clean and honest, and carried on the air the comforting smell of damp mother earth.

"Today, life was good."

The following morning I was not so sure. I was convinced that even taking my student days into account, I had never spent such an uncomfortable night in my life. My back ached, a stiff neck and an excruciating pain stabbing in my hips which a hypochondriac would have sworn was the onset of crippling arthritis had kept me from a fitful night's sleep. Added to that the sound of a fox screeching and the occasional hoot of an owl set my ears on edge and my heart thumping. Oh for the familiar disturbances of city life and the joy of modern double-glazing that protected you from the sounds of the outside world!

Much to my annoyance the boys had slept the sleep of the innocent and had awoken as the sun had touched the canvas walls of the Yurt. Nature's alarm clock showed no respect for decent folk and had gently prised their eyelids open at five-thirty. Shortly afterwards they had got up, dressed and rushed out to play, shouting and yelling and then after five minutes all was quiet again.

Firstly I had wanted to shout at them to shut up, but knew that the effort of shouting would have fully woken me up, making it impossible to drift back to sleep, no matter how lightly. This inability to get back to sleep was further aggravated by their continued shouting and me continuing to promise myself that if they yelled just once more, I would give them what for. The words charged around my mind, building up pressure as they begged to be let out, lest I explode. Then all went quiet, save for the enthusiastic singing from birds as they greeted the new day and my pulse was on its way back down when I started to panic about what the boys were doing, to cause them to be silent. It usually spelt trouble and this final straw forced me to unzip my twisted body and stagger out of the sleeping bag.

Keeping the short-term goal of that first cup of coffee firmly in my mind, to stop my body from collapsing in protest, I ran through a few basic stretching exercises to help warm and nurse the muscles to life. Better, though still feeling sore and extremely sorry for myself, I was at least then able to stagger the few yards to the cooker, then over to where we had stacked our bags to slip into jeans and a T-shirt.

Fortunately I had just taken my first sip when the door of the Yurt burst open and the boys charged in.

"I'm hungry, what's for breakfast?" Tom threw himself onto his camp bed and much to this own amusement tipped it straight over and jammed himself up against the canvas wall.

"Idiot." Freddie shouted at him, ignoring Tom's hand waving helplessly over the green canvas of the camp bed. "My trainers are soaked and so are the bottom of my jeans. And my feet are freezing" He moaned, sinking into one of the chairs to remove the offending articles.

"Tom, once you've finished mucking about, perhaps you can lay the table for breakfast. There's cereal in the box under the table with the plates and mugs and milk's in the coolbox next to it." It was a comical sight that on any other morning would have had me laughing as well, but after such a depressing night's sleep I was in no mood for high jinx or anyone else's self pity. "And Tom, stop being such a big girl's blouse. Take your trainers and socks off, jeans too and put them by the wood burner. Then put on a pair of shorts and go around barefoot and once you've had some breakfast you can both go and fetch some wood that we can put in this contraption." I pointed to the new wood-burning stove in the centre of the floor.

"Cool. Can I go barefoot as well?" Tom had managed to extricate himself and kicked off his sodden trainers to leave wet footprints on the groundsheet wherever he trod.

"But I don't want to go around without shoes on," Freddie whined nasally. "My feet will get all dirty and wet."

"Enough Freddie. I'm not getting into an argument over this. There's not a lot of choice in the matter. Either you can spend all day in the tent waiting for them to dry, or you can go barefoot."

"I'm going to go barefoot like Huckleberry Finn. Come on Freddie, don't be such a sissy," Tom baited his elder brother and threw his own socks onto the pile with his trainers.

"Shut up idiot, pea brain," Freddie warned, his pale face turning beetroot with suppressed anger and indignation.

"Get them off, Freddie." I kicked out in frustration at the stove standing in the centre of the Yurt and even before my foot connected I wished I hadn't been quite so hasty, as the wind between my toes reminded me that I too was shoeless.

Cursing and swearing, I hopped and hobbled around the wood burner, its grate seeming to smile at me through the reinforced glass. Tom took this as his queue to let loose his sense of humour.

"Look, Dad's an Indian." And he proceeded to dance around the stove, albeit at a safe distance behind me, whooping and yelling when his laughter would allow.

"Idiot," Freddie shouted at his brother again, but this time unable to restrain a smile and snort of laughter before tagging on to the end of the human chain behind his younger brother.

"That's it!" I yelled as soon as I could put any weight on my foot and like Captain Hook trying to catch the elusive and shadowy form of Peter Pan I lollopped after them. In the end, out of breath and with tears of pain and mirth blurring my view, I collapsed somewhat dramatically on the floor and was immediately mobbed by two wannabe Indians who set about trying to scalp me.

"Surrender, surrender, surrender!" the boys chanted, pinning me to the floor.

"Okay, I surrender." All strength was sapped by laughter.

With breakfast over, the argument long forgotten and trainers drying in front of the wood burner, the now barefoot boys spent the morning exploring down by the river. I sat peacefully outside the tent, legs stretched contentedly out in front of me, watching the sun burn off the hazy mist hanging in the valley and attempted to draw up a list of things we were going to need now we had settled in. With the boys out of sight I phoned Jo's mobile but after ringing briefly it went to her voicemail; to hear her warm, familiar voice brought a smile to my face, though I didn't leave a message. What could I say?

This time apart gave us the chance to make a clean break. Things should never have continued for as long as they had and now we had the opportunity to put things right and get back to how things used to be.

An hour or so later with clear blue skies overhead and a warm breeze tugging gently at my T-shirt I watched the boys making their way slowly back up the hill to camp.

"Oh no," I groaned. They were walking about twenty feet apart, Tom striding ahead, his natural inexhaustible energy showing in his every bound. Freddie lagged behind, walking slowly, his bare feet stepping cautiously on the ground; but with his arms stretched out like a scarecrow, there could only be one explanation.

"Freddie fell in the river," Tom laughed as soon as he was in earshot, throwing himself on the grass at my feet.

"No I didn't, you pushed me!" Freddie wailed, jumping on Tom, fists flailing.

"Dad, get him off me!" Tom was still laughing, though he had brought his arms up to cover his head from an accidental strike.

"Freddie, stop that. Get off him now!" I yelled, leaping to my feet and wary of flying fists, I scooped Freddie up in my arms and dragged him, still trying to lash out with his feet, away from his brother.

"Now calm down and tell me what the hell's this all about?"

His chest heaving with effort and trying desperately to hold back the tears he sobbed. "I was kneeling on the bank looking at a pond skater when peabrain came up behind me and pushed me into the water. I hate him."

"Freddie, now I know you don't hate him—and will you stop calling him peabrain."

"Well, he *is* a peabrain," he interjected.

"No, he's not, and how would you like it if people started to call you names?"

"I wouldn't care," Freddie pouted defiantly.

"Yes you would. Now go and take your wet things off—use some of the water to wash off all that mud, then put some dry clothes on. We're going to go shopping in a minute. Oh, and Freddie, it looks like you've got some duckweed or something green and slimy in your hair." I couldn't but help smile at the bedraggled sight before me.

"What about Tom, what are you going to do to him?" he shouted back at me, my smile only infuriating him further.

"I'm going to speak to him while you're getting changed, so don't you worry," I tried to placate him.

"I bet you won't. I know he's your favourite. You don't care about me, I might as well be dead." The dam of tears so bravely held back now started to flow uncontrollably.

"Hey, hey, where'd that come from? You know that's not true Freddie. I love you both, lots and lots, you know that." I soothed and hugged him to me. I held his shaking, wet body, seemingly so frail and defenceless until the tears subsided and I felt him regain his steady even breathing. Gently I tried to separate us, to look into his face and smile reassuringly at him, but his wiry arms held on tightly about my waist, refusing to budge.

"I want to go home, I hate it here," Freddie muttered into my T-shirt.

"No you don't. We've got your tent here, which I think is absolutely brilliant by the way. And I thought that when we go shopping, if we can find a bookshop you might like to pick up some books? You seemed pretty keen on the wars and things that the General was talking about yesterday. Would you like that?"

"Okay, whatever." The lure of books had brought him around and though it was a grudging acceptance, that was Freddie and off he went to get changed.

"Right." I turned to Tom who was now fully engrossed in stripping the bark from one of the logs they had stacked up for the fire. "You carry on like this and I'll have you spending the rest of the holiday chained up in the tent. You do not treat your brother like that. Now I want you to go and say you're sorry, get some shoes on, then get in the car—we're leaving in five minutes."

Like water off a duck's back, Tom smiled, shrugged his shoulders and skipped off into the tent.

To a Londoner, Monkhampton was a quaint, picture postcard, country market town. It was built around three main streets running in parallel, connected by a network of narrow, worn cobbled alleyways filled with coffeehouses and curiosity-cum tourist shops. Where animals and horse-drawn carts once filled these streets, they had now been blocked off at each end to traffic and pedestrianised and, despite the aggressive, pulsating and all-consuming pace of modern times, Monkhampton had retained its slow, ponderous lifestyle—a small blessing to the locals who to the increasing annoyance of myself would stop and chat wherever they pleased, forcing the rest of us to walk around them, immune to my stares of disbelief and incredulity.

We had inadvertently chosen to come into town on Market day, of all days. It had taken half an hour to find a space to park the Landrover and the streets were packed with people and that's where the comforting similarity with London ended. The streets of this old market town were filled with the noise of people talking, laughing and shouting out to greet friends. This was far from the hustle and bustle of London street life: heads down, avoiding eye contact, the street a means to get from A to B. Here the street was a place to gather to meet friends, perhaps do a little business and, as a bonus, buy your wares.

"Christ, they used to send people to relax and recuperate in the country! This pace of life would drive me up the wall," I thought to myself as we sidestepped another group of men in flat hats and checked shirts who had stopped to discuss things of no consequence, relevance or interest to me.

Nonetheless, we patiently threaded our way through the main streets picking up the necessary essentials, which included the purchase of an inflatable mattress, sheets and duvet. I was not going to suffer another night like that again.

We dropped our purchases back at the Landrover and had taken one of the narrow lanes, to bring us back on the main high street close to one of the major book retail stores we had spied earlier, when we found ourselves passing a small second-hand bookstore. We were not able to gain much of an impression of the shop by peering through the window, though a small bookshelf on the windowsill filled with rather tatty, well-thumbed novels that one usually sees outside a charity shop indicated this was not the sort of establishment we were seeking. With my eyes firmly ahead I walked past the entrance, but before I could stop him, Freddie had pushed open the door and, deep inside, a bell announced his presence.

"Bloody hell, Freddie," I mumbled somewhat selfishly to myself. Two things were going to now happen. Either it was going to be a complete waste of time and I was already irritated by the slow pace that had bored me to the core and I resented wasting anymore of the day; or Freddie was going to be in there for hours. At least in these modern retailers, their rather clinical set up to focus on punters buying and getting out kept time to a minimum, rather than these potential time traps that were suited to the avid reader. Come in and browse, the trap was set; the odd threadbare armchair discreetly placed to make it a more comfortable and relaxing experience. Not hovering over your shoulder, but engrossed in another part of the shop, an older man or woman would let you know where they were if you needed their assistance, or indeed if you wished to give someone your cash. These easygoing literary sirens always appeared to have little understanding of sales targets and a sales training course would be an anathema to them. And just when you had been lulled into a false sense of security the wolf burst forth from the belly of the sheep, for their passion for literature was only equalled by their desire to spend all day talking about all things books with a fellow booknut. It was kill with niceness and, worst of all, Freddie attracted this type of person like wasps around the sweetest jam.

He peered at the window, smiled and with the eyes of a religious zealot, who courtesy of a ball of hashish had gone in his head to a better place, beckoned us in; this was going to be painful.

The staff must have thought it was their lucky day as the bell rung for the second time in a minute as I pushed the door open and ushered Tom inside.

The powerful and unmistakable smell of leather and old books assailed the nostrils before I had even put one foot in to the room. Not an unpleasant odour and with the morning already warming up it was surprisingly cool inside. Books of every size and colour crammed the shelves from floor to ceiling, overflowing into neat rows along the Persian runner down the side of the longest wall in the room. Even the perfunctory worn armchair hidden in one corner had a stack of books in the seat, precariously balanced and only prevented from toppling by one of the stained wings.

A veritable honeytrap for the innocent bookworm. I needed to find Freddie quickly and rescue him, before his mind was completely taken over and my wallet subsequently emptied.

I found him sitting cross-legged on the floor, in the military history section, already absorbed in an old A4 sized book. The pages were turning slowly, so clearly Tom and I were now in trouble.

"Freddie, come on, let's go," I hissed. "We're going to the other shop, remember, and I can get a paper as well?"

"This shop is brilliant, dad!" Freddie beamed up at me. "I've already found one book and look, there's more upstairs as well."

"Great! Well, one's enough to be getting on with, so let's pay for this one and get going," I urged, trying to convey that a sense of urgency was required, but it fell on deaf ears.

"I just want a quick look around, dad. I won't be more than five minutes, I promise." And without waiting for an answer he had shot around my legs and disappeared down another row.

"Dad, I'm bored. Can we go yet?" Tom piped up from the doorway.

"Five minutes, Tom," I promised him. "Tell you what, why don't you come with me and we'll see if we can find a book on survival in the wild? You never know, it may come in handy."

Trawling the faded subject topics at the top of each row, we had just reached the S section when I heard a woman's voice.

"Oh shit," it moaned in frustration. "Shit, shit and more shit."

"Hello?" I called out uncertain as to the location of the voice, "Is everything okay, or can I help?"

Silence.

"Hello?" I peered down a couple of rows and eventually saw a woman, her back towards us, seated somewhat inelegantly upon the floor with books scattered all about her.

"Hello, can I help?" I tried again, advancing down the aisle.

"That's very kind, but I think I can manage," she replied in a warm friendly voice as she tried to get to her feet, an ankle length gypsy style skirt hampering her efforts. Finally on her feet, she turned to face me. "It's this bloody thing." She waved her left arm at me that was encased in plaster from wrist to just below the elbow. Its once pristine white shell was now a grubby brown, though one could see that writing and brightly coloured drawings filled almost every available inch of the surface. "Comes off in ten days, can't wait; it's been such a nuisance."

"I can imagine, I broke my right wrist as a teenager and typically guess what?"

"You're right handed!" she laughed easily.

"Sure am. Couldn't do anything myself. My mother had to help with getting dressed, doing up laces, cutting up my food. I recall bath time being particularly embarrassing for a spotty teenager." I recalled the distant memory, shaking my head.

"I've got the same problem but left handed, though fortunately I've been able to do most things on my own. The only thing I've not been able to do and don't imagine it was a problem for you, was to get a bra done up. I've had to wear these rather uncomfortable vest tops for weeks. Haven't dared try and run anywhere—give myself black eyes." She looked directly into my eyes and laughed again.

Red faced and lost for words, I wasn't sure where to look or what to do.

"I'm sorry," she said seriously though the laughter still danced in her eyes. "I've embarrassed you. Here, I am talking about personal things to a complete stranger. And I'm also sorry." She noticed Tom and gave him a little wave with her plastered hand. "For earlier, for swearing, I mean. It's not the sort of thing I usually do and I'm extremely embarrassed about it—please forgive me?"

I could have said many things about her, but embarrassed was not one of them.

She tugged at the baggy, white shirt that lapped over the top of her lovat green skirt, then pushed the long blonde hair away from her face to reveal clear, blue eyes and a pair of round glasses perched upon a small slightly upturned nose.

Composed, self assured, flirty, perhaps, but definitely not embarrassed.

"Don't worry about it, no apology necessary," I stuttered slightly.

"Now it's my turn to ask if I can help you?" she asked after a moment's silence.

"What, oh, yes please. Tom here's looking for a book on outdoor survival. My eldest is also around here somewhere, but he needs no assistance when it comes to books and suspect he will reappear with an armful of them pretty shortly." I was still flustered by our conversation and this was further complicated by my compulsion to want to stare at her chest.

"Are you here on holiday?" she inquired, beckoning us to follow her.

"We're camping," Tom said proudly.

"You've got some excellent weather for it. Which site are you staying at?"

"Actually, we're camping on the Woodholme Park estate," I replied.

"How wonderful! I mean, I've never been in there of course, but from the road it looks like a beautiful place." She stopped at an aisle, thought about it for a moment, then walked straight to a shelf marked Outdoor Pursuits.

"It is. Very peaceful and so quiet compared to London."

"We've got a great big tent and a real fire and everything!" Tom beamed up at her.

She patted his head fondly. "Then I'm not surprised you want a book on survival. You can learn all about knots, making shelters and all kinds of things."

She pulled a large soft-backed book from a lower shelf and smiling, handed it to Tom. "I think this is what you're looking for."

I then found myself an outsider to the conversation between her and Tom as they discussed the merits of the book. By accident or design she had cleverly picked out a book with plenty of pictures and drawings, which would keep a boy's attention, especially one with such a short span of attention and boredom threshold like Tom.

There was something about the way she spoke to him that I couldn't quite put my finger on. Not patronising or maternal, but encouraging, friendly, experienced and confident in gaining a child's trust. Tom who needing little encouragement warmed to her and was soon asking her about how she had broken her arm, did it hurt, did the doctors have to cut her open.

Crouched as she was beside Tom as they leafed through the pages, I tried to peer over their shoulders at the book so I could join in the conversation. Instead I found myself staring down this woman's cleavage, which after trying and failing to be a gentleman and overlook such distraction, I went in search of Freddie. It was definitely time to go.

"Thanks Dad." Freddie's tantrum was now but a distant memory as he swung his plastic bag containing his book on swords, another on American Indians, down the high street. "That's a really cool bookshop, it had everything. We'll have to go back again before we go home."

"Yeah," Tom agreed, surprisingly. "And the lady was very nice too. Did you know she broke her wrist when she was putting some books away and she fell off the ladder in her shop? She said you could hear the bone go snap!"

"Very nice, Tom," I muttered. "We'll have to see."

We stopped at a street café and had lunch in the sunshine, before heading back to the Landrover. Not wishing to go back past the bookshop again, I steered the boys down another side alley and found myself staring into the window of a music shop. A trumpet in pristine condition hung in the window, distorting the faces of people who stopped to peer inside.

Ten minutes later we stepped back out on to the cobbles. Freddie had persuaded me to buy him a penny whistle, Tom was clutching a set of second-hand bongo drums and myself a book of traditional and modern folk guitar music.

Back at the campsite, trousers and T-shirts were discarded for the freedom of shorts and suncream, and even though

Freddie's trainers had dried, he chose to go barefoot, albeit at a more cautious pace than Tom's full pelt.

With fingers crossed for no repeat of this morning as the boys disappeared back down to the river, I put the kettle on the cooker and settled down into my chair to enjoy the relaxing peace and quiet and soothing sensation of the warm breeze on my pasty body. It was not a pretty sight; office fever as we used to call it. Not just bags, but a matching set of suitcases hanging under the eyes and in turn a pot belly hanging over skinny legs; all a rather ghastly shade of white.

I didn't remember closing my eyes, but the next thing I knew the kettle's piercing whistle cut through the air. I made myself a cup of tea, grabbed both my guitar and my new purchase and returned to my chair.

Some time later the boys returned, both soaking from head to foot, but this time both grinning from ear to ear.

"Come on dad, come exploring with us." Putting the guitar down just in time, I was hauled unceremoniously to my feet and dragged a short way until my slow walking pace got the better of them and they ran ahead, stopping to turn back every so often to ensure I hadn't sloped back to the tent.

Down at the river, the boys had found a gentle slope down to the water.

"I bet you that this would be a natural place for animals to come down to drink," Freddie said thoughtfully. "If only we had some of those glasses that can see in the dark, we could come down here and watch."

"Well Freddie, as it doesn't get really dark until quite late, we could, if you wanted, come down about nine-ish, bring a blanket and plenty of mosquito repellent and see if we can see anything."

"Can we dad? That'd be really great! I bet we'd see badgers and foxes and everything." Freddie could hardly contain himself, jumping up and down in the river, his mind already far away from the worries of stubbing his toe or hurting his feet.

Like three intrepid explorers, we followed the winding, gently flowing water down through the valley, Freddie running here and there, stopping to stoop and look at something that had caught his eye before running on again. Tom running, walking, skipping with the occasional cartwheel thrown in for good measure. Simply happy to be active, unrestrained by boundaries, his only chains being the laws of gravity that prevented him from soaring through the blue skies and light white clouds above.

Having set out at my usual brisk London pace, I soon found my stride begin to falter and within half a mile it had become a slower, less strenuous amble. After all, what was the hurry? There was no end goal, no diary arrangement, no torrent of heaving, sweating people to fight through with loathing; there wasn't a destination, it was an application of time. Time to spend with the boys, time together to roll the dice and follow the consequences, away from the pressure, strains and distractions of our day-to-day existences.

The river turned as slowly as the age of time, its clear cool waters leading us through a small copse, where the air was permeated by the smell of wild garlic and the river began to deepen, its grassy, gently sloping banks giving way to steep earthy walls that held out the light and warmth of natural daylight.

Feeling the shift in temperature, we retraced our steps and were soon enjoying the warmth of the sunshine on our backs. Taking a shortcut across a bulge of grassland formed by a natural ox-bow bend, we were soon back to the point in the river where we had set out.

It was Tom who found our hot tub, though naturally by accident of course. Scouting ahead with water up to his knees, there was a sudden shriek of surprise and he had disappeared up to his chest.

"Help, I'm drowning!" he yelled as I hurried towards him as quickly as the water would permit. Even Freddie had dropped what he was doing and waded bravely in to help his younger brother.

With the water up to my waist I grabbed Tom under his armpits and dragged him back into shallower waters.

"Are you all right?" I asked with concern. "You gave us one hell of a fright there."

He nodded back sheepishly, angry with himself for having given way to fear.

"Look, it's like someone has dug a pit down here and then surrounded it with large rocks, like a dam." Freddie beckoned us over.

Tom with the excitement of discovery, immediately forgot about his scare and charged back to where his brother was standing, peering through the silty, brown water that had been stirred up by the recent commotion.

"Hooray, I bet we could build it back up again; then we could have our very own outdoor Jacuzzi!" Tom was delighted at the find and keen to go to work immediately.

"Idiot," Freddie muttered under his breath. "A jacuzzi has bubbles in it; you mean a hot bath."

"Hot tub." I corrected them.

"No, I'm going to have a jacuzzi because I'm going to guff in it." Tom roared with laughter at his own joke.

Freddie shook his head sadly at his brother; a lost cause in his eyes.

"Language, Tom Meredith." I kicked water at him. "Besides which, it's time to get back to camp, if you want any supper tonight."

"Oh dad, please can we stay for a bit longer? Please, please, please?" both begged.

"We can come back tomorrow and build it. Come on, what about your new books? Don't you want to have a look at them?"

Freddie, reminded of his purchase, was immediately back on side and even Tom gave up the protest at the prospect of learning how to catch animals, skin them and put the entrails to all kinds of interesting uses.

Later that evening, after a more successful supper, sitting around the blazing camp fire, Freddie reading quietly, Tom flicking to the sections that caught his interest and occasionally asking for help on some of the words, I picked up my guitar. Resting my newly acquired music book on a table, I clicked my knuckles, an unattractive habit of old, and finding the page that I wanted, started to play.

I played through the song, occasionally tripping over various notes, stopping and repeating until I had a chord or section to my liking. Finally with the familiar ache in my lower back from a poor posture hunched over the guitar to watch where I was placing my fingers, but otherwise much to my own satisfaction, I managed to play through the entire song. Not perhaps as fluidly as I would have liked, but without a glaringly obvious mistake.

"I've heard that before," Freddie piped up. "At home, it's on one of your CDs."

Surprised but also quite pleased with myself, I said, "It's by a brilliant and very famous singer songwriter called Bob Dylan and the song's called 'The times they are a changing.' Let's see if I can add the words in as well this time."

At the end of the song and despite a hacking cough halfway through as I attempted to mimic the gravely voice, I received mixed feedback from my audience.

"Cool dad," Tom clapped enthusiastically.

"You need help, dad." Freddie smiled thinly, rubbing his sleepy, smoke filled eyes.

"I guess I'll have to teach you the words tomorrow so you can help me out with the singing bit then." I laughed. "Come on, let's get off to bed and guess what?" I pointed to the skyline. "Red sky…"

"At night…" Freddie took over

"Shepherd's delight." We all said together, but with varying degrees of enthusiasm.

"Dad?"

"Yes Freddie?"

"You're not going to say that every night are you?"

"Shut up Freddie and go to bed." I ruffled his hair fondly and gently pushed him in the direction of the tent.

Chapter Five

A s nature had promised, we woke early to a glorious morning. Mist still hung over the trees and somewhere in our valley, down towards the ox bow bend we had crossed the previous day and could normally see from our site, a bird was singing. Its drawn out, melodious song, similar to that of a flute, was far more pleasing to the ear than an alarm clock or radio presenter's voice, as we lay in our beds allowing our minds to float through the transition between dreams and conscious thought of the day ahead.

"I wonder what that bird is that's singing?" Freddie noticed I had my eyes open.

"Probably a Blackbird, or a lark, or something like that." I took a wild guess, whispering in case Tom was still asleep, but I need not have bothered.

"I wish I'd bought a book on birds in that shop yesterday," Freddie continued seriously. "I've seen lots of different types of them and they all make different noises and I don't really know much about them."

"I bet you know more than you think you do. I mean, you know what a Robin looks like, a magpie and pigeons—you've seen plenty of those."

"And even I know what a duck and a penguin looks like," Tom said in earnest, propping himself on an elbow to join the conversation.

"Ha-Ha idiot," Freddie replied caustically.

"Freddie, enough. I've told you I'm not going to permit you to keep calling people nasty names. It stops here and now, do you understand?"

"Yes, sorry dad," he replied sullenly. "But everyone knows what a penguin looks like. He's just being stupid," Freddie retorted, not knowing when to keep his mouth shut.

"Tom is seven years old, Freddie, and don't you forget that. You are two years older than him." I wondered whether I was suffering from Déjà vu and that this morning was going to be a repeat of yesterday's start to the day.

"Yeah, but he's always calling me names and things. You don't have a go at him when he's horrible to me."

"Freddie," I was by now quite exasperated. The relaxing wake up had come to an abrupt ending. "Have you thought that perhaps he has learnt that from you? Younger children look to those older than them to know what to say and do."

"Yeah, but…" Freddie had to have the last word.

"No more 'Yeah buts' Freddie. Stop right now and give some thought to what I've just said, else I can promise you no more visits to the bookshop and we certainly won't be going to build that pool in the river today."

"Okay dad," Freddie replied, though the tone suggested he was not happy with being blackmailed and still wanted to argue the point.

"I'm off to get some wood," Tom broke the silence, unzipping himself from his sleeping bag to throw on shorts and a sweatshirt.

"Wait for me," Freddie said and, dressing quickly, followed his brother outside.

They stood for a moment and I could hear them talking to each other. Their voices, no more than whispers, were indistinct and words were carried away on the breeze, but it was the tone of the voices that made me sit up and tilt my ear towards the door.

Then, either forgetting it was mere canvas between us, or the anguish inside made Freddie raise his voice, but I heard quite clearly…

"…It's not fair, dad always picks on me. I can't wait to get back home and then we can go and stay with Guy and Dominic."

Then there was silence and a moment later I heard Tom say, "I'll race you." And then they were gone, their bare feet running silently over the wet grass.

"Well, Laura, after that silly argument yesterday morning, we had a really great day, or so I thought. And today, back to where we started. Is it me, or is this the way things are meant to be? Oh, I wish you could tell me what to do." I willed my thoughts up through the crown of the Yurt and into the heavens above. It wasn't a prayer. I still hadn't forgiven God, if he even existed at all, for taking Laura away from us, but I needed the understanding, the calm, rational insights and honest answers. Someone to tell me I was the idiot, but that they loved me for it anyway. To stop being so priggish, lighten up and to remind me how to let go and laugh at myself.

There was no response, of course; I would perhaps have thought I had gone insane if there had been, though without conscious thought the image of that woman in the bookshop talking so readily and easily to Tom filled my thoughts. I bundled the memory quickly to the back of my mind and slid out of bed; the jealous feelings it raised were petty minded and quite unforgivable.

I stretched tentatively and felt fine and, compared to twenty-fours hours ago, I was a man reborn. A night on the mattress with the freedom to roam beneath the duvet had worked wonders.

"Yes," I sighed. "Today was going to be a good day."

And so it was, as were the following three days. The sun shone brightly down upon us, turning our pale bodies, through red and then to a healthy light brown. We built our very own private hot tub in the river with seats and even a small ledge for soap and for once the boys didn't complain about bath time. We became intrepid explorers and fought our way through thick, dense jungle in search of lost treasure; or under Tom's guidance we were Mohawks setting traps to fill our stores before winter set in. Thankfully we still had a cool box filled with sausages, bacon, bread milk and cereal to fall back upon.

In the evenings after supper we sat around the campfire and as promised I taught the boys the words to a couple of songs, which filled the still night's air. My own voice started to find its pitch, deeper, perhaps more resonant than I could remember from my youth; Freddie carrying the high notes with his clear, moving treble voice, whilst Tom brought his joie de vivre and gusto. Once their attention had turned to other things, or sleep beckoned with welcoming arms and their cries for encores had died away, I would turn the pages and quietly pick my way through a new tune until nature and the dying embers told me the day was over and it was time for bed.

On the seventh morning, we woke to the sound of rain falling upon the canvas roof. It was not a heavy deluge, but constant and sufficient to delay the planned trip to Devizes to see the site of a Civil War Battle.

The patter of rain upon the canvas above us added to the comforting, cosy and warm feeling inside. Spacious and surrounded by natural light that penetrated the canvas walls, we spent the morning quietly reading, writing postcards to friends and playing a couple of board games the boys had brought with them. Laughter, shrieks of delight or mock disgust bounced off the walls of the tent at the roll of dice and movement of counters around the board. Gentle conversation and good humour. Tom thumping on his bongo drums, no co-ordination, merely content to make a loud unholy racket. Then Freddie taking his turn on the penny whistle. Following instructions to the word, patient and determined to master. Delicate fingers covering holes, a shrill note followed by a shriek, another breath followed by a wavering warble, then perfection; a note conquered, then a further finger raised and on to the next note.

How different it was to a rainy day at home, I mused. Either we would have been ensconced in sofas glued to some mindless drivel on the television, or a DVD; or in completely separate rooms the boys hypnotised by computer games. The effects of the modern world had crept up on us unawares—breaking down the tribal support and ultimately the family unit, isolating us as individuals; weakening the art of conversation and human interaction, denying the learning of life skills, to stunt mental and physical growth, to send our children undeveloped and unprotected into a savage and cruelly conniving world. The only outcome of exposure to such an existence demanded that we fail to live a full and productive life, spitting in the eye of the miracle and inspiring wonder of life itself. The world of the modern day couch potato, civilisation regressing at pace with no sign of slowing up, never mind a recovery.

Around the world we were cutting down jungles, destroying nature's blanket, to replace it with another jungle; manmade, deliberate, yet more fundamentally flawed and destructive than nature intended. Man was playing God and that did not bode well.

I shivered at what had just passed through my mind. Sat before me, happy and contented, mentally satiated, Freddie on his penny whistle, Tom, head down, engrossed in his survival book, and I was going to willingly take them back into that world? There appeared to be no alternative and that was truly depressing and demanded further thought.

I was prevented from sinking into further depression by a knock at the door and upon investigation found a young man in a worn waxed coat and matching wide brimmed hat.

"Mr Meredith. Name's Andrew Ponsonby. I'm the estate manager cum general factotum here at Woodholme Park." He raised a hand to his hat in salutation.

"How do you do." We shook hands. "Come in, come in, won't you?"

He stepped inside and removed his hat, then proceeded to stand in the doorway uncomfortable and ill at ease, conscious that his coat was dripping water onto the ground sheet.

"Don't worry about that. Here, let me have your coat and have a seat. Freddie, get Mr Ponsonby a chair, there's a good lad." I took the wet clothes from him and hung them over the top of the doorframe and put a towel on the floor beneath them.

After I had introduced him to the boys and he had settled into a chair, his frame relaxed and whilst waiting for a cup of coffee his eyes flicked about him taking in his new surroundings with great interest.

"This is one hell of a tent you've got here, Mr Meredith. I don't think I've ever seen anything like it before."

"Freddie's idea. And I have to agree with you, it really is a home away from home." I passed the credit to my eldest and saw with delight, the pride in his face at the compliment.

Taking the time to study our visitor, I found a short, stocky man in his early thirties with a ruddy, weathered complexion and a crop of unruly blond hair creeping over the back of his collar. His every pore screamed country gentleman—a man who found the streets of London alien and depressing; and the laws emanating from our capital city an affront to those who spent their lives and made their livelihood in the countryside.

We chatted about the estate and he gave us directions to an old folly, built by one of the General's ancestors that might be of interest. He also warned us about an old chalk pit we must keep away from—a honeycomb of tunnels and holes that over the years had partially collapsed, leaving the immediate surrounding area unsafe and a danger to be avoided. Lastly, if we needed anything, to drop in on him or his wife as they lived in the gatekeeper's house on the estate.

Finishing his cup of coffee, he put it on the table and went to collect his coat and hat.

"Look, I must be getting on." He jammed the hat firmly down on his head. "The general asked if I would drop by to remind you that he's expecting you for dinner tonight, about eight?"

"Thanks for the reminder, we'd quite forgotten." I shook hands warmly with him, thankful for the reminder for what would otherwise have been an embarrassing faux pas.

"Bye boys." He shook hands with each of the boys, then turned to leave, but paused, turning back, to add, "While I think about it, how would you both like to come up and help me feed the deer one day?"

"Yes please!" they both blurted out together.

"Marvellous, that's settled then. Pop up to the house any day next week just before four o'clock." He gave a brief wave and swung himself into a battered old Landrover and roared up the track at a far greater speed than I would have dared.

"I want to do what Mr Ponsonby does for a job when I grow up," Tom said firmly.

"I thought you wanted to become a pilot?" I replied in amazement. For the last two years whenever asked what he wanted to do when he grew up, all he wanted to do was fly planes, preferably fighters.

"Well, I've changed my mind."

"What made you do that?" I enquired.

"I like being outside and I like playing in the fields and the river and looking after animals." Tom set his jaw out stubbornly, his mind made up.

"Well, I think that's a brilliant idea and I expect you'd make a great estate manager. I expect there are some other things you have to do as well, like having to be outside in the pouring rain and wind and no doubt there's loads of paperwork to do. You ought to ask him next time we see him."

"I will."

After lunch the rain had not abated so I decided to take the boys back into Monkhampton to get fresh supplies and, because I'd not heard the slightest derogatory comment escape from Freddie's lips, I relented and agreed to a visit to the bookshop.

Going around the local fruit and vegetable shop, the boys were fascinated by the boxes of carrots, potatoes and other assorted vegetables, still covered with a fine layer of earth, denoting good, honest fresh food. Along with curved cucumbers and apples of all shapes and sizes, the sights and wholesome aroma was a pleasure I had long forgotten. The ease of the supermarket, especially the advent of being able to order on-line, had moved us further away from the food chain frontline—sterile, where uniformity of size and shape, colour and without nature's blemishes were more important than the feel and taste of good food.

This prompted a serious discussion with Freddie about organic food, pesticides and the benefits of the big corporate giants versus the small individual grower trader.

Digesting the information whilst I handed the money over for the fruit and vegetables we had purchased, Freddie came to the point. "So if this food is better for us, why don't we buy it when we're at home?"

"Well, you're right, we should really," I replied, self-conscious in the presence of the shop owner who was smiling, whether at my discomfort or Freddie's honest questioning I wasn't sure. "But it boils down to having the time to do the shopping. And the supermarket food may not be as fresh but it tends to last a bit longer."

"Then we should make the time. I think we should find our local shop and go there instead from now on." Freddie had spoken.

"Well said, sonny, that's the way to go." The smiling owner wiped his grubby hands on blue butcher's apron tied loosely around his large girth and applauded. "You support your local fruit and veg shop, they'll never let you down. An' what's more, you'll grow up healthy. Now take these carrots 'ere. Twenty-four hours ago they was still in the ground. Short of nicking 'em from the farm, you can't get fresher and with none of that muck them big supermarkets put on 'em neither."

"These are delicious." Tom had already delved into a brown paper bag and with the juice running down his chin had already tucked into an apple.

Whilst hopeful that the boys would have forgotten about this crusade by the time we got home, I thanked the shop owner; and with a firm reassurance that we would seek out the nearest shop as soon as we got home, I pushed the boys out the door and headed to the butchers.

The butchers elicited more of the same from Freddie, though this time with Tom's full support. Freddie was delighted with his brother's backing and folded his arms as if to say, "Well that's decided then." He overlooked the obvious fact that Tom's loyalty was not motivated by the desire to have a healthier diet and support local business, but more a morbid delight at seeing pigs heads and a variety of different game birds and rabbits hanging up out the back of the shop. And after Tom had shown such an interest in what he was doing, the butcher had taken Tom quite to his heart and as a special treat, let him take a quick peek into their freezer area to see the larger carcasses awaiting the butcher's cleaver.

It was therefore quite a relief to head down the cobblestone alleyway and after jumping over a large puddle of water that had formed outside a new age shop, to push open the door to the bookshop. At least I knew what to expect from the boys; or rather I thought I did.

"Well, hello again." The woman smiled in welcome from behind a desk piled high with books that she appeared to be cataloguing, though I could not immediately determine any logical methodology. "You bought the book on survival. Are you enjoying it?" she asked Tom.

"Oh yes, and I've made some traps just like the pictures in the book, but I haven't caught anything yet," he replied sadly.

"Well, maybe there aren't any animals around where you're camping?" she answered kindly.

"No, there's lots of them. Foxes and badgers and loads of rabbits. Mr Ponsonby told us and he should know because he works there. And I'm going to be just like him when I grow up."

"And what does Mr Ponsonby do?" she asked, coming around from behind her desk to kneel beside Tom.

"He looks after the animals and the land for the old General. He's very clever." Tom enthused with great admiration of his new hero.

"Well that's wonderful," she replied delighted for Tom, her enthusiasm coming out so naturally and effortlessly. "It's a very important job to look after the land, because it, in turn, looks after us."

"That's what we've just being saying to the man in the vegetable shop and we're only going to buy organic food from now on," Freddie added solemnly.

"My my, it sounds as though you've been learning lots whilst you've been camping." She seemed genuinely happy for us.

"How are they going to take the plaster off your arm?" Tom asked, no longer able to contain himself, his inquisitive brown eyes falling upon her cast.

Tom was thrilled to hear they would be using a small circular saw to cut it off, though surprisingly relieved to hear that it wouldn't hurt her. He had obviously decided she was now a friend; for had she still been a stranger he would have wanted perhaps a little pain so he could hear all about it afterwards.

"And hello to you too." She smiled up at me. And as she rose, so the blue skirt she was wearing appeared to change colours before my eyes. The dress was made up of a multitude of different shades of blue; from a deep royal blue through to the lightest turquoise. And thus as the long wide bottomed skirt swirled and danced to her movement, so the light caught it and accentuated the different shades.

"That's a beautiful skirt," I blurted out without thinking.

"Why thank you kind sir." And laughing, she curtsied, much to the amusement of the two boys. "And what can I do for you today?" she asked, her blues eyes still smiling behind her glasses.

"Have you got any books that tell me about all the different birds? It's got to have pictures of them as well," Freddie asked eagerly, coming up on to his toes with anticipation.

"And I want a book that shows me the different footprints of animals. They leave *tracks* and I want to be able to tell what they are." Tom proudly emphasised the new word he had learnt from Andrew Ponsonby earlier that morning.

"Come with me and I'll show you where they are." She nodded seriously at their requests and led them off to the back of the shop.

"It sounds like you're having a marvellous time where you're camping. Where was it again?" she asked me over her shoulder.

I told her.

"Oh yes, I remember now. How fantastic. I bet it's full of wildlife." She sighed wishfully.

"They've got their own herd of deer," Freddie spoke up. "There's a white one and they're very rare."

"And Mr Ponsonby is going to let us feed them," Tom verbally genuflected.

"I'd love to see them, you are lucky."

"Maybe you can come out and visit us one day and we'll show you them," Tom replied.

"Well, that all sounds lovely. We'll have to see, but I expect you're going home soon aren't you?" She turned and looked at me directly.

"We've got another week. In fact I can't believe how quickly this one's gone, absolutely shot past." I said non-committedly.

"Will you come and see us?" Freddie asked.

"You'd really like it," Tom added.

"Well, I don't really know?" She looked at me helplessly, not wishing to let them down, but aware the decision was not hers to make.

"Oh, please say you will." Tom reached up and held her hand in both of his as if in obeisance.

"We would love you to come and see us—if you would like to, that is?" I bowed slightly as if offering a formal invitation. We had already spent half our holiday and were now on the home run, and though we had yet to achieve the full bonding and healing experience I was seeking, we seemed to have made some progress and I could refuse them nothing.

"If you're sure?" She scanned my eyes, uncertainty in her own as she tried to fathom the sincerity of my invitation.

"Absolutely. The sign on the door says that you shut at lunchtime on Saturday. Why not come straight over and if you don't mind your food being a bit hit and miss, then you must stay for supper as well." I applied the full Meredith charm, though deep in the pit of my stomach a large snake was writing and turning itself in knots. Truly, I could not believe that here I was, inviting a complete stranger to dinner.

"Hit and miss is my favourite." She broke into a grin, her eyes suddenly shyly fixed on the floorboards at her feet.

"Hooray!" The boys both exclaimed in jubilation.

With my brain still in free-fall at my rashness, I followed the boys around in something of a daze as they found the books they were looking for and, after giving her directions to the camp, we said our goodbyes and headed back to the landrover.

"Meredith, do you drink port? I've got a very good bottle that needs drinking up and I'm not one for drinking on my own." Without waiting for a response the General took two glasses out of a fine mahogany corner cupboard and, pouring one for himself, he passed the heavy glass decanter down the table to me.

"Good man," he said as I took a sip, enjoying the rich, full-bodied port, and though I made all the right noises, as no connoisseur, I suspect I failed to fully appreciate the quality of the grape and the meticulous and long maturation process.

"Philip gave it to me when he came to stay at Christmas. Brought one of his harem with him. Incredibly long legs and wore a skirt that left nothing to the imagination. Came down a couple of months ago, completely different girl. He may not be able to keep them for long, but by God he can pick them, what."

Supper had been another splendidly entertaining time. The General's cook had put in a brief appearance to place on the table a large serving dish groaning under the weight of a large succulent joint of pork. After depositing various bowls of steaming vegetables she bade goodnight to the General and closed the door quietly behind her. As the aroma hit the taste buds, the boys positively drooled in anticipation as the old man took up an old bone-handled carving knife and expertly started to cut off the crackling. It was our first proper meal all week and even I found myself returning my plate for a second helping.

"All that fresh air, always brings on a good appetite. Nothing like being under canvas. Now, did I tell you young cubs about my time in Korea?" And that was it—the meal's conversation was monopolised by the General recounting his own memories, as well as numerous anecdotes from various campaigns he recalled studying as a young serving officer.

Though both boys and I declined the dessert, there was a selection of cheeses and biscuits that the General attacked with as much aggression as he had done the Koreans. Freddie used this brief moment to tell the General about the book on swords he had bought and this replenished the General's enthusiasm for further evocative accounts of swordsmanship through the ages and the different strokes used by a cavalry officer versus that of an officer on foot.

I was sorry that the General lived such a solitary existence, though he would not have thanked me for my sympathy. He was an extremely dignified yet amusing man and despite his gammy leg and a slight stoop, his grey eyes still twinkled brightly with the joy of life and a sense of mischief. And clearly he loved to be in and amongst people and irrespective of the relationship he had with Philip, he had a natural talent for engaging children.

After the cut and thrust of another enjoyable meal with the General and a further invitation to lunch on our last day had been most cordially accepted, we were making our way back down the poorly lit hallway to the front door when he picked up three packages. He handed two to Freddie, the other to Tom.

"These are for you. A staying present, if you will. Don't open them now—wait until you get back to your camp." And lightly brushing off our thanks as though embarrassed, he stood under the light in the porch and waved us farewell until the rear lights of the Landrover were lost to his sight.

Despite their tiredness the boys were revitalised by the presents and as soon as we had stepped back inside the tent, they tore at the brown paper and string with gusto.

"Oh my God!" Was all I could say as Freddie was the first to unwrap a long, thin present.

"It's the Tulwar!" Freddie exclaimed in delight, brandishing the glinting blade about his head with glee.

"What the bloody hell are we going to do with that?" I exclaimed in despair at the General's idea of a present for a nine-year-old boy in this day and age.

"I'm going to hang it on a wall in my bedroom."

"No you're not!" I exploded.

"Yes I am. The General's given it to me. Look you can read what the card says and he handed me a small white notelet. 'A blade, from an old one to a young one'."

"And look what he's given me." Tom was almost breathless in awe at what he held in his hands.

"Oh my God," I repeated for the second time in as many seconds, slapping my forehead with both hands. "An air rifle."

Though in beautiful condition and filling the tent with the smell of gun oil, the worn, wooden stock suggested it was an old rifle. However, it still sported a telescopic sight and against my deepest hopes and prayers, the General had even been thoughtful enough to add a tin of two hundred pellets.

Freddie finally unwrapped his second package to find an old leather case and inside a pair of binoculars.

"I can use these to watch the birds!" Freddie was ecstatic and immediately slung them around his neck and though it was still raining, went outside to put them to use in the fading evening light.

"No!" I shouted at Tom as he pulled the lid off the pellet tin. "Put that back right this instant!"

I quickly poured and drained a glass of scotch to calm myself down and help me think. "Mad old bugger," was all I could come up with initially, though once the first throttling grip of stress had left me I came to realise I had two options. The first was to return the presents to the General with a 'thanks but no thanks' reply. This would have given me the least stress as a caring parent, but would have offended the General. I could have lived with that, though was loath to do so after such generous hospitality to a family of complete strangers. But more importantly it would have been a tremendous upset for the boys and no doubt the one lasting memory of the camping they would harbour in later years.

The second option was to grin and bear it. Lay down some very firm rules, with the threat of returning them to Woodholme Park at the first whiff of a misdemeanour. That would see us through on a temporary basis whilst we were camping, but upon our return home that was another matter. Gun laws, knife and blade laws—that would need to be investigated further, but could wait for the time being.

The following day, the sun and clear blue skies had returned to our valley and we were once more able to slip into shorts and roam the green fields and meadowland at will. With some reservations I taught them both to shoot, though not before they had memorised a long list of rules I laid down and they could recall them on demand. With Tom proudly carrying the broken gun under his arm as I had showed him, we went into the woods where I had found an ideal spot for their extra-curricula education, courtesy of the General. In a clearing, dominated at one end by a high bank, once inhabited by a set of badgers, I placed some of our used cans of fizzy drink on a log and set to their instruction. Having set the sights I knocked each can off in turn, each hit earning me a round of applause from the boys standing behind me. Breaking the rifle and getting back to my feet we returned the cans to their places and the boys, with ten pellets apiece, took it in turns to shoot away.

Unsurprisingly, Freddie was the first to score a direct hit; his second shot sending the can spinning away behind the log with a high pitched *ping*, which elicited a round of applause from Tom and myself. Tom took a little longer, despite the keen hand-eye co-ordination of the sportsman. The rifle was still heavy for a seven-year-old, so we found another log upon which he could rest the barrel, and soon enough and much to his delight, a can crashed against the bank.

That evening after a quick dip in the pool the boys went happily to sleep whilst I read a children's short story to them. I couldn't recall the last time I had read to them, not for some years and even I had to join in the laughter at my efforts to use different accents and voices for each of the characters. By the time I finished the last page both boys were fast asleep, serene and content; it had been another good day.

I must have been asleep for only an hour or so when my sleep was shattered by a terrified scream from Tom.

"Tom, Tom, don't worry, everything's all right, daddy's here," I tried to soothe in the darkness as I fumbled around the mattress for the lamp and soon the tent was bathed in light, casting distorted shadows against the canvas walls.

"Daddy, I had a horrible dream!" Tom's panicked heart was thumping in his chest.

"Hey, hey, it's all right, it was only a dream. Come over here and tell me all about it."

His warm body slid under the duvet and he snuggled up to me, his hand resting on my chest, feeling my own heartbeat.

"Daddy, is Tom okay?" Freddie asked sleepily, though not without brotherly concern in his voice.

Reassuring Freddie that Tom was fine and he could go back to sleep, I left the light on to keep the demons away and looked down at my handsome youngest son.

"Better?" I asked and he nodded bravely. "Do you want to tell me about it?"

He shook his head and pulled himself tighter against me.

"It'll make you feel better," I reassured him.

"You won't be angry?" Tom checked before progressing.

"Of course not. Why should I be angry?"

He shrugged and after a little more encouragement he began. "Well, when Freddie and I were our playing down at the river today, we were playing a game about people."

"What sort of game?" I wasn't sure where this was going though it was clearly troubling Tom.

"It's when you say what you like and what you don't like about people. You take it in turns to say someone's name and the other person has to say." Tom explained this new game to me, drawing out the detail in order that he could delay telling me what had scared him so greatly.

"We'd done all our friends and I then said your name, so Freddie had to say things about you…" He halted, unsure as to whether to continue.

"That's okay, Tom." I brushed the wild locks away from his eyes so he could see that I wasn't angry with him, but he hadn't finished.

"And then Freddie said mummy's name, but I couldn't remember anything that I liked about her." He started to cry, the tears running freely down his little brown cheeks as he continued. "And in my dream, I dreamt we were back home and mummy was there and I rushed in to see her, but I couldn't find her. And when I woke up I couldn't remember what mummy looked like." He buried his head into my chest and I could feel his tears fall upon my skin. Brave Tom, so honest and true. His pain tore into my heart and I felt my own tears welling in my eyes.

"Tom, don't you worry." I hugged him back. "I tell you what—shall we try something?"

"What?" his muffled voice replied, his breath warm against my side.

"I want you to shut your eyes and keep them shut. Now I want you to breathe nice and deeply for me, okay? One, two, three in, one, two, three out… That's it." His breathing gradually came under control.

"Now I want you to picture yourself lying in bed at home, can you do that?" He nodded.

"Good, now you can hear mummy and daddy coming upstairs to say goodnight to you and Freddie. Can you hear us?" He nodded again.

"Now Daddy's told mummy a silly joke and mummy's laughing, can you hear her laugh?"

With his eyes still tightly shut, he smiled and nodded once more.

"Now I come into your room first and you are all snuggled up in your bed, under your duvet and I say, 'Goodnight darling, sleep tight, see you in the morning.' Then I lean over and give you a kiss on your forehead." My lips touched his forehead and he smiled again.

"Then mummy comes in and she sits on your bed and does that thing where she fusses with the duvet to make sure you don't get a chill around your shoulders." His eyes are screwed up in concentration as though watching a film inside his head.

"Then she leans over, gives you a kiss and says, 'Goodnight Tom-Tom, my beautiful big boy. Sleep tight and don't let the bedbugs bite. I love you.' You give her a great big hug and you can smell that lovely perfume she used to wear. Do you remember the one that you said made her smell like a party?"

I looked down at Tom; he was tranquil, relaxed, his eyes no longer screwed up, but shut as though in deep sleep, a wide contented and reassured smile upon his face.

"I can see her now." He spoke for the first time. "I loved how she always smiled and she gave me such warm hugs. And when I got hurt, she'd put on a plaster and kiss the pain away. And she did smell like parties; I love parties." He had hardly finished the words before he was asleep.

"Night night, Tom, I love you," I whispered to his sleeping form and gently, so as not to disturb him, reached over to switch off the light, then lay back in the bed.

"Daddy?" I heard in the darkness.

"Yes Freddie? I thought you'd gone back to sleep. What is it?" I raised myself up on one elbow, unable to keep the concern from creeping into my voice.

"Daddy, I just wanted to say thank you for bringing us here and I love you. Night."

"Night, night, and I love you too, Freddie, with all my heart." I could hardly get the last words out.

I lay back and let my tears fall silently and unchecked upon the pillow.

The following day was Saturday, the day of the visit. It caused a frantic scurrying around inside the tent as we sought to tidy up and show our home off in the best possible light. We lowered one side of the canvas to give the tent a good airing. The odour of three males mixed with the smell of the wood camp fire now heavily impregnated in all our clothes was a powerful combination, not that we could tell. Wood for the fire was stacked up neatly in preparation and I nervously checked the cool box several times to ensure we had all the food for the evening's meal.

"Do you know something, boys, I don't even know her name. Do either of you know it?" I stopped checking the cool box for the third time and shook my head in amazement. They didn't know either, but then the ease with which children so often make friends, names are the last things that are discovered.

We passed a further hour down at our pool, screams echoing down the valley. In vain I ran a comb through the boys smoked and matted hair and even after donning clean shorts they still looked like a couple of feral children.

Why I was so anxious to impress I could not determine. It was a campsite, for heaven's sake—things were meant to be messy, and the boys feral perhaps, but tanned, healthy and enjoying the stimulation of the great outdoors. It wasn't a visit by royalty or a health visitor, but by a woman who worked in a bookshop. She wasn't what I would have called beautiful, certainly not in the same league as Laura or Jo; but there again she wasn't unattractive and had a certain way with her that was appealing and, to cap it all, I didn't even know her name.

The sun had passed overhead and was working its slow ponderous way down the valley when Freddie espied a figure carrying a wicker basket walking down the hill towards our camp.

Both he and Tom shouting madly, raced up to greet her and escort her proudly back down to our home. I remained standing beside the tent, shielding my eyes from the sun, a lurching, hollow sensation in my stomach as I watched them approach.

She looked the very epitome of summer. She wore a light, white sleeveless dress embroidered with a pattern of small, pale blue flowers, the hem dancing gaily above her bare feet as she walked. A pair of delicate leather sandals held loosely in her plastered hand and a sensible, wide-brimmed straw hat turned up at the front covering her blonde hair completed the essence of a summer's day.

She was laughing at something the boys had said as she arrived, bringing with her the delicate scent of roses.

"Hello." She smiled, slightly out of breath, wisps of blonde hair flirting with her warm red cheeks.

"Hello, I'm Meredith by the way." I took her good hand in mine and despite the warmth of the day, it still felt cool in mine.

"Dad," Tom shouted mid cartwheel, "her name is Imogen, but some people call her Midge, or Imo, or even Moggy."

"Hello Meredith." Her blue eyes held my own for a moment longer than an encounter between two perfect strangers before she turned to admire the valley stretching out before us. "It's beautiful. You are lucky to wake up to this view every morning."

"Yes, it's quite beautiful, isn't it? And the boys love it here as well." I nodded, strangely proud on behalf of the General and the tenuous link that merited such a special opportunity.

Whilst I stored away the strawberries and cream that Imogen had brought and poured her a refreshing glass of lemonade, the boys gave her the guided tour of the Yurt. And much to the boy's pleasure she nodded and made appreciative noises and gestures at all the right moments.

"Would you rather sit inside, it's a bit cooler?" I noticed her dabbing at the perspiration at the point where her collarbones met.

"No thank you. I see so little of the sun these days cooped up in the shop that it's a joy to be out in the sunshine." She savoured each sip of the refreshingly chilled lemonade as it slipped down her throat.

I refilled her glass and followed her outside. She was already sitting in a camp chair, the hat redundant on the grass beside her, legs stretched out before her, the skirt hitched up above her pale knees.

She drank deeply from her second glass. "I needed that. Hadn't realised quite how unfit I was."

She explained that with the weather as good as it was and a little uncertain as to whether her car would stay in one piece, she had left it at the top of the track and elected to walk down to us.

"I hope you're up for a little more exercise. The boys are dying to show you around the valley."

"Five minutes and I promise I'll be as right as rain."

The hottest part of the afternoon slipped past in pleasant conversation; though encumbered with shy reservations on both sides, it was full of social niceties and self-imposed boundaries. The boys would occasionally drift towards us and enquire whether it was time to take Imogen for her tour, but even their enthusiasm had been dulled, brought about by the lethargic heat and they soon disappeared inside the tent to play quietly out of the burning sun.

It turned out that Imogen did not own the bookshop, but that an appeal for casual help from a friend some two years previously had simply stuck, though the pittance she received was now encouraging her to find a different and more permanent employment. Fortunately she lived with her mother, who suffered from arthritis, and thanks to a copy of Common Illnesses and Ailments for her bedtime reading, she also seemed to be debilitated by just about every known virus, germ and malady going. Beyond the implications that she was young, single and footloose and had no deliberate hobbies other than a passion for reading, especially anything historical, Imogen remained coy and elusive about the rest of her past. Very much an enigma wrapped up in a puzzle. And despite her many attractive qualities, this trait held a mysterious appeal that made one naturally wish to draw her closer in the hope she would unravel further glimpses of her past.

With the arrival of longer shadows and a cooler breeze, we managed to shake off our indolence and soon were headed down the gently sloping hill.

It was during this lazy stroll, the grass flicking at our ankles and occasionally catching between toes, that we cast adrift our shy, nervous fencing as we started to get to know one another beyond this unusual relationship built to date.

Beyond the cool and composed exterior within her own literary habitat, we soon found a woman of quick intelligence and a mischievous sense of humour. And though outwardly confident to the point of uninhibited frankness, it did not sit naturally with the rest of her personality, more a defence mechanism, a well-practised protective layer from the true person beneath.

The boys steered us down to the pool where Imogen looked on enviously as we took a refreshing plunge.

"Come on in, Imogen!" Freddie splashed at the water playfully.

"I've not got my swim suit with me, but it looks very nice in there." She lifted the hem of her dress up to her thighs and contented herself with wading in as far as her modesty would permit.

"You'll have to bring your swimming things with you next time!" Tom yelled out, naturally assuming there would be a next time.

"You bet I will," She replied gaily, finding a spot on the bank where she could sit comfortably and dabble her feet in the water.

"You're all so brown and disgustingly healthy," she moaned after I had briefly run a towel over my head and chest before joining her on the bank.

"You wouldn't have said that two weeks ago. We looked like anaemic zombies." I recalled our pallid states and our minds and nerves stretched as tight as piano wire.

"Well, so long as you know that I'm very jealous and it won't help when I go back to work on Monday, to that dark, musty, airless shop and think of this wonderful place and you lot running through the fields and cooling off in your pool."

"We've only got a few days left," I said sadly. "Then it's back to the real world and the Big Smoke."

"You'll miss it," she laughed, a warm uninhibited laugh as she watched the two boys frolicking in the pool below. "They certainly will."

I nodded. "I think they're already half wild and wouldn't be long before they became completely feral. And I'd like to think they've enjoyed themselves; it's certainly been better than they thought it would be."

"Oh, come on." Imogen pointed at them with her small, polished toes. "You've only got to look at them to see they're having the time of their lives."

"I hope so, and I won't bore you rigid with the detail, but it's been a difficult last year, so it's been important for us to spend some real time together." I smiled at her.

"I would say they've probably had a better time than even if you went to Disney. They've had unconstructed playtime using their imagination and initiative. Talking to both of them, they've learnt and seen new things that they wouldn't even have covered in school, and I should think they've had more sustained physical exercise than they've ever had in their lives before. And to cap it all, they've had your undivided attention as well. Not bad for a holiday I would say." Imogen reached over and in a motherly way, touched my arm as if to physically reassure me of the truth in her words.

Later after supper and despite the still warm night, the mandatory campfire was lit, we sat outside watching the sun slide over the bloodstained horizon chatting without the constraint or uncertainty of people newly acquainted, but almost as if old friends.

The boys begged me to play a couple of songs for them, roping Imogen in to apply greater pressure, and despite my initial embarrassment we had a great time. Imogen joined in with a clear, sweet voice laced with honey that filled the night air and startled the birds swooping and diving for their evening meal.

"I haven't had so much fun in years!" she laughed as we escorted her back to her car.

"We've enjoyed having you, haven't we boys?" I raised my voice to be heard by the boys running ahead and they shouted out in agreement.

We walked slowly up the track, almost deliberately slowing the pace so we could spend more time together, delaying the end to an otherwise perfect day.

"When are you going back?" she asked with sadness in her voice, though the tilt of her silhouetted chin showed she was not going to allow this inevitable separation to find a chink in her armour and get through to hurt or scar.

"On Wednesday," I whispered back, afraid to say it out loud and wake me from this utopian dream world.

She sighed in disappointment but said nothing, just looked straight ahead to where the outline of her car could now be seen.

"Could we see you again before we go? The boys would love to see you!" I blurted out, my tongue becoming thick and swollen as though stung by a bee as I added, "And I'd like to see you again as well."

She stopped suddenly. Two glittering diamonds stared quizzically at me through the darkness. "Would you?" She sounded surprised, but elated. "I'd like that too."

"When can you come? Tomorrow?" I couldn't help the eagerness in my voice.

"I've got to take mother to church, but I could come over after that." Was it me, or did she sound disappointed that she couldn't spend the whole day with us.

"I don't want to sound too forward, but I'm going to take the boys to watch the badgers tomorrow night. Why not bring a sleeping bag and stay the night? We've got plenty of room."

"That's very kind of you, Meredith, and whilst I've had a lovely day today, I think we'd better let's see how things go." It was a strange tone in her voice. Pleasure, tempered with a certain coolness, as though she had come close to a precipice and was now trying to back away.

It was even more confusing when we said goodbye and I reached out and took her hand to find her pulling herself against me and reaching up to kiss me lightly on the cheek. And then she was in the car, her backlights temporarily blinding us as she made her way slowly down the drive.

That night I lay in bed, my mind racing with the day's events. I wasn't looking for love, I wasn't even looking for a fling. Hell, we were going back home in four days time, so what future would there be between us? Long distance relationships, especially those built on such sandy ground as ours, would never have worked. Still, there was something about her, something compelling, addictive. But what was it that I found so attractive about her? She wasn't beautifully stunning, she was in her mid-thirties and whilst far from being as thin as a rake, neither was she fat; in fact, she was wonderfully wholesome. She was comfortable with and confident about her body, and yet she also seemed unaware of her sexuality.

And then there was Laura. How could I find anyone to replace the love of my life? It wasn't possible, and yes of course we had had our spats, our arguments and our differences, we were individuals and I had loved her for having her own opinion. But underneath it all we had been soul mates; a binding union that was stronger than any words spoken in a church and a tie that crossed the mere boundaries of our own mortality. I had already arrested, tried and judged Imogen by the law according to Laura and found her to be wanting. So what did I think I was doing with her, why had I been so pathetically eager to see her again, as tongue-tied as a teenager with their first hesitant, sweaty, fumbling declarations of love?

I did not fall into an easy sleep and the dreams when at last they did come, stayed like nightmares, half in the shadows filling me with angst and trepidation.

Chapter Six

The following evening whilst waiting for dusk to fall I had sent the boys to rest in the tent until it was time to go down to the badger set. Imogen and I sat outside enjoying the view and relishing the silences that we now felt comfortable to allow between us.

I watched her surreptitiously from the corners of my eyes. It was hard to take in, but I was growing dangerously fond of this woman. In my eyes she had grown more beautiful overnight. Not in the physical sense, but in her aura, her being. It was no one particular thing, but a hundred small things that made her so attractive, so appealing on both the physical and mental planes. It was in the way she carried herself, the way she wore her clothes. The way she casually tucked a loose strand of her blonde hair behind her ear that had escaped her ponytail; the way she had thrown off her bookshop austerity to giggle like a schoolgirl and enjoy walking barefoot through the meadows. Shakespeare's Puck had cast a spell and was no doubt sitting back to await the chaos and pandemonium that would ensue.

"You're very good with the children." For someone with no children of her own I was quietly amazed at her uncanny ability to relate to and interact with the two boys.

"What's that?" In a now familiar gesture, Imogen pushed a curl of blonde hair that had escaped from her ponytail back behind her ear.

"I said, you're very good with the children."

"Oh it's not me, it's Freddie and Tom. They're very easy to get on with. They're a credit to you." She fended off the compliment, not abashed but seemingly defensive of a scar not properly healed, a wound still open and suppurating; but now was not the time to attempt such invasive mental surgery.

After a light lunch the boys had insisted on giving Imogen a display of their marksmanship. Having preened their self-confidence by clapping and acknowledging their skills with the newly acquired air rifle, she had promptly demanded a go herself. And ignoring the potential mess to her turquoise summer dress, she dropped to the leaf covered ground and proceeded to raise herself to the same level of hero status that only the General enjoyed in the boys' eyes, by sending the now shredded cans spinning away one after the other.

"One of the benefits of growing up in the countryside and having two older brothers," she had laughed casually and left it at that.

Then, amidst screeches of laughter and snatches of conversation that drifted away in the wind, she had raced them to our pool, leaving me to lollop along behind as best I could, encumbered by the air rifle and a large bag filled with towels and cool drinks. From a distance I could see Imogen, unabashed, pull her dress up over her head and discard it on the grass before disappearing down the riverbank.

Even from where I was standing I could not miss that it was done with such innocence and so casually, yet was filled with grace and sensuality.

I joined them some minutes later to find Imogen sitting quite regally in a one-piece swimming costume matching the colour of her dress, the arm with the plaster cast resting upon her head chatting away merrily to the boys, sitting quite still either side of her.

And with the water lapping just below her chest I could not but help notice how admirably her breasts filled her swimsuit.

"My, my, Grandma, what big eyes you've got." She put on a pseudo Marilyn Monroe voice and pretended to cover her assets with her good hand.

As I took my place in the pool, though, it may have been my imagination or did I notice a glint of mischief in her eyes and that her shoulders were pushed a little further back, encouraging the discomfort that I was already feeling in my cut off jean shorts.

"A penny for them?" she interrupted my thoughts, bringing me back to the present and the sun settling quietly in front of us.

" I was just thinking how much I've enjoyed today."

"Me too, simply heavenly," she replied, shivering slightly.

"Come on, let me get you a warm fleece jumper; then we ought to raise the boys and see if we can find those badgers."

We stole quietly down the hill and five minutes later I had spread a blanket upon the ground just on the top of a ridge looking down an embankment into a natural bowl amongst the trees where Andrew Ponsonby had told us our best chances of finding the badgers would be.

Lying down to ensure our outlines did not show up over the ridge, Freddie and Tom took turns on watch with the binoculars. Imogen lay face up watching the stars, pointing out in a whisper some of the names of the formations that she knew.

"You're quite a mine of information," I whispered close to her ear. "Birds, trees, plants, geography, shooting, history; where did you learn it all?"

"I used to be a teacher, a lifetime ago. Maybe one day I'll tell you all about it," she whispered back, revealing another layer of her past, but equally revealing yet more intrigue and mystery.

"*Ssh*, I can see them," Freddie hissed with excitement, the binoculars glued to his face as he pointed to the far side of the embankment.

Infected by his excitement, we slithered as quickly as we dared to the top of the rise and peered down into nature's theatre.

Below us were what appeared to be a family of badgers, led by a large, handsome male cautiously emerging from the darkness. He paused every few yards to peer blindly around and sniff the air for scents and any sign of impending danger. He was followed by two small cubs, frolicking and playing together whilst a female, smaller than the male, brought up the rear, never straying far from her cubs.

The male and female would rush forward with an ambling gait that made you want to laugh out loud, then snuffle the ground, occasionally driving their powerful claws into the ground searching for their evening meal of earthworms and insects. The cubs copied their parents for a while until, like all children, their attention span wandered, causing them to rush off in another direction, nipping at each other with small, sharp teeth and rolling around in a play fight tussle. Relishing the freedom of the open air, though still not fully comprehending the dangers that lay above ground, they caused their parents to tread with trepidation and caution.

"Isn't this exciting," Imogen whispered in my ear, shuffling closer to me until our bodies were touching. "I've never seen anything like this before."

"Me neither." Her hair brushed my cheek and I caught the heady scent of her perfume.

Whether it was the excitement of the scene that played before us, or perhaps something else, neither of us moved, and from shoulders to feet our bodies pressed firmly against one another, the electricity palpable in the air.

Eventually the badgers had had enough and the larger one snuffled the air and with a rustle of the dry leaves beneath his paws, led them all away, their round bottoms wiggling away into the dark protection of the copse and their set that lay within.

"Dad, did you see that?" Tom was awestruck by what he had just seen.

"That was really great," Freddie agreed, putting the binoculars safely away in their case.

"How cute were their little bums!" Imogen giggled as I helped her to her feet.

Without waiting for us the boys raced on ahead, back to the tent, attempting to mimic the hoot of an owl that we had heard earlier as it hunted down its evening meal.

We walked slowly, feeling the damp grass beneath our feet, the smell of the earth clean and fresh filling our nostrils.

Without saying a word Imogen danced around from my left to my right side and slipped a warm hand into mine and without breaking our stride we walked back to camp.

"Now then, young lady, are you going to accept our invitation to spend the night in this fine auberge so that I can offer you a glass of whatever you fancy, as long as it's wine or whisky?" I asked her in a joking off-hand manner though my every fibre willed her to accept.

"Yes, please stay!" the boys shouted from their beds.

"Be quiet, boys, you should be asleep." I stuck my head inside the tent to admonish them lightly, though secretly pleased about the additional support.

"So what's it to be?" I continued nonchalantly, studying her face for any indication of her decision.

"I'd quite like a glass of wine," she replied, causing my heart to somersault with delight.

"Red or white?" I called out to her from inside the tent once I was confident my voice would not betray me.

"White preferably, but whichever is easiest," she replied lightly.

I handed her a glass and raised my own in salute to her.

"I must warn you," she giggled, "I'm not a big drinker and am liable to get very tipsy after a couple of glasses, so I am trusting your honour as a gentleman not to take advantage of me." Her eyes flirted playfully at me over the rim of her glass.

"Your virtue is safe with me, mademoiselle, though if you don't mind I'm going to get a small fire going or your blood will not be safe." I swatted pointlessly at the horde of insect nightlife that had started to gather around the lamp hanging from a pole behind our chairs.

I soon settled back into my chair as the kindling wood took hold, sending the occasional spark coughing and spluttering into the dark night. The smoke spiralling lazily upwards from the glowing base providing us with some protection from the irritating gnats and mosquitoes.

"I've only just realised it's Sunday today. God, you'll have work tomorrow. Are you sure you're okay to stay tonight?" I sat up with a start, almost spilling my drink.

"Not to worry, I've taken the day off." She turned her head to smile at me. "I've only taken a few days holiday this year and I don't have anything else earth shatteringly exciting planned, so thought why not take a few days now whilst I'm enjoying myself."

"And are you, enjoying yourself, I mean?" I probed.

"Oh yes, I'm having a great time. It's been a long time since I laughed so much, and just to run through the fields with bare feet, the sun on my skin. I feel like I've been in hibernation for so long and am just coming back to life. It's a truly magical place."

I nodded in agreement. There was little more I could add to explain how I felt.

"Can I be extremely nosy? I mean, I know it's none of my business so tell me to butt out if you like." She shifted in her seat so she could look directly at me, her cheeks glowing from the heat given off by the fire.

"Go ahead, I promise I won't take offence."

"Why have you come here? I believe in fate, destiny, karma, call it what you will. But with all the thousands of people who have walked into that bookshop, or whom I have met recently, none have come bounding along and turned my cosy little world upside down. And here you are—a father of two fabulous boys, living in London a hundred miles away and shortly to return. I mean, why and how has this happened to me?"

Staring deep into the fire I told her our story; about Laura, the problems we had had since, that the boys had not mourned their mother's death, my work-life balance and even intimated at my brief relationship with Jo.

When I had finished I realised I had tears in my eyes and Imogen was kneeling beside me, her good arm slung comfortingly about my shoulders.

"Bloody smoke," I wiped my eyes, leaving dark smudges upon my cheeks.

"Oh you poor boys." And I noticed she too had wet cheeks. "You've had a terrible time."

"And that's why chance, fortune, fate, or maybe just the wind, has brought us here." I pulled myself to my feet, not wishing to break away from her embrace, but suddenly feeling the need to replenish my glass.

"Do you think your time here has helped? Are you now on the mend, so to speak?" Despite her frank questions, there was a soft velvet wrap to her words that took away the sting of such personal introspection.

"Christ yes. Two weeks ago the boys and I hardly knew each other, let alone spoke to one another. I've been running like mad on the hamster wheel of life and didn't have time to think what the bloody hell was going on. I was hurting people without even realising it, perhaps not even caring. Bloody hell, I even had an affair with my wife's sister, I was that screwed up. So the last ten days have been a rest beyond measure; to disengage the brain and allow it to idle in neutral and then to spend some time thinking without all the other crap that gets flung at you back in the real world."

"Did it help? Did the affair with your sister in law help?" she asked in her frank manner.

I thought about it for a moment. It seemed all so long ago now. "Yes, yes, I suppose it did, though don't ask me to explain quite how."

"Well, I don't see a problem with that then, as long as her husband doesn't find out. Mind you, that doesn't mean it was a good idea to do it whenever the mood took you. But if it helped to get you through the pain of bereavement, then you shouldn't lose any sleep over it."

Her simple reasoning made sense; there was enough still to resolve about the future, never mind worrying about the past. That was done, over, it couldn't be changed, altered or even deleted, but it could be buried in some dark forgotten recess in the mind to be left to rest in peace.

"You're right, and much of the last ten days has helped put some of those skeletons to bed; though a couple of new ghosts have now arisen."

"Like what?"

"Tom is having nightmares because he can't remember what his mother looks like. In his dreams, that is; he's fine when he wakes, but he's had a couple of sleepless nights so it's obviously playing on his mind."

"Poor mite, he's such a cheerful, happy-go-lucky boy, and he makes me really laugh with some of the things he comes out with." Her infectious chuckle made my mouth crack into a grin.

"And do you know what bothers me most? It's having to go back to our normal lives, back into the rat race without all the answers." The frustration was evident in my voice.

"Well, don't go back then, stay here." Imogen's simple way of looking at a problem cut right through to the chase. It really was that simple.

"We could, I suppose. I've taken the whole summer off, but I promised the boys we'd only be away for two weeks; they have a hectic social life awaiting their return." I shrugged helplessly as though events were already in motion and the matter was out of my control.

"Well, I think you should stay, but that's for very selfish reasons—to want to spend more time to get to know you and your wonderful boys. You have stormed into my life and I think it would be very unfair for you to just bugger off again without so much as a by your leave." She ran her hand through my hair and gave me a peck on the side of the face before regaining her seat to warm her feet in front of the fire.

We talked until the glowing embers dulled and died in the ashes. Then, with the threat of the birds announcing a new day, we retreated inside to our respective beds and I did not even feel my head hit the pillow before I was asleep.

The following morning the boys were unforgiving about the late night we had had and demanded with menaces our fullest attention. It was in fact Imogen's attention they sought and this was achieved both immediately and directly by plonking themselves down on her inflatable mattress and teasing her nose lightly with a feather. Chatter and laughter ensued; though from listening to her attempted hoarse and slightly dopey whispering, Imogen was clearly suffering as well. With no hope of getting back to sleep, my tastebuds like a hungry baby demanded their caffeine fix so I dragged myself out of bed and, ignoring the cheap shot wolf whistle from Imogen, I staggered in just my boxer shorts to the cooker and put the kettle on.

Slipping a T-shirt on to ensure a modicum of decency was preserved, I stepped outside to see what the day had in store for us. It was going to be hot, damn hot! The air already lacked oxygen and felt warm in the back of the throat and the view down the valley was clear, each contour ridge and feature clearly defined in the landscape, the colours so crisp and stark.

"Sleep well?" I handed Imogen a cup of coffee and settled myself down at the end of her bed.

"Mmm, like a baby, thanks. All that fresh air and exercise, quite wonderful, though I seem to ache in places I didn't know I had places." She sat up in her bed and guarded her coffee from the boys' boisterous nudging and pushing. She looked remarkably well considering how late we had gone to bed. Her blonde hair hung down onto her shoulders though a rather endearing tuft sprang straight upwards before cascading down over her eyes; and despite her grooming, it refused to comply and with a small shrug, she gave it up as a lost cause. With all that said and done I was the first to admit I was not doing credit to the male of the species—with tousled hair, sleep lines down one cheek and bags under my eyes, giving me a sad, hangdog look that had gone out of vogue with Humphrey Boggart.

"Now then, one and all, a day like today needs a cunning plan, so not a moment is wasted; so how about feeding the deer this afternoon?" I enquired roughly.

"Great idea, dad." Tom bounced up and down, threatening to spill Imogen's coffee at any moment.

"Count me in!" Freddie bounced on his knees beside her, sending a stream of coffee over the side of the mug to land on the white cotton vest top, the brown stain immediately spreading out over the area partially covering her cleavage.

"Are you all right?" I asked as she scrubbed quickly but fruitlessly at her top.

"I'm fine, not to worry, it'll come out in the wash." She laughed and gave up on the task to ruffle the boys' hair. "You two must have ants in your pants."

"Sorry Imogen, I didn't mean to." Freddie looked forlorn at the mess he had caused.

"That's okay, Freddie, don't you worry, nothing's broken and it sounds like you're going to have a fab time feeding the deer, so I'm not surprised you're excited."

He smiled shyly back at her. "Aren't you going to come and feed the deer with us?"

"I've got to go home soon. I've got to clean the house, do the washing and get ready to go back to work tomorrow," Imogen replied with a sad face. I wasn't the only one who had cornered the market in the hangdog look.

"Imogen, you cannot be indoors doing such boring things on a day like today. I simply insist you stay with us," I protested, aghast at the idea of us losing her so soon.

"But I can't, I mean I haven't even got any fresh clothes to wear and then I've got the hospital tomorrow morning to have this removed at last." She waved her plastered arm in the air.

"Look, I tell you what, we'll do a deal. We've got to do some shopping in town or else we're going to starve tonight anyway; so, you let us drive you home and whilst we're shopping you can do whatever beautiful young women do. Then throw some clothes into a bag to stay overnight and we'll pick you up and it's back to the deer for teatime. Then tomorrow, if you like, we could come with you to the hospital, I'm sure it's completely illegal to drive immediately after having your cast removed anyway."

The deal was on the table and I sat back, not realising I was holding my breath. Forty-eight hours ago I would never have offered and now here I was shamelessly throwing everything including the kitchen sink to get her to stay a while longer.

Her face screwed up in concentration as she deliberated the pros and cons of the suggestion. Did she want to stay and was therefore checking to make sure every avenue was covered; or did she want to leave and was trying desperately to find a loophole that meant she could escape our clutches.

"Okay," she said simply, "but you must let me bring the wine. Whatever we had last night tasted like a bonfire." She giggled at her own joke, which immediately set the boys and myself off till the tears were pouring down my cheeks and my sides ached.

We pulled up outside a modest three bedroom bungalow with a well-kept front lawn, its short driveway lined with alternate red and white roses and my eye was drawn to the net curtains twitching in a bay window. From the outside it presented a neat and tidy front, sparse, practical yet cared for. Though I sensed that what had been achieved to inject some life into the dull, drab brown building with the array of colours, carefully edged lawn and weeded flowerbeds had been achieved in the face of adversity. This, coupled with its dark interior, made the place seem austere and inhospitable. And despite the searing heat of the day, it felt cold and soulless causing goosebumps to rise in protest on my bare legs and arms

"Oh dear, mother's on her one woman neighbourhood watch campaign; you'd better give me an extra half an hour before picking me up." She smiled wanly, suddenly deflated of all happiness and enthusiasm.

"That's a scary house. I bet someone died in there, horribly murdered." Tom peered ghoulishly through his open window.

"It gives me the willies," Freddie added a touch of class to the shared sentiment.

"That's the house where I live and I promise you, Tom, no one has died in there—well, at least not to my knowledge."

Imogen tried to laugh but it sounded hollow and even the sparkle had gone out of her eyes.

She got down from the Landrover and without looking back she took a breath, squared her shoulders and was swallowed up by the ugly, toothless mouth of a front door.

An hour and a half later, with our shopping safely stored in cool bags in the boot and a couple of bottles of rather splendid wine wedged between the seats, we pulled up outside the bungalow. The only noise and signs of life came from a couple of young children listlessly kicking a plastic football in the road, the ball skidding off the hot tarmac and occasionally hitting cars parked on either side of the street. All else was silent. There was no visible movement within the house of horrors as it had been named by the boys and I rather felt that a sign should be nailed to the front door proclaiming 'Abandon hope all ye who enter here.'

I recalled Imogen's parting words: "That's the house where I live..." She was right, it was just a house, a shell with four walls and a roof, where people endured an existence; it was not a home where people lived and loved.

Ten minutes later, just when I was thinking I was going to have to muster up every ounce of courage and knock on the entrance to Hades, the door swung open and Imogen was spat back out into the land of the living. Squinting against the sudden assault of glaring light, she made a lonely figure as she approached the car. She had been crying and by the looks of things for some time. Her usually clear blue eyes were bloodshot and puffy and there were streaks down her lightly tanned cheeks where the tears had fallen unchecked.

"Boys, shut your eyes, I'm going to kiss your father," she announced immediately upon hiking herself up into cab next to me.

And before I knew what was going on she had planted a long lingering kiss on my lips.

"There, that should give the old bag something to think about," she said defiantly as the net curtains twitched furiously from within.

The more distance we put between us and her house, the more she relaxed. The tension around her eyes and mouth slowly dissolved and the mischievous glint returned.

"Sorry about that," she said at last, her hand reaching out to momentarily touch my thigh. "But sometimes she drives me completely around the bend and though a murder hasn't yet happened in that house, there could be one shortly."

"Do you want to talk about it?" I asked, my eyes straying to where she was sitting.

"No, maybe later. First of all I need to feel the grass beneath my feet, the sun on my skin and to run through those fields like a dog chasing it's tail. Do we have time for a quick dip in the pool before we see the deer?"

"I don't see why not. Fancy a dip, boys?"

"You bet, I'm so hot you could cook an egg on my stomach!" Freddie wiped the sweat from his hot, beetroot face.

"Yeah, and my bum's all slimy," Tom sniggered quietly to his brother, though loud enough to reach our ears.

"Tom Meredith!" I shouted over Imogen's uncontrollable laughter. "You are incorrigible."

Chapter Seven

"Now you can see why I don't take holidays and spend so much time at the bookshop. It's not much of an alternative, but it's a damned sight better than spending one minute more in that place than I have to." Imogen finished her second glass of wine and held it out for a refresh.

As soon as I had pulled the Landrover to a halt beside the Yurt there was a mad, ungainly yet exhilarating stampede down the hill, with arms flying in all directions to keep ourselves from tumbling arse over tit as we raced to the pool. The gentle current washed the heat and dust from our bodies, cooling the blood and calming the brain. For Imogen it was a therapeutic cleansing, washing off the stench of decay and depression to leave her body a healthy glowing light brown. She left her damp hair to dry naturally whilst also keeping the back of her neck cool as we returned to the camp at a more relaxed and sedate pace.

The innocent beauty of the deer also worked wonders on us, Imogen more so. Their large intelligent, alert and yet trusting eyes blew away the last vestiges of her pent up angst and frustration. She slipped into a far more mellow, almost Zen state as she cooed and aah'd like a mute simpleton if one of the deer so much as twitched a muscle. Nature's medicine chest had delivered up the perfect treatment.

"Why do you stay if it's that bad?" I refilled her glass and passed it back.

"Complete and utter blackmail, that's what it is. She gives me this 'I'm not going to be around much longer' crap: 'I've now got such and such a disease and with the pain of the arthritis I can't leave the house. I love you, this is your home and we've got each other. Now can you come in here and wipe my bum'." She mimicked in the voice of an old crone.

"Is she really dying?" I asked without much tact.

"Oh I don't know, I don't think so, though I do sometimes realise I've been wishing that she were. Is that terribly bad of me?"

"To be honest with you it was the same with Laura. Towards the end she was in so much pain, drugged up to the gills and didn't know me or the boys from Adam. I prayed to God that if he really was this all-loving master of creation and he wasn't going to cure her, then he should take her quickly. I sometimes think that Laura wished it as well. In her more lucid moments I am sure I saw it in her eyes, if you know what I mean. But she had such a strong will to live and such a love of life she could never come to terms with the idea of just giving up and willing herself to death." I had never told a soul before about my unforgivable thoughts, but now that I had said them out loud, in public, I realised I no longer felt any guilt. I had and still loved Laura. I had mourned her death even before she had died and who would begrudge anyone for not wishing to see the person they loved suffer beyond belief?

"So what are you going to do now? Your plaster comes off tomorrow and you mentioned it was time to get a move on with your life. Does your mother feature in your new life?" I threw another log on the fire.

"I really don't know, I haven't got that far. I just know what I don't want in my life and dear mumsy heads up that list."

"Would you consider going back to teaching?" I chucked a line out in the water to see if she would bite and unravel the mystery she had revealed the previous night. But she wasn't biting.

"Might do; there again, I've always wanted to go travelling as well, maybe even live abroad for a bit; somewhere hot where I can feel like this all the time." She stretched her arms out as if trying to embrace the setting sun. "What about you? What are you going to do when you go back home?" She cast her own net out.

"Go home, try to work less and spend more time with the boys." I absentmindedly plucked at my guitar strings; the future sounded weak and not particularly exciting, or hopeful, given everything that I had learnt over the past weeks.

I stopped suddenly and leant forward towards the fire before saying quietly, "I'm scared shitless about going back, truth be told." She sat up, suddenly curious, but patient enough to allow me to explain in my own good time. "I can't go back to the way life used to be. I mean I could go back, but it would be the death of us. I mean I feel I've changed, in here." I tapped my chest over my heart. "Things that were important to me aren't anymore. I've come to my senses and realised that my values have been so out of whack for so long. But to reshuffle those priorities and values means that my life has to change, dramatically; though not unlike your good self I haven't figured out how. Pretty weak, huh? Perhaps we should open up a bookshop together, in Tibet?" I joked, then immediately wished I had kept my mouth shut as the implications of what I had said hit like a lightening strike.

"No chance." Imogen laughed it off, though she had not missed the inference. "Tibet's too bloody cold and I want to get as far away from bookshops as I possibly can. Don't get me wrong, I love books and I love reading, God I could do it all day. But I can't stand talking about them. The people who come into the shop and drone on for hours about this and that book they've just read and instead of telling them to go away, I smile politely and ask another damn stupid question that keeps them at it for another ten minutes. I don't have much of a life I know, but that's one cross I am definitely going to be well rid of."

I laughed. The moment had passed without issue and I took up the guitar once more. I played from memory and after a few false starts, the chords clicked and a familiar tune emerged. Imogen started to hum as she tried to place the tune, then smiled with satisfaction as her memory didn't desert her.

"The times they are a changin'. How apt." She chuckled, then added her soft melodious voice.

Just after midnight, Imogen cried enough for one day and went to her bed, though paused behind my chair to wrap her arms around me and give me a kiss on the cheek, before slipping quietly inside the tent. Despite the enticing thought of throwing caution to the wind and joining her, wanting to feel her lips against mine once more, I knew it would cause more problems than the momentary feeling of pleasure it would give. So casting less gentlemanly thoughts aside I listened to her dress being drawn up over her head, the inelegant sound of someone settling on an air mattress and finally once I heard her shuffling down into her sleeping bag, I extinguished the lantern and went inside to my own bed.

It had been a good day.

The next morning, clouds hung on the horizon making their way steadily towards us bringing with them the unmistakable heavy, oppressive heat and electrical build up in the air that forewarned a thunderstorm. The boys and myself stood outside the tent watching the impressive cracks of lightening rent the darkened landscape in two, the grumbling, rumbling sound of thunder growing louder by the minute.

"In here a minute, boys," Imogen called from inside.

"What's that?" Freddie pointed to a curious object that she had just suspended from one of the roof poles. It looked like it had been made from a very flexible type of wood and was shaped like a circular net with two feathers hanging beneath.

"I hoped you might have been able to tell me, Freddie, what with you doing your project on the American Indians. Any ideas?" Imogen looked at each of us in turn and received a blank response.

"It's called a Dreamcatcher," she said emphatically as though everyone should have heard of such a thing.

"What is it?" Freddie asked, circling beneath the object to view if from different angles as it rotated slowly in the gentle breeze.

"They were invented by the Native American Indians who believed that they were a spiritual protector."

"A what?" I raised an eyebrow, though realised from her voice she was absolutely serious.

"They believed that if you hung the Dreamcatcher above the sleeper they could separate out the good dreams from the bad and thus protect your positive spirit."

"So how does it work?" Freddie asked in wonder.

"Well," she continued earnestly, "there are several theories, but the most widely held opinion is that good dreams pass through the hole in the middle whilst the bad are caught up in the web. A bit like a fly getting caught in a spider's web."

"Do they work?" Tom wore his sceptical expression though also there was an underlying desire to be convinced and that it wasn't just some hocus-pocus, mumbo-jumbo."

"I've got one above my bed at home," Imogen sealed the matter. If it was good enough for her, it was good enough for the boys.

"So whoever sleeps under this will have good dreams?" Tom asked just to be clear.

"That's right, Tom," she replied, ruffling his already dishevelled hair.

"But there's only one and we need three." Voicing the outcome of his logical thought process.

"Ah-ha, well spotted." She laughed and reached into an old soft leather bag that she had brought with her. "I thought your Dad could have this one and we can make one each for you."

One after the other, she placed on the table strips of willow, a long ball of string, a box of coloured beads and, lastly, half a dozen assorted feathers.

"Cool!" both boys shouted in unison and in no time at all Imogen was giving a lesson on Dreamcatcher making to two highly attentive pupils.

"I bet you've never paid so much attention to a lesson in school as you are now," I chuckled, coming to stand beside their chairs.

"Ha-ha Dad, very funny, not," Freddie said wearily, rolling his eyes at Imogen, much to her amusement.

Tom didn't reply and gave no indication of having even heard my jibe. His face contorted in concentration, the tip of his small pink tongue protruding from his mouth as he threaded the string around the willow circle he had already created.

Half an hour later three Dreamcatchers hung from the roof poles, one over each of our beds.

"I can't wait to go to bed tonight!" Tom said excitedly.

"Saddo," Freddie muttered, though his eyes frequently returned to his own creation with a mixture of wonder and anticipation.

"You're so clever knowing about all these things, you are quite wasted as a bookshop manager." Without thinking about it I was standing next to Imogen and had placed my hand around her upper back to rest lightly on her bare shoulder and squeezed it affectionately.

In response her arm had slid around my waist and together we gazed at the boys and their Indian spiritual creations.

"Thank you," I said quietly just for her ears. "I'm sure it will do Tom the power of good."

"My pleasure, but it's the least I could do for you, having me to stay and letting me share your holiday and this beautiful place with you." She rested her head in the curve of my shoulder and there was a trace of sadness in her voice.

"Oh crap!" She suddenly blurted out, breaking the spell, forcing us apart and causing the boys to stare at her in alarm as she started to rush around the tent stuffing her things into bags. "Hospital. Gotta fly."

Though Imogen insisted on driving herself to the hospital, we followed behind in case she did not feel up to the drive after the cast had been removed. I suspect that Tom would also have sulked for weeks if he had missed the chance to watch her cast being removed.

"Don't even think about laughing," she warned us as the cast was finally removed and she stared in dismay at the pale, wrinkled skin from her wrist to her elbow, contrasted against the healthy, honey brown of her upper arm.

"Would you like to take your mum's plaster home as a memento?" the doctor asked after finding everything to his satisfaction.

"She's not my mummy. My mummy's dead, this is Imogen." Tom was quite forthright in his response, leaving the young doctor more than a little embarrassed and looking for the nearest black hole to swallow him up.

"We're just good friends," she laughed it off, though the look she gave me with those deep blue eyes said so much more and yet I could interpret nothing.

After a celebratory lunch in a pub in town, we bade a sad farewell to a heavyhearted Imogen, demanding that we came to see her at the bookshop before we departed. Once again her absence from the camp left a noticeable gap in our ranks. It was not just the gap where her bed had been, where just over twenty-four hours previously she had sat and spilt coffee on her bosom, but it felt as though the lines read by a fourth character in a play had been omitted from the performance. If felt strange and even though the boys still made a good impression of a horde of the whirling dervish, the place was emptier; the lush grass was not as green, nor the sky above so blue.

I was sitting in the tent, playing the guitar quietly to myself when a small cough caught my attention.

"Hello boys, what's going on?" Standing side by side to attention, shoulders touching for moral support and wearing the most serious faces I had seen in ages, the well-tanned boys clearly had something important to say, so I put the guitar down to give them my full attention.

"Daddy, Tom and I have been talking and well, we were wondering whether we could stay a bit longer."

"What about seeing your friends, computer games and TV?" I was completely taken aback.

"We like it here more. It's more fun and there's so much to do and it's all gone so quickly," Freddie's words tumbled out.

"And I like sleeping outside in our tent," Tom added earnestly.

"And we haven't been to watch a cricket match."

"And you promised to take us to Stonehenge and we haven't done that yet either, so we can't go home." Freddie wrapped up the case for the defence and both hopped up and down with anxious anticipation, eyes shining with the hope of youth that expects disappointment but still demands the delivery of miracles.

"Well, I'm not sure, I mean Mrs Fry will be expecting us." The surprise was still evident on my face and in my disbelieving voice.

"You can call her," Freddie parried.

"You don't want to disappoint Guy and Dominic, do you?"

"Yes!" They both shouted out laughing. "Please, please, please can we stay?"

Thinking quickly on my feet I realised that with all that was going on in my mind at the moment and with more questions than answers, coupled with us all getting on so well, it would be an ideal solution for us to stay on longer.

"Well…" I looked at my two wild haired, tanned, fit, healthy and impossibly handsome boys. I toyed with them um'ing and ar'ing to stretch out the tension a little longer before continuing, "I think that would be an excellent idea and if the General says it's okay with him, then we can stay."

"Hooray!" they both cheered and proceeded to dance around the woodburner whooping and hollering.

So early the next morning, we dropped in on the Manor house and hammered at the door. The General feigned a nonchalant air that we could do as we wished, though underneath seemed quite delighted that we were staying and a further invitation for lunch was accepted as eagerly as it was offered.

The now familiar ring of the bell announced our arrival. The shop was cool and a welcome relief from the heat of another fine day.

"I suppose you've come to break my heart and say farewell and have a nice life?" Imogen sniffed, the tears already starting to well up behind her glasses.

"May I say you are looking quite beautiful this morning?" She had chosen a simple long sleeved, white v-neck top that hid her deathly white forearm but showed off her tan to perfection. She was also wearing her hair down rather than the more formal ponytail and with a wide belt drawing in a bright yellow skirt and accentuating her waistline, she was, I realised, a very attractive woman indeed.

"You complete sod. You can't come in here and say nice things like that to me and then leave." She was now crying openly. "Oh damn it all to hell, and I promised myself that I wouldn't cry."

"Shall we tell her, boys?" They nodded conspiratorially.

"Now then, you are going to have to moderate your language, young lady, if you are going to be in the presence of young impressionable children for any period of time." I wagged a finger at her in mock-admonishment, then broke into a huge grin.

"What? Why? What's going on?" She fumed at being left out of our little secret; then the meaning of the words sank in. "You're not staying, are you? Are you? You *are*." Her voice rose in both pitch and level of excitement until we could hardly understand a word she was saying.

"We're staying, we're staying!" the boys chanted.

"Quiet boys, this is a shop," I tried to temper their enthusiasm.

"Oh stuff that." Imogen came around from behind her desk in a swirl of yellow and gave each of the boys a hug and a kiss on the cheek. "How wonderful! I'm so pleased for you, you're going to have a smashing time."

"And what about me?" I opened my arms and with a great deal of reluctant pretence she came. She pressed herself against me and reached up on tiptoes to touch my lips with a kiss that said more than just good friends.

"Daddy and Imogen sitting in a tree, K.I.S.S.I.N.G." Tom shouted out the children's rhyme and clapped his hands in delight.

"And I can't say how happy I am that you're staying," she whispered in my ear before turning on Tom and planting a further kiss on his cheek amidst howls of mock protest.

"So how long are you going to stay for?" she asked once things had calmed down and a rather indignant elderly gentleman had left without buying.

"We'll play it by ear, but I would have thought for another couple of weeks, till the end of August at the latest," I replied.

"When can I come out and stay again?" She stopped and rephrased her question. "Rather, can I come out and see you all again and, if so, when?"

She was as excited as a schoolgirl having passed her exams, and after swapping mobile phone numbers so we could keep in touch, we agreed to meet in a couple of days time.

I was elated and equally I was worried. To be blunt, I was bloody confused. The words "It was the best of times, It was the worst of times" sprang to mind. I could not refute that I was deeply attracted to this woman. I was not looking for love, marriage or any long-term relationship. A quick summer romance would have been fun, but on the other hand, deep down, did I really want more? And at the end of it all the practicality of the real world meant that I could only say goodbye.

I was trying to simplify my life, not over complicate it; to strip away the layers of stress that had built up, not add more. She made me smile; I longed to see her and missed her when she was not beside me. My stomach tied itself in knots when I thought of her and my heart jumped when our eyes met, irrespective of reason. She brightened up my life, yet I could not have her, because I could not promise her anything.

Much to think about, I thought to myself as we returned to camp.

"Dad, we've decided to form a tribe," Freddie announced importantly the following evening after supper.

"We're going to call it The Fighting Merediths," Tom confirmed proudly, jutting out his chest.

"So, we're going to have a ceremony tonight and we're all going to have Indian names and we must promise things to each other in the tribe and if you break them then you can get thrown out," Freddie continued.

"Well, right, er, fantastic." Once the immediate images of college initiation ceremonies, drinking races and various other sado-masochistic tests had passed through my mind, I was left intrigued as to what was planned for later that evening.

I was not to be disappointed.

Once the campfire was crackling and the flames were flicking their tongues up into the dark night sky the first tribal meeting was called to order by Freddie. He was bare-chested and wore feathers in his dark hair. He had found some wire and fashioned this into a bracelet that gripped his upper arm. Tom, like his elder brother was also bare-chested with feathers in his hair, but had used a burnt stick to cover his torso in charcoal circles and non-symmetrical lines. He sat cross-legged around the fire and with a serious-faced nod from his brother, he started to thump on the drums in his lap. There was no discernible rhythm—volume was obviously the key—and after a minute the drums stopped and Freddie applauded his brother's efforts.

Oaths were sworn to look after each other, be kind to one another and always to protect any member of the family against someone not in the tribe. More charcoal was then daubed on our faces and we each received a lucky charm. This took the form of a leather bootlace threaded through a small stone with a naturally made hole that the boys had found in the river.

This was followed by the naming ceremony where we were given our tribal names. Freddie had chosen Running Bear and Tom with great gravitas accepted the name of Runs like the Wind. I without time to give much thought to the matter could only conjure to mind Howling Wolf and so it was that I entered the tribal family, The Fighting Merediths.

The last part of the ceremony was to dance around the campfire three times in each direction, with Tom bashing away madly on his drums, then a mad dash in the dark, down to the pool to complete the test of courage. This involved edging ourselves into the cold water accompanied by some fairly unheroic shrieks and screams, where we had to submerge ourselves fully for ten seconds before the ceremony was considered complete.

With teeth still chattering uncontrollably despite the warm night air, I lay awake in bed long after the boys' even breathing let me know they had fallen asleep. I had been tempted to laugh at the juvenile minded seriousness of the whole affair, but this would have hurt both boys to the quick and made my cruelty quite unforgivable. I did not however fail to recognise the importance of the ceremony both to them and for myself. They were making a statement that shouted out that they wanted to be a part of this family; that they were proud of who they were. I, in turn, felt equally proud and relieved that they had felt confident in allowing me to be a part of their ritual and that this in turn meant the rifts of the past had been healed. We had reached a landmark; we were a family reborn. And I was now Howling Wolf Meredith, tribal chief of the Fighting Merediths; now that was something to put on my business card when we got home!

I swear I slept with a smile on my face the whole night through.

Chapter Eight

The next two weeks maintained their blissfully slow pace; the weather held and we enjoyed the full benefit of the outdoor life. Tans darkened and I noticed that even Freddie's stomach muscles were starting to stand proud when in certain positions. Even without realising it my own potbelly, the infamous office workers' ailment, had diminished; not entirely but sufficient to warrant a trip to the shops to purchase a belt to keep my shorts from slipping around my ankles.

I felt healthy, happy and relaxed. A month ago I would have been satisfied with any one of the three and though answers still eluded me, not least of all those surrounding Imogen, it was more than I could have dreamed of.

Hell, I didn't even know what day it was unless it cropped up in conversation. We didn't miss Television and I couldn't be bothered with newspapers. There was never any good news anyway, it was either scandal or political-religious war and insurgency and ultimately there was nothing I could do about it, except get angry and stressed.

It was only upon giving Imogen my number that I realised I had left the phone in the Landrover glovebox and its battery had run down. I had several missed calls and a message from Jonny gruffly letting me know that all was going well, but I had no inclination whatsoever to make contact with anyone in my day-to-day life back home.

I no longer woke up in the morning reluctant to put my feet on the floor, my mind already spinning with worry, trying to juggle a dozen work and home life priorities. The churn in my stomach from feeling physically sick as the day spiralled out of control until I fell into bed mentally exhausted, with a whisky addled brain still trying to resolve problems and issues keeping me awake until the early hours. And then the cycle would commence again. The day ruled by electronic bells, alarms, bleepers and buzzers, assaulting already neurotic nerves and negating the need for thought, they demanded I adhere to a schedule that was no longer of my choosing.

Now I awoke to the soothing sound of the lark or a blackbird, revitalised and eager for the day. The day unfolded with a sense of calm chaos as we roamed the valley, or went on day trips. I spent time thinking about what I wanted, about others and what they wanted. We enjoyed the simple beauty and miracle of watching the sun settling over the horizon, we bought a book from Imogen and learnt some of the constellations in the night sky, pointing them out to each other with delight and wonder at the mystery of the heavenly stars. Then to end the day I slipped into bed and slept, physically tired and mentally relaxed; a perfect combination.

To say it was a perfect worry free existence was perhaps a stretch too far. The boys and I would still bicker and argue occasionally, though far less frequent and explosive than before. We were a family after all, living in close proximity to one another and had our own opinions and would have generated even greater concern perhaps if we didn't get a little heated under the collar every now and then.

The main concerns monopolising my mind were centred around two questions—two questions that were easy to say, quick to say in one breath; in fact, you could say both questions in one breath, they were that simple.

"What should we do after the holiday and what about Imogen?"

A further layer of complexity sat below these conundrums and added to the dense cloud that hovered over our future. Could one be resolved independently of the other, or were they both so closely intertwined that they were in fact one and the same question? Or more worrying, were they so diametrically opposed that only one could be answered at the expense of the other?

In fact, the answer to the second question partially resolved itself one evening after I had taken the boys down to Somerset so Tom could finally get to watch his game of cricket. Not being cricket fans, Freddie and I found the day terminally boring and had brought books to help staunch the utter tedium and heavy lidded fatigue that quickly descended once we had settled in. Once the game got underway, Tom, to my surprise, stayed in his seat with only his eyes roving around the grounds from crease to bowler to scoreboard. The only movement being the frantic, spasmodic waving of his boundary card, followed by mimicking the umpire's strange heathen hand language with an accompaniment of raucous cheering and unrestrained laughter to celebrate any number of boundaries that were scored by both sides.

If Tom had been particularly pious or religiously inclined, this was the equivalent of being taken through the doors of Westminster Cathedral. He was bowled over by the size of the ground and was quite in awe of the white clad popes who defended their altars with a zealous fervour whilst the philistine tried to smite them down. Heroes of legendary and mythical proportion were created that day in a child's mind. Though on the way home, his constant chatter of "Did you see that shot, didn't so-and-so bowl fast, what about that catch?" nearly gave me cause to dump him on the side of the road and let him seek alternative sponsorship to see him through to adulthood.

Imogen was already back at the campsite, her battered hatchback parked at the top of the track and I fondly imagined her relaxed stride barefoot through the meadow, her leather sandals swinging casually in one hand and a long flowing skirt swinging seductively around her legs.

"I thought I'd get here early and surprise you with a special meal to say thanks for all the times you've had me over." She straightened up from leaning over the cooker, stretched her aching back and delicately flicked a damp lock of blonde hair off her red face. "Unfortunately I forgot that my culinary skills never match the effort I put in." She held up a piece of rump steak that now looked like a hockey puck.

I laughed. "It's the thought that counts and for that I say a thousand thanks. Firstly though, I've spent the last three hours promising myself a reward of the coldest bottle of beer in Wiltshire. Can I get you anything?"

"No thanks, I've already helped myself to a glass of the old vino. But why a reward, was it that bad?" she laughed quizzically.

And I proceeded to tell her the events of the day and that my sainthood should be in the post.

"That's what dads are for, though, isn't it? Tell me you'd rather have been at work today?" she challenged my thinking.

"Fair point, you're right, I wouldn't have wanted to have been anywhere else today," I conceded willingly.

"Yeuch, we're not eating that, are we?" Freddie and Tom turned their noses up at the burnt sacrifices still in the frying pan, with a look of suspicion and disgust. "I'm going to become a vegetarian if we are," Freddie added, giving it a prod with a fork.

"Sorry boys, like good old King Alfred I've burnt the food." Imogen picked up the blackened frying pan and shovelled the contents into the bin with a sickly thud.

"Who is King Alfred and what did he do?" Tom enquired.

Imogen then proceeded to give the boys an autobiographical account of the legendary King of Wessex. The boys sat enthralled on the log whilst she brought the ancient kingdom and its history to life. Their ears pricked up with excitement when she told them that the very area where they were now sitting could have been the site of a battle against invading Viking hordes. Their eyes eagerly scoured the ground when she talked of flint arrowheads, ornaments, chain mail and even skeletons found on archaeological sites and even by amateurs with metal detectors.

She had a way with words that brought the subject vividly to life; they could see, feel, touch, smell and hear the sound of battle raging around them. She adapted her language and her style to suit her audience. Her hands drew pictures, her body re-enacted and her voice took on different accents and colloquialisms. And her audience was hooked and clamoured for more. King Alfred was seated around this very fire with Freddie and Tom literally peering over his shoulder as the cakes began to smoulder and burn.

"I think I would have become a historian if you had been my school mistress," I complimented her afterwards as I served up a simple tuna pasta dish.

"Steady tiger. Well, you certainly wouldn't have become a cook if I'd tried to teach that." She laughed and started to eat. "Fantastic. It must be so nice to be able to cook."

I didn't need to ask her what she did for food at home. Earlier conversation made it abundantly clear that her mother didn't lift a finger around the house and if Imogen couldn't cook, then it could only be cans and TV dinners; the electronic *ping* of the microwave, stir, pour and eat.

"Dad's a great cook," Freddie muttered between mouthfuls. "My favourite is when he does toad in the hole."

"Why, thank you for saying so, Freddie." He blushed at the compliment that was still visible even through his darkened skin.

"We haven't had toad in the hole for ages," Tom spoke with his mouth full of pasta. "Can we have it tomorrow Dad?"

"Haven't quite got the right cooker to make it, but I promise I'll make it for you when we get back home."

"Sounds like I'm missing out on something if I haven't tasted the world famous Meredith toad in the hole," Imogen added, a smile touching the corner of her lips.

"I guess we'll have to invite you up to London to stay then." I laid the serious invitation before her.

"A two hundred mile round trip just for toad in the hole. It had better be good." She giggled.

"Just wait and see, you won't be disappointed, I promise."

"Right, you've got yourself a deal, Meredith." And to seal it, we shook hands across the table.

The boys cleared the plates away before pulling out my guitar and Cole Porter must have been turning in his grave as I played his timeless classic *Don't Fence Me In*. This had become the boys' favourite; a song they could relate to and they never seemed to tire of singing it over and over again. In the end it took the good luck of a broken string to bring the song to a close.

After I had received a strength-sapping hug from Tom in thanks for his memorable day, the boys slipped inside the Yurt and half an hour later their quiet whispers had ceased and all was silent within.

"Fancy a midnight stroll?" Imogen asked quietly, getting to her feet to fetch a fleece jumper from her pack. "I need to walk off that lovely meal you gave us this evening."

In no great hurry, we walked down the hill in silence, enjoying the peace and quiet around us. Imogen slipped her arm about my waist and so like young lovers, happiest and fulfilled when together and guided by the silvery light of the moon, we strolled towards the river.

"Let's have a dip!" Imogen suddenly burst out eagerly.

"But I haven't brought my trunks," I replied somewhat prudishly.

"Have you never been skinny dipping before?" She danced ahead of me, spinning around in the shadow darkness as a cloud passed slowly in front of the moon, lighting it up like a white negative.

"Yes, but it'll be bloody cold in there as well at this time of night," I lied quickly, feeling as though to admit I hadn't would have been a slur on my status in her eyes.

"Worried I may not see you at your best?" she teased, her hands flirting playfully at the buttons on my shirt.

"Okay, okay, you win, but let me do it." I slapped her warm fumbling hands away and pulled the shirt over my head and dropped it at my feet. Then without pausing in case I considered what I was doing was both stupid and immature, I slipped my shorts off to join the shirt.

The cloud passed silently overhead and with no interference the moon's beams exposed, like a theatre curtain reveals the actors to the audience, our silhouetted outlines.

"Have you taken your clothes off yet?" Imogen asked brazenly.

"Yes, I'm standing here as naked as the day I was born."

"I bet you're not. Oops, sorry, yes you are." Her hands quickly darted out to touch warm skin and quickly withdrew.

An erotic rustling of clothing and then silence once more.

"Have you taken your clothes off, or is this just a trick?"

In response her hand reached out of the darkness and took mine, guiding it down her ribcage. My trembling fingers felt the smooth ridges of each rib; then moving further down, my hand briefly cupped a soft love handle before finding the hard hip bone and then something else.

"What's this? You've got your knickers on!" I protested strongly, my fingers investigating elastic and embroidery, so coarse to the touch after the soft smooth skin and contours of her body. "You can get those off for a start," I demanded amiably.

"Oh drat, I hadn't meant to let you go down that far. I don't know what came over me." She was slightly breathless. Her small fingers hooked into the sides of her knickers and bending quickly at the waist, with an added wiggle of her hips my fingers were able to continue their sensuous journey unimpeded onto her thigh.

"Come on, last one in makes the coffee." She whirled away and with a brief flash of her white bottom she was completely swallowed up by the night.

Her feet disturbed the silent running water as she waded over to the pool, ending in a large splash as she decided it was better to get it over with rather than ease her body slowly into the chilled water.

"Jesus Christ that's cold!" she shrieked between gasps.

Cautiously feeling my way over the smooth stones and silt, I bit down hard on my cheeks, determined not to scream, berating myself as something between a tortured groan and an unmanly squeak escaped my lips as my private parts touched the water then sank beneath the surface.

"Is this your idea of fun?" I muttered through chattering teeth.

The moonlight cast a pale reflection on the water that highlighted ripples on the surface caused by our shivering bodies, yet I could not make out any features of Imogen's face, though two small, twinkling pools let me know that she was watching me.

"Stop being such a wuss," she chided, her words coming out in fits and gasps. "Don't you feel so alive?"

"Yes, but probably not for much longer," I quipped in return as I felt every fibre in my body scream out for mercy, every goosebump raised in protest, every hair follicle standing erect.

"I think you may be right, it seemed a good idea at the time." Her smooth wet body brushed past my legs, sending small waves to cover parts of my chest that had not been submersed, driving further gasps of breath deep from within my lungs.

I reached out and circled her waist, pulling her to me, her body slippery and rubbery in my hands. Slowly and without protest she came to me, bringing her legs up so as to sit on my lap, her fleshy buttocks nestling comfortably on my thighs, her arms wrapping about my neck. The two shimmering pools looked directly into my face and I thought I could detect through the shadows and half-light, a smile of triumph.

"Imogen, are you smiling?" I asked quietly.

"No, I'm forcing my teeth together to stop them biting off my tongue!" she giggled. "Yes of course I'm smiling," she conceded.

"Why?"

"Well, I don't think I've ever been so happy as I am at this moment in time. Ever!" She reinforced the sincerity of her words. "Thank you." She pressed herself against me, forcing the water from between us until her breasts were squashed against my chest before kissing me on the lips.

A long lingering kiss, passionate, sensuous and unhurried; the twin stars temporarily extinguished as she closed her eyes and a soft moan escaped her lips.

"Oh, this is no good. Come on, the coffee's on me." She gently but firmly prised herself from my hold and slipped from my lap. Then holding hands to steady one another over the slippery stones and rocks beneath our feet, we made our way up the bank. After a brief search we found the piles of clothes and without bothering to dress, walked still hand in hand, still naked, back to the tent, under the all auspicious gaze of the celestial heavens.

"I need you to know something." Imogen blew on the steaming mug of coffee and sipped at the hot dark liquid. "I don't know what's going on at the moment, between us that is. One minute I think I've fallen head over heels in love with you. God I can't believe I've just said that. Do mature adults really say things like that?" Ignoring my open mouth that was about to reply she carried on. "Never mind, it's out now. Well, as I said, one minute I think I'm madly in love with you and the next I think don't be such a stupid old woman, it's a crush, a holiday romance, a fling. A shooting star that will burn brightly for a moment and then die out."

I had just taken a sip of my whisky-laced coffee, but before I could swallow and speak she had started again. "Now don't get me wrong, I like sex as much as the next person, probably more since I haven't had it for so long and, well, to be honest, I'd like nothing more than for you and I to take a rug right now and well, you know what." For once her frank and blunt words faltered and glancing across I noticed she was watching me shyly, her chin hidden in the folds of the red fleece jacket, her blue eyes still twinkling at me through the fringes of her hair.

"But I don't just want to be a notch in one of your tent poles, a holiday shag and I don't think that you're ready to give me more." Imogen's coarse words were a brave defence against the pain and anguish she was so keenly feeling.

"Don't look at me, Meredith." She warned. "I can't believe I'm going to cry." And she buried her head in the warm fleece and sobbed uncontrollably.

"Imogen," I hugged her to me, stroking the fine blonde hair that shone brightly in the light of the lantern. "Hey, come on, cheer up, you said this was the happiest time of your life, remember?"

"I was lying," she sobbed.

"Come on, let me have a look at that beautiful face of yours."

"No, go away."

I took her head in both my hands and lifted it up out of the protection of the fleece.

"I look awful now," she wailed and tried to bury her head once more, but I wouldn't let her. Instead, I knelt in front of her chair and used my handkerchief to dry her wet cheeks, before kissing her gently on the lips.

"You look beautiful," I said truthfully from the heart.

"Give me that handkerchief," she ordered and blew her shining nose in an extremely un-ladylike manner, before folding it inwards and handing it back to me.

"Thanks for that." I put the wet cotton square back into my pocket. She laughed half-heartedly.

"That's more like it. Right now it's my turn to talk." I dragged my chair next to hers and placed my arm about her shoulders. She turned her head and nestled into my shoulder, her hand resting lightly upon my chest.

Taking a swig of coffee, the whisky fumes further fuelling the warm liquid as it slid down my throat, I began to speak. They were words born, nurtured and driven from the heart, accompanied by a warm, caring voice, soft and full of tenderness.

"I came here looking to bring a family back together; to mend so many fences, broken over time and some I thought almost irreparable, that I didn't know where to start. I believed that by putting the boys first and foremost in all that we did, my own personal happiness would be reborn. And so far, it has proved to be the case. We are closer now than I ever could have dared believe was possible and, as I mentioned the other night, I now dread having to go back to a world that will demand a wedge is driven between us once more."

I finished the coffee and affectionately kissed the top of her head before continuing. "My wife died less than a year ago, though I mourned her loss long before then. At the time I felt that my heart was ripped apart during the day, then was repaired overnight to be ripped apart again the next day. And I believe that if it weren't for the children I would not have survived; gladly, at times, I would have taken my own life to be with her just one more time. Since then I have woken up in the morning, I have remembered to breathe in and out whilst trying desperately to keep up a losing battle against a world that seemed to want to crush what little life was left in my body and soul."

"And then we bought this tent and came here. I was n't looking for love and I wasn't even looking for a holiday shag." I chuckled quietly. "It would only have added complication to the chaotic world I was and still am trying to resolve."

"I know, my dearest Meredith, and my deepest pain is that I understand and that it is hopeless for me to believe anything good could ever come of all of this for us," Imogen lamented.

"But," I continued, "I hadn't counted on meeting you. I hadn't counted on meeting a beautiful woman who has made me laugh out loud when I believed all laughter had been wrung from my body. A woman who makes my stomach churn and my heart leap with joy when we are about to meet and causes such sorrow and wrenching pain when we part. And above all a woman who can respect and love my children as her own."

Imogen had pushed herself away from me, her eyes openly staring at me, a look of shock and disbelief upon her face. "Tell me, what is it you're saying? Are you saying what I think you're saying?" she demanded forcibly from me.

I laughed warmly. "What I am trying to say and badly at that, is that I believe two things. Firstly, that it is all right for mature adults to say, I think I've fallen head over heels in love with you. And secondly that I have fallen head over heels in love with you."

Imogen appeared to have gone into shock. Her mouth opened and shut but emitted no sound. I kissed her on the lips in an attempt to break the spell, but it was some moments before she was able to speak.

"You're not playing with me, are you, Meredith? If you are, that would be the cruellest joke in the world and I would never speak to you again." There was hope, doubt, caution and warning all mixed up in her voice and she punched me hard on the arm to ensure she had my attention.

"Darling Imogen, I love you—now will you shut up and kiss me." Still sitting in my chair I flew over backwards as she threw herself into my open arms, knocking over the pole that held the lantern, plunging us into darkness save for the majestic, white light of the moon.

I loved Imogen and she loved me. But the burning question still remained—what to do about it?

Chapter Nine

Much to our joy, we persuaded Imogen to take two weeks immediate holiday and spend it with us, staying in the Yurt. She had phoned the bookshop owner and after threatening to just leave there and then, he grudgingly agreed to her request. Sadly but not unsurprisingly, her mother had accepted the news with even less good grace. After her initial pleading and begging had failed to move Imogen though tears flowed freely on both sides, she had become quite vitriolic. And despite her debilitating arthritis and her self-diagnosed blood clot in her legs, her mother brought her poisonous scorn out into the open and harried Imogen all the way from the front door of her house to the Landrover. It was shocking to watch and even I felt intimidated by this large grey haired woman with an enormous, unsupported chest that drooped around her midriff and made her appear physically deformed. Once she realised her verbal abuse and disgusting language was falling upon deaf ears and Imogen had thrown her bags into the back of the Landrover, the vicious old hag turned to more physical abuse. She raised her stout walking stick over her head and with surprising strength rained a torrent of blows on the bonnet and side panels of the Landrover.

Not even waiting for Imogen to clip in her seat belt, I had put my foot to the floor and the Landrover had shot down the road. With a sense of morbid horror I checked the rear view mirror expecting to see her running alongside with a large knife in her equally large callused hands. Instead, she had taken a few laboured paces after us, then hawked and spat a large globule of phlegm after us and stuck up two fingers in farewell.

The boys were terrified and even Freddie took a moment before bedtime to blow on his Dreamcatcher to remove any dust that might impede any bad dreams from getting caught by the net.

"I still have nightmares, you know," Imogen said, her words noticeably slurred.

Imogen had been quite inconsolable immediately after the traumatic scene and even the thought of an unprecedented two weeks holiday had failed to lift the black dog hanging over her. We agreed after the boys had gone to bed to get very, very drunk. With three bottles of white wine now standing empty on the table and the bottle of scotch about to join them, we were both trying hard to live up to our agreement.

"The kind that wakes you up screaming, covered head to toe in sweat, your bedclothes soaked through and terrified of the dark."

"Can you remember what they're about in the morning?" I asked, my own words thick upon my tongue.

"Oh yes, it's always the same dream." Despite the warm night, she shivered at the images in her mind and leaned forward to warm herself on the crackling campfire.

"What are they about?" I asked innocently.

She thought about it for a moment, then took a breath. "Do you remember I told you that years ago I used to be a teacher?" she asked.

I nodded.

And still staring into the flames she told me her story.

"When I went to university I became a bit of a party animal. I flirted with all the boys, had a hangover every weekend and occasionally found myself in someone's bed that I regretted the moment I opened my eyes and they told me their name was something nerdy like Barry, or Clive. I suppose it was the story of the naïve country girl going to the big cosmopolitan city and doing everything to excess. Well, just before graduating I met a man at a party. He was a teacher at a school up in Leeds and he seemed so suave and sophisticated; so educated." She laughed a hollow painful cry that made me want to reach out to hold and reassure her, but I restrained myself.

"To cut a long story short, I graduated and moved up to Leeds to be with Bill. We moved in together and lived the life of the suburban middle class. Dinner parties, summer barbecues and the odd political rally just to keep our revolutionary blood on the boil. You see, we were going to change the world, change the way that children were educated. Instead of the stuffy noses to books, we knew children learnt more if they enjoyed what they were doing. Christ, thanks to the Attenborough film they could all spell Jurassic and tell the difference between a tyrannosaurus rex and a velociraptor, but couldn't do their ten times table. And worst of all so many parents were indifferent to their children's situation; they just didn't care. 'It never did me no harm and its not like there's any jobs out there anyhow,' she mimicked a voice from her past.

"Then I started feeling violently ill and I just couldn't shake it off. So after a few days I went to the doctors and lo and behold, like a bolt out of the blue I was pregnant. I went straight out of the doctors and straight into the nearest wine bar and had several gin and tonics to get over the shock. By the time I had finished my second G and T I realised I was overjoyed at the prospect of becoming a mother, creating a family, setting up a proper home, completing the circle of life. And I rushed home to tell Bill." She sighed sadly and shook her head at the flames.

"Bill was furious. How could I be so careless, how could we bring a child into this evil uncaring world? It was entirely my fault. I had never felt so alone in all my life. The one person who I thought I really knew, who I looked up to, adored and wished to please more than anything in the world, wanted nothing to do with it. He demanded that I have an abortion and I told him where he could stick the needle. He moved into the spare room and whenever we spoke to each other it always ended in a blistering row with him storming out and me in floods of tears.

"Then one day, I was in my seventh month of pregnancy we had an argument. About the colour of paint for the nursery of all things." Silent tears started to roll down her cheeks but I realised it was important for her to share this heart-wrenching and personal part of her life with me, so made no move to offer her my comfort and sympathy.

"I wanted yellow, cornflower yellow. And Bill, well Bill just didn't care; didn't give a damn. I suppose looking back on it now we should have broken up way before then. It was an impossible position that neither of us would, or could in my case, back down from. It was February. A cold Saturday morning, the frost lay on the ground, so pretty. I remember thinking how beautiful it was, nature masking the mess and destruction that man has made with his careless, thoughtless search for a more civilised world. Bill stormed out with his now familiar slam of the front door; a friend was picking him up to go off on a protest march. CND, anti-vivisection, human rights, one or the other. I didn't think about it at the time but it makes me laugh now that he was so passionate about all those bloody rights movements. Stop the seal murders yet wanted to terminate his own child.

"Bugger you, I thought, and after sticking two fingers up at the front door I jumped in the car to go down to the DIY store to get the paint. Never mind the warning, don't drink and drive. Don't drive when you're so angry that you can hardly breathe and you're crying so much that your tears are filling up the car footwell."

She paused for a moment to take a deep breath and wipe the tears from her cheeks with the back of her hand.

"I didn't see the ice, the car spun off the road and the next thing I know I wake up in hospital and a lovely old doctor tells me how lucky I've been to escape with concussion, two fractured ribs and a broken collarbone. Then before I can ask, he breaks the news to me that I've lost my baby. He had such a kind face and I could tell by the way his face was all creased up that it was terribly upsetting for him as well and all I could do was apologise for being such a nuisance. Bill came to see me and told me how sorry he was but perhaps it was fate that it just wasn't meant to be. I spent a week in hospital with lovely nurses trying to be kind to me, but I didn't want to know. And as soon as they released me, I went straight home, packed my things, pushed the door key back through the letterbox and took the first train back home to mum. I lost my job of course, but I can tell you that things like that kind of wash over you when you're in a catatonic state. I just sat in a chair, my mum in another though I hardly knew she was there, and stared out of the window.

Eighteen months later I went off to join one of those philosophical, hippie soul-healing camps. You know the sort, where you all sit around cross-legged and after a bit of chanting you talk about things. In fact, it helped clear a lot of the bullshit out of my head. But sometimes you can get to a point where you can talk all you want, but what you really need to do is just get on with life and accept that some memories are going to be with you forever. So I left and guess I've been falling in and out of things ever since. And the dream I get, though not so often these days, is a swirling, black void and white lines that come from nowhere and take the shape of my baby, just like the pictures you see when you go for your scans. Then the baby takes its thumb out of its mouth and points a half-formed finger at me and its transparent, eyeless skull starts to cry out, but I can't hear what it's saying. And I know it's in pain and trying to tell me something, but I can't reach it, it's like my feet are stuck in porridge and as I reach out my arms it sinks down into this dark vortex of nothingness."

I rose from my chair and went to her. She clung to me as the sobs racked her entire body and I held her safely in my arms until they subsided.

"You see, I've never let a man get close to me since. I haven't been able to trust a man again, to open myself up to that amount of pain once more. I just know that my mind and soul would not be able to cope with another betrayal, it would kill me." She whispered: "Or rather I would kill myself. I suspect that maybe I'm not all there, perhaps even just a little bit mad."

I said nothing but continued to hold her, to let her know she was safe in my arms.

Later as I lay in bed listening to the peaceful breathing of Freddie, Tom and Imogen, surrounded by the serenity of mother earth and protected by the white canvas overhead, one thing was now clear in my mind. All doubts were removed. Whatever direction the winds of change blew for the Fighting Meredith tribe, Imogen was going to be a core part of that future.

Chapter Ten

The following morning after breakfast I took the boys aside to have a quiet, surreptitious word and with vigorous head nodding in response, they smiled and slipped inside the Yurt, the door shutting conspiratorially behind them. I then invited Imogen, somewhat forcibly as she was suffering the after effects of a night on alcohol, for a long walk. With events of the previous night seemingly forgotten, we strolled hand-in-hand down through fields of long grass, its lush green carpet broken up by thousands of bright yellow buttercups that attracted the soft, unmistakable buzz of bumblebees already labouring in the heat of the morning sun.

"What are the boys up to?" she slyly slipped into our general conversation.

"Now that's a secret," I replied, tapping the side of my nose.

"Come on, do tell," Imogen pleaded.

"Not even under extreme torture, you'll just have to wait and see." I laughed and led her into yet another small copse where Andrew Ponsonby had advised we would find an old folly, built by one of the General's ancestors at the time when they were very much in fashion.

"What if I were to throw myself at you and let you do wicked things with my body?" she suggested huskily.

With a look of playful innocence upon her face, Imogen lightly gripped her low cut, plain linen camisole top and coquettishly fanned the loose material, each time revealing a little more of the deep cleavage and curves of her unfettered breasts.

"Stop, I'll tell you everything! The tunnel is under the hut. We were going to break out at midnight and make our way to the nearest port using counterfeit coffee machine tokens," I joked, though much to Imogen's amusement and pleasure, she noticed that I was talking to her chest.

"Do you find me attractive, physically that is?" She caught up with me and looped her arm through mine. "It's just I know that I'm a little on the larger side, comfortable, I believe one might say."

"Why do you ask that?" I was taken by surprise, still not used to her direct and often frank approach.

"Well, you saw me naked last night; hell, I even sat on your lap and yet you didn't, you know. You didn't try anything on."

"Much to my lasting regret I didn't see you naked last night. It was as black as hell and I couldn't even see my own hand, never mind yours. And besides," I added, "I want us to make love when we're both ready, physically and emotionally." My eyes now held her own blue gaze.

"Pinch me," she suddenly commanded.

"What? Why? Are you some kind of pervert?" I replied, astounded at where this one was going.

"Pinch me, because I can't believe you are for real." She laughed gaily and gave me a quick hug before elusively dancing away from my tentacle like arms that wished never to let her go.

We climbed a short steep rise, using the trees to pull ourselves up, then jumping for the next one and repeating the process. It was hard work and both of us found ourselves slipping back down the hill on more then one occasion, brushing ourselves down, picking crisp brown leaves and twigs from our hair and to the amusement of the other, starting the climb once more.

Eventually we reached the summit and down on the other side in a glade sparsely populated with young birch and larger, more mature ash trees, lay the now derelict folly. The roof was long gone and two of the walls had collapsed, the brickwork still lying where it fell, though now heavily covered with a rich green moss and stinging nettles sprouting up through the gaps. A mass of ivy clung up the remaining walls, dooming them to the same ultimate fate as those already fallen, as their roots buried deep within the plaster, undermining the stability of the structure. As we descended I noticed that the arched entrance was still intact and part of its rotten lintel remained, precariously held in place by a couple of strands of fence wire and some rubble that had been hastily put in place by a previous visitor, though clearly some years before.

"Come inside, it's just like a carpet—no, more like a mattress!" Imogen squeaked with delight as the thick bed of moss cushioned the impact of her bare feet, springing back into place once she shifted her weight.

Even though I didn't need to, I automatically ducked my head as I walked through the arched doorway. The floor was just as Imogen had said, completely covered from wall to wall in a thick spongy bed of moss. It was so inviting I wanted to lie down, *perchance to sleep awhile*. The same idea must have flicked through Imogen's mind for the next thing I knew I was being dragged down to lie beside her, to gaze up through the open roof to the sun-dappled, verdant foliage in the tree canopy above. I could well understand why the old General's ancestor had built in such a location. It was secluded and as a result peaceful, with only the intermittent calls of the birds in the branches above to prevent us listening to what would otherwise have been complete and utter silence.

Some five minutes later, and strangely refreshed as though I had awoken from a deep sleep, I felt a weight descend across my abdomen and opened my eyes.

"Imogen, what are you doing?" I enquired suspiciously, noticing the mischievous glint in her eyes.

"You never answered my question." She giggled down at me as she reached behind her and removed the grip that was holding her ponytail in place, releasing a cascade of blonde hair to fall seductively around her shoulders.

"What question was that?" My breathing was laboured due to the pressure from above, but it was an enjoyable sensation and I made no effort to move her. Besides which, if she were to move the chances were likely that she would have slid further down to straddle my thighs and there were certain things in that direction I did not want her to be feeling right now.

"Do you find me attractive of course, silly?" she repeated her original question.

"I find you both beautiful and attractive, dearest Imogen. Your eyes so blue, intelligent and kind, yet a warning of a mischievous sense of humour and fun. The way you put a curl of your hair back behind your ear. So natural and unassuming, yet such a sensual gesture. The way you wear your skirts so that they flirt so disgracefully around your legs. And how you carry yourself, so confident, almost brazen were it not for the innocence and vulnerability in your eyes and that you don't even know that you are being so alluring and seductive. Your body so soft and smooth with such tantalising curves that you hide so frustratingly beneath your dress. Oh Imogen, I could talk all day about how attractive and bewitching you are."

"Would you like to see the tantalising curves that I hide beneath my dress?" she whispered in my ear, the rush of breath against my skin so intimate and personal. My throat had gone dry and no saliva would come. I could only nod my confirmation.

Smiling demurely, her eyes not wavering from my own, she rose to her feet and stepped back a pace. Her small, delicate fingers undid each of the buttons on her camisole in turn, revealing a narrow strip of pale skin that ran unhindered from her neck down to her waist. She then turned her back to me and shrugged the light linen from her shoulders where gravity then did the rest, its unseen hands caressing the material down her arms until it fell at her feet. Her hands then reached behind her and located the hidden zip of her skirt, which she lowered in one movement, the sound unnaturally loud in this quiet place. She eased the skirt easily over her hips to reveal the top of her buttocks and with the smallest of wiggles her skirt joined the top around her feet. She was naked underneath.

Still with her back to me, she stepped daintily out of the circle of clothes, the curve at the top of the back of her thighs smiling briefly as the contours of her body reacted to her every movement.

Slowly and gracefully she turned to face me. A nervous smile now replaced the mischievous grin as she stood before me, one arm wrapped protectively across her breasts, the other hand at the top of her thighs.

"Ready?" The nervousness was now apparent in her voice. It was only then that I realised we had not spoken and still my voice would take no command and I nodded once more.

Imogen let her arms fall to her sides to reveal her unashamed nakedness in all its glory. She was majestic and imperious in her beauty, a Nordic goddess from the valley of dreams.

Still bewitched, I could only hold out my hand and she came to me lying beside me on a bed prepared by mother earth herself. Her curves and contours once more changed with her graceful movement hypnotising my mind like a pearlescent paint subtly changes colour in sunlight.

"You are beautiful." The spell was broken as I smiled at her, my hand caressing a curl of her blonde hair back behind her ear.

And at that moment her beauty blossomed throughout her. Confidence and reassurance filled every pore of Imogen's being and her smile radiated warmth and love.

"You realise we can't make love, don't you?" I whispered huskily, afraid that if I did not speak now, I might never speak again.

"Yes," she groaned in frustration. "Though half of me says damn the consequences. But on the other hand?"

"What?" I moaned, angry both at my conscience for this self-imposed constraint and for my own stupidity in not having any protection to hand.

I caught a glint of playfulness in her eye. "Let's just take a small moment in time to spend some time together, just as God intended." Imogen raised her eyebrows suggestively, then still smiling, slipped on top of me and began to undo the buttons on my shirt.

Still picking bits of moss and leaf from our clothes and hair, we ran the last part of the way back to the camp, collapsing with laughter and out of breath into the chairs around the campfire.

"By God, Miss Imogen, you will be the ruin of me." I wheezed with euphoric pleasure.

"Oh, I hope so, my darling Meredith, I do so hope so." She reached across and entwined her fingers with mine, satiated and at peace with all about her.

Once I had caught my breath, I filled the kettle and put it on the ring to boil, then slipped inside the tent.

"How's it going, boys?" I spoke quietly so as not to be heard by Imogen.

Neither Freddie nor Tom looked up from the task in hand and with the serious expressions upon their faces I could see they had put a great deal of effort into their work.

"Nearly ready, Dad." Freddie whispered back, thoroughly enjoying the clandestine secrecy.

"Two minutes, Dad." Tom said before trapping his tongue between his teeth in concentration.

"Well done boys, it looks brilliant. You've really done yourselves proud. Come and get me when you're ready." I winked at them, though neither would have seen the gesture as their heads were already back down focused on finishing Imogen's surprise.

I had just passed Imogen her cup of coffee and taken a quick sip from my own when the door to the Yurt opened and Tom beckoned me inside.

"Back in a moment," I promised Imogen and followed Tom back under the cool protection of the canvas.

"Imogen, can you come here for a moment?" I called out two minutes later.

Imogen opened the door and stepped inside, her eyes immediately falling upon me and two smirking cherubs standing either side of me in front of her bed.

"What are you three up to?" she asked suspiciously, trying to look behind us at her bed and the surrounding area.

Seeing nothing immediately out of the ordinary, her eyes scanned the rest of the tent, even taking a furtive look behind her, but found nothing circumspect.

Freddie, Tom and I all looked at each other, nodded to one another and then as one, pointed above our heads.

Imogen's eyes quickly followed our directions and there, floating above her bed, was her own Dreamcatcher.

Her hands flew to her mouth and tears started to fill her eyes.

"Well," I broke the silence, "you kindly brought one for each of us and as our most honoured guest we realised you didn't have one. So the boys thought we should make one for you."

"And I haven't had one single bad dream since I've had mine," Tom shouted happily.

"Nor me," Freddie added, though with more restraint in his voice.

"They must really work. So we made one for you, so you don't have horrible dreams. Come and see." Tom rushed forward and grabbing a hand he pulled Imogen to where we stood so she could take a closer inspection.

"Oh boys, it's perfectly beautiful. Oh thank you, thank you, thank you." With tears of joy still in her eyes she knelt down and scooped them both into her arms and kissed them both.

The boys both laughed with delight at seeing Imogen so happy and returned her hug with gusto until they over balanced and all three became a mass of tangled limbs on the floor.

Once the boys had helped Imogen back to her feet they proudly explained every step in her Dreamcatcher's creation, each taking over from the other in a continuous stream of chatter. Then with full agreement on a pub lunch and the promise of large ice creams for dessert, the boys charged out of the Yurt to give us five minutes peace and quiet to get ready to leave.

"Oh Meredith, this truly is the best present anyone has ever given me. And you and your boys are the best things that have ever happened to me." She wrapped her arms around my waist and kissed me. "Thank you," she added and I realised she was remembering our conversation from the night before.

"Darling Imogen, I want you to know," I looked down at her, my eyes suddenly serious, "that whilst you are under this canvas roof, you are safe. You are protected from everything that this shitty world throws at us and, what's more, you are loved more dearly than you may ever realise. You aren't alone in this world anymore."

Like a dam bursting from deep within, Imogen cried. She mourned for the sadness and loneliness of her past, she cried for the happiness of the present and she cried for the dreams of a future that might be.

From that day forward though powerful memories never quite leave us, Imogen never dreamt her nightmare again.

Chapter Eleven

August slipped past as slowly and inevitably as the river ran through the valley. Happy sun-filled days turned into halcyon memories. Much to their delight, Andrew promoted Freddie and Tom to the important position of joint head deer warden and they would disappear with him for hours to watch or help with the herd, leaving Imogen and me to spend a blissful few hours together. If we felt like it we would go for long walks or simply down to the pool; slowly, intimately washing and exploring each other's bodies with gentle, languorous caresses and kisses. Often just lazing around the camp, sunbathing in silence, or quietly talking whenever the mood took us, allowing the warmth of the sun and gentle breeze to wash over our bodies. Sometimes our hands would reach out to touch one another, to reassure that this was no dream, at other times to prod and poke, starting a play fight that would usually end in us making love, slowly and tenderly under the cool, white canvas of the Yurt.

Once if not twice a week we would all walk up to the manor house to take lunch with the General. Despite the extended invitation, Imogen was initially reluctant to intrude upon this all-male club, but half an hour into her first visit she had become engrossed in a debate with our host over the strategies deployed during the Crimean war. The battle raged on throughout lunch with both parties thoroughly enjoying themselves. Eyes gleamed and commands were issued and challenged as a regiment of peas attacked a sweetcorn gun battery, their salt and pepper grinder generals watching on dispassionately from napkin hilltops. The boys cheering as the enemy were heroically swept away before the thin red wine line, crying out in disbelief at the scandalous yet outrageous bravery of the light brigade.

"My word, Meredith, I tell you something, that gal's got spirit and by God she knows her Sebastapol from her Inkermann. What a catch m'boy, what!" he chuckled, his eyes still blazing; the smell of cordite and gunpowder had got his dander up as he slapped me paternally on the back as we made our way through the hallway at the end of lunch.

"My dear, how about the Zulus day after tomorrow?" He hurried ahead as quickly as his gamy leg would allow, catching up with Imogen and the boys as they descended the steps.

Imogen readily accepted both the challenge and a whiskered kiss on both cheeks. "From Lord Chelmsford or King Cetshwayo's perspective, General?"

"Good Lord, you do know your stuff. Lord Chelmsford, of course."

"In that case you have just met your Isandlwana," Imogen laughed back in return.

"Splendid, splendid, better sharpen your assegais then, eh!" the old man roared back in delight.

"He pinched my bottom!" Imogen giggled as we started back down the track to the camp, rubbing the spot through her dress. "Just as well I was wearing knickers or he might have got far too excited."

"Dirty old sod, serve him right if he dropped down with a heart attack," I laughed. "Come to think of it, I wouldn't mind if it was the last thing I laid my hands on before I snuffed it. But don't you think he's one hell of a character?"

"Oh, absolutely wonderful. It's characters like that, belligerent, bloody minded old buggers who once made this country great. Though I do feel so terribly sorry for him, all alone in that great big pile; must be awfully lonely."

"I'm sure you're right and he obviously enjoys our visits; seems to take years off him and he's so good with the boys. God knows what I'm going to do with the bloody sword he's given Freddie." I shook my head in amusement.

Upon our return to the camp, Freddie, much to Imogen's pleasure, demanded that she recreate the battles and talk him through, blow by blow, the reasons leading up to the war and all it's machinations. Causes, strategies, alliances and tactical manoeuvres, all were brought back to life with Freddie enthralled by every word, rarely interrupting, but when he did it was with intelligent questions way beyond his years.

Once she had finished and he in turn had impressed her with his knowledge of Florence Nightingale and the nursing conditions of the time, he begged to hear about the Zulu war. She clapped her hands in delight at his enthusiasm, but pleaded for a half-hour respite to regroup her troops. He gave her a quick hug, but before he could charge off and join Tom, Imogen sent him into a paroxysm of ecstasy when she promised to take him into Monkhampton later in the afternoon to buy some toy soldiers and other supporting paraphernalia to help visualise the battle scenes.

"I bet you a pound that when he grows up, if Freddie doesn't join the army, he will become an eminent military historian. Teaching officer cadets at Sandhurst Military Academy, that sort of thing. He's got a natural aptitude for it and clearly loves the topic and by God he asks some tricky questions." Imogen puffed out her cheeks with relief at the temporary armistice, though clearly relishing the role of tutor.

Imogen must have covered two if not three of these lessons cum re-enactments a week throughout the remainder of the month, further fuelled by additional visits with Freddie to see the General, who had become a fervent Imogen fan. Though much to her amusement her bottom became peppered with small, blue-black bruises from the old man's attention. And whilst I needed no urging, it also provided at her regular bidding, a coy excuse to lay my healing hands upon her.

It also gave Tom and me the perfect opportunity to spend quality time together. I couldn't recall the two of us ever spending time alone, for as second born, we had always done things with the boys together.

We poured over his survival book, then tramped through the woods laying traps, that despite his enthusiasm but to my great relief, failed to bring anything to the cooking pot. We placed our shirts ten feet apart and I allowed myself to be battered black and blue as he assumed the mantle of Wayne Rooney and kicked ball after ball at a goalkeeper who really was over the hill.

Much to everyone's relief he had also grown bored of his drums and passed them on to Imogen and though a little bemused but willing none the less, she proved to have a good ear and quickly picked out the beats of our favourite fireside songs.

This however proved an enormous irritation to Tom as he hated to be left on the sideline when the rest of us, irrespective of how badly, were picking our way through a tune or two. Typically Freddie had picked up the penny whistle with effortless ease, two years of enforced recorder lessons at school finally paying off.

And with this jealous irritation pricking him, Tom dropped into conversation one afternoon whilst trying to catch fish with string and hooks I had fashioned from a nail and a paper clip, whether I would teach him how to play the guitar.

Biting back my immediate reaction to laugh and point out that he would neither concentrate nor stick with it long enough for me to teach him a chord, I agreed and prepared myself for a battle of tolerance I knew had but one conclusion.

Much to my lasting surprise and to everyone's delight, not least his own, Tom proved both diligent and disciplined, often dragging my guitar off to some quiet spot down the hill to practise. I had long forgotten the determination he had shown learning to ride his bicycle without stabilisers. Envious of his brother who had a two-year advantage, fuelled with a self-motivating concoction of envy and a highly competitive spirit had firstly worn me down as I pushed him around a park one summer's day. Then seemingly immune to the pain and anger of scuffed knees and injured pride, he had left me behind in a hot sweaty heap and continued to master his balance. Two hours later he had returned to where Laura, Freddie and I were sitting patiently on a picnic blanket, cycling past us with a huge, cocksure smile on his face, as steady and confident as though he had been bicycling for years.

With this same determination blazing behind his chocolate brown eyes and his tongue sorely chewed in concentration, he persisted. And with each conquered step further fuelling his enthusiastic appetite, he made tremendous progress and was soon capable of working his way through the simple nursery rhymes and ditty songs that I could remember.

Needing to absolve myself of the shame of not having faith in my youngest and recognising the biggest discouragement for a child once they have learnt to play a little is a guitar that is too large for their small hands, I undertook a sneak raid on the music shop. I bought a second hand child's guitar and an easy-to-learn songbook and for myself one on fifties American rock and roll.

With one of Laura's important lessons on child management ringing in my ears ("What you do for one you must to for the other") I dropped into the bookshop. Though the bell rang with its familiar sound, the shop felt less welcoming and friendly. A disinterested man in his late fifties, who I presumed was the owner, barely looked up from his book to greet me and without moving from his chair pointed me in the vague direction of what I was looking for.

"What's that dad?" Tom asked excitedly as I pulled the bags out of the back of the Landrover and staggered inside the tent.

"Just you wait and see," I chuckled, careful to keep the blanket over the most obvious item.

Lining the boys up like children visiting a shopping centre Father Christmas grotto, I handed Tom his present first.

"Thanks dad, this is fantastic." He immediately dug the guitar into his abdomen and started to strum madly like a rock star.

"Pretty cool huh?" I said as I handed him the songbook.

"Dad?"

"Yes Freddie?"

"Can you not say cool, please?"

"What, why?" I replied, thoroughly perplexed at his odd request.

"Well, it doesn't sound cool, when you say it," Freddie answered apologetically. "You're a bit old to say things like cool."

Imogen roared with laughter, setting off both the boys, and I, though feigning hurt, could not hold the pretence for long and soon joined in the laughter.

Freddie's pleasure in his book on Famous Military Battles through the Ages was evident, as he disappeared inside the tent and had to be called for supper several times, several hours later.

Though Imogen and I had agreed to keep our relationship a secret from the boys for the time being, I was troubled by this decision, though it added a greater sense of excitement and spice to our budding new love. Stealing a kiss or a playful caress when they weren't looking sent the blood rushing around the body and the heart to palpitate as wildly as any immature teenager's; or to relax by cuddling up to watch the sun slip slowly over the horizon once the boys had gone to bed. On the downside I could not go to bed with Imogen held tenderly in my arms, nor would her kind, beautiful and loving face be the first thing I would see when I awoke. Whilst we weren't lying to the boys, we weren't exactly being honest with them either and though caution prevailed, it still did not sit well with me.

In the end after much debate and indecision I decided to throw caution to the wind and tell the boys. We agreed to wait until Imogen had returned to work so it gave me plenty of time to talk privately with them and allay any fears or concerns they may have.

The night before I was due to tell the boys was the first time in a long time I did not sleep well. Imogen likewise, despondent about returning to work, tossed and turned until the luminous clock showed one o'clock. With sleep thus avoiding my despairing clutches I gathered up the picnic blanket, duvet and pillows and made my way quietly out of the Yurt.

"Where are you off to my lover?" Imogen whispered through the darkness.

"Can't sleep, so I'm going outside for a bit," I whispered back.

"Bit of what?" A stifled giggle at her own humour. "Hold on, I'm coming too."

We settled down beside the dying embers of the fire and though it was a still hot night, we huddled up next to each other, protecting and reassuring one another from the fears in our minds.

The rising sun touched our faces only a few hours later and, not wishing to give the game away, with sleep still heavy upon our eyelids, we crept quietly back into the Yurt to our respective beds and were soon asleep.

With the boys still deep in the world of dreams, protected by the powerful medicine from their Dreamcatchers, I slipped outside and put the kettle on to boil, returning to watch Imogen get dressed. She pulled her clothes on with visible loathing and resentment, then with careless speed ran a brush through her blonde tresses and scooped them expertly into a tight ponytail, the face of professionalism, the actor's costume now complete and ready for the curtain call.

"You don't have to go. Just give him a call and stay here," I said quietly, removing the kettle from the cooker before its shrill whistle could wake the boys.

"I don't want to go, but I have to, I gave him my word," Imogen groaned.

"Excuse my French, but I met him last week when I bought Freddie's book; he's a complete tosser. He's a lazy sod who's taking advantage of your friendship and you should tell him to get stuffed." My voice low but vehement.

"I know, but I promised, it won't be for long and I'll be back before you know it. We'll then find out whether there's any truth behind the saying that absence makes the heart grow fonder. And if there is, then I may even let you ravish my poor defenceless body." She smiled thinly, bolstered by the thought of being back at the camp for a dip in the pool before supper.

"Okay but so long as you know that you don't have to go, I'll look after you." It sounded lame and I knew it.

"I know you will, dearest Meredith, but it's important to me that I do things on my terms. I'm never going to let another man like Bill take over my life, dominating the very way I think, controlling what I can or cannot do." Her words were strong and the message clear as she took my head in her hands and kissed me lightly. "You are my man and I am your woman. We will be together." Then she smiled, drained her mug, slung a bright red leather handbag that was bulging at the seams, over her shoulder and walked purposefully up the track to her car.

I watched her go with a heavy heart, my hand half raised to wave in case she should turn around, but she kept on walking and shortly had disappeared over the rise and then was gone.

It was the closest we had come to an argument since we had met and on the very morning of her parting and my telling the boys we wanted to be together, I wondered whether it was an omen. A sign that perhaps we were not meant to be, or that our relationship would not work. Either way it fanned the nervous flames of fear that had already been lit in the pit of my stomach.

The boys were late to rise for a change. Telling myself that there was no hurry for them to be up for we had no other plans that morning, I was not even fooling myself for I knew the reason that my heart thumped harder every time I heard a sign of movement or noise within the tent. I was worried about what to say and how to say it and deep down, I was absolutely petrified about how they would respond to my news.

The longer they lay in, the worse I felt and the tenser I became. The tenser I became, the worse I felt. Like an eternal torture from Greek mythology devised by the gods as punishment for mortals, it was a wicked and unforgiving self-perpetuating circle. Subconsciously I tried to take my mind off the matter and started to clean out the Landrover; removing crisp packets, empty drink cartons, sweet wrappers and various objects which had no place in the vehicle. Long overdue it was therefore with a sense of satisfaction that I finished and celebrated by slamming the boot door shut in a gesture of closure. Immediately regretting the loud noise, I crept up to the tent wall and not daring to breathe, I listened intently for any sign of life within.

I cursed my stupidity as quiet groans and movement came from inside.

"Dad?" Freddie asked in a sleepy voice.

"Yes?" I whispered back guiltily.

"Why are you standing so funnily next to the tent?" From the puzzled tone, Freddie clearly thought I had gone quite mad.

"Just cleaning out the Landrover, nothing to worry about." I cursed myself again and quickly moved away from my half-crouched position against the tent.

"What's it like outside?" Tom's loud enthusiastic dawn chorus filled my ears.

"Miserable and it's raining." I said the first thing that came into my mind.

"Rats." Tom was disappointed, but before I could rectify matters, Freddie called out, having already analysed the situation. "Liar. Don't listen to Dad. If it were raining we'd be able to hear it on the roof of the tent. He's just being stupid."

"Sorry boys, can't help it," I replied, trying to brush it off as a joke, but failing dismally.

"Idiot," Tom muttered as I heard zips being undone and footsteps head towards the door.

"Lying to your children even before they've got out of bed, on the day you're going to have the conversation of all conversations. Nice one, Meredith," I castigated myself.

I left the boys to their breakfast and went to check my phone in case I'd received a text from Imogen. I switched my phone on; there were no texts, but an icon let me know that a voice mail was waiting for me. I called the service and was shocked to hear Jo's dulcet tones asking that I call her when I had a moment. I deleted the message and turned to confront my fears.

"Boys, I need a quick word. Come and sit with me, it won't take long." My throat was dry and constricted.

Innocent and unaware, they came and sat on the grass at my feet; Tom's impatience immediate as he started to pull at the ground and drizzle blades of grass over his and his brother's outstretched legs.

"Right, now where to start?" I stammered nervously, wishing that the words I had so carefully memorised over the previous days had deserted me. "Have you enjoyed your time here?"

"Oh yes, it's been fantastic—I want to stay here forever," Tom enthused, his brown eyes looking up at me as faithfully and trusting as a puppy.

"It's been great, dad," Freddie said more cautiously, his eyes wary and guarded, somehow aware that there was more to come.

"What have you enjoyed the most?"

Tom thought about it for a moment before replying. "Feeding the deer, having our own pool and not having to go to bed until we want to."

"And you, Freddie?"

He twitched his nose in careful consideration. "I think it's been learning about all the wars and finding out about the different birds and plants and things like that."

"It *has* been a great time, hasn't it," I laughed. "And you remember that you didn't want to come?"

Taking a deep breath as my stomach constricted, I continued: "And have you liked meeting Imogen and having her stay with us?"

It was Tom who again replied first; almost before I had finished my words his open and honest mind had spoken. "She's cool and she makes me laugh, she's so funny. And she made us the Dreamcatchers," he added as an important afterthought.

I smiled and looked to Freddie. Again I could see from the look on his face that he was not only considering his response, but also trying to determine where the conversation was headed.

"I really like her and she's very clever. She knows lots of interesting things; I wish she was one of my teachers because she makes things so interesting and fun. And she joins in with the things we're doing and she always seems so happy. But I'm sad that she has such a horrid mummy." Each word deliberately weighed and slowly spoken.

Here we go, I thought to myself; the serpent contracted and squeezed my abdomen in its vicelike grip. "I like Imogen as well. And do you know, Imogen really likes us as well. And daddy really wants Imogen to be his special friend." The words were pathetically poor and badly spoken, little more than a whisper. I studied my toes carefully whilst thinking, "How can a mature adult be reduced to a gibbering, inarticulate wreck by two children?"

"Like boyfriend and girlfriend?" Tom giggled, his fist in his mouth.

"Well, yes, that sort of thing." I could feel myself starting to blush with embarrassment, but at least the serpent had slackened its grip.

"Will she be coming to live with us at home?" A note of worry in Freddie's voice; the snake writhed and constricted once more.

"I don't know, we haven't discussed it, but maybe, later," I answered truthfully.

"Would she sleep in the same bed like you and mummy?" he continued anxiously.

"Well, yes," I nodded. "We would sleep in the same bed, Freddie."

"So does that mean you and Imogen are going to get married?" Freddie's gaze never left my face, ignoring the embarrassed sniggering coming from his younger brother.

"I want Imogen to come and stay with us," Tom interrupted, clapping his hands in delight and, pulling up tufts of grass, he threw them up into the air like exploding celebratory fireworks.

"I've no idea, Freddie, and even if we did, it wouldn't be for a long time." I could not help but be impressed with how far reaching my eldest son's thinking went as he considered the implications of the bombshell I had dropped on them.

"I don't want another mummy!" He looked crestfallen and his chin sank to his chest as tears welled in his eyes.

"Hey, hey Freddie," I tried to console him. "Your mummy is and always will be your mummy. No-one is going to try and replace her. I wouldn't let them."

"Mummy's in heaven," Tom stated simply.

"That's right, Tom-Tom, mummy's in heaven and I miss her as much as you do, because daddy loved her so very much." My heart heaved at the sudden memories of her lying in her bed, so pale, in such pain, yet still with such loving eyes.

"But daddy's lonely and he wants Imogen to be with him, to share his life. To be a part of all our lives." I felt the tears well in my own eyes.

"But you're not lonely, you've got us, you don't need anyone else!" Freddie cried out in anger and pain.

"And I love you more than anything in this world. You are the most important things in my life and I wouldn't do anything to make you unhappy. But I also love Imogen." I tried to explain how I needed someone to share my fears, my concerns, as well as the fun and joy of good times. To help me bring them up, to ensure they lacked for nothing and never felt alone or unloved. And through my tears, I could see that Tom had become upset at my distress and had started to sob, whilst Freddie's face was still buried in his chest, though from his shaking shoulders I could tell that he too, though for different reasons, was crying.

Wiping away the tears with the back of my hand I gathered my thoughts and spoke once more, though firmer and more clearly than before, using short statements like swearing an oath of allegiance, to help them understand and gain a reassuring foothold in this sudden torrent of upheaval.

"You must know that I love you so much and I always will. Nothing is going to come between us and no-one is going to take my love for you away. I have never enjoyed myself as much as I have since we came to stay in your Yurt, Freddie." I smiled at him, though it was not returned. "The time we have had here has made me realise how important and special you are to me and how much fun we have together and that is not going to change. All those things we have done and learnt and all the fun we have had with Imogen. How lucky we are to have met her. Remember what you were saying about how much fun you've had with her learning about all those battles? And Tom, think what she's showed us about the plants and animals."

Tom nodded and realising that his brother had stopped crying, he dried his eyes, but was not ready to offer a smile.

"I want Imogen to stay with us and keep making us laugh and being kind to us and being our very special friend. But neither she nor anyone else will ever try to take the place of mummy, I promise."

I don't think I had ever loved my children as much as I did in those moments. Their honesty, fears and strength had all been laid bare and I felt my heart break at the pain I was causing. The bottled up emotion since Laura's death, the utter sadness, their desperate loneliness and terrifying fears of being deserted poured like a pregnant river breaking its banks. The love and attention so recently given since our time in the Yurt, initially received with suspicion, had become a warm reassuring comfort blanket in which to wrap themselves; a protection against those deepest fears. And now they saw that comfort and reassurance threatened, to be stolen back, once more to be emotionally exposed and physically ignored.

I hugged them to me as though our lives depended upon it, my arms enveloping them and gripping their small light frames tightly, almost painfully.

"Hey, don't you ever forget we are the tribe of the Fighting Merediths, remember?" I could feel their heads nodding against my chest.

A while later, Freddie pushed himself away from my chest to look me directly in the eyes. He had stopped crying, though his lip still trembled and the streaks of tears down his cheeks cut deeply into my heart. I smiled at him and using my thumb I rubbed his cheeks gently until the tracks disappeared.

He smiled bravely in return, though it did not match the tremor in his voice. "So if Imogen isn't going to come home with us, how is she going to be our special friend?"

I chuckled as Freddie, clever beyond his years, had hit the one big unknown that I could not answer. "Do you know, that's one thing we've not been able to figure out yet, but we wanted to talk to both of you first before we started thinking about making any plans. So how did you get to be so clever, Freddie? They don't teach you to be clever like that at school. It must come from your mother, she was clever like that." I sighed in wonder.

This time he smiled, proud to be compared with and linked to his mother, perhaps also happy that we were at last talking about Laura. Happy that she was not to be forgotten, but would stay with us for all time, permanent and comforting in the forefront of our minds, not rubbed out and forgotten like a beautiful picture on a chalkboard.

"So what do you think then?" I asked gently.

"I want Imogen to stay with us," Tom repeated, happily still nestled in my chest.

"Freddie?"

"I like Imogen lots and I think I think it's a good idea, but I'm not sure. I need to think about it." The wise head on such young shoulders nodded sagely. "I think I'll go for a walk."

And like an old man with the weight of the world upon his shoulders, Freddie strolled ponderously down the hill, Tom skipping and flitting around him.

"Great job, Meredith, you really loused that up, you blithering idiot. You put the fear of God into your children and reduced them to tears." I swore at myself out loud as soon as the boys were out of earshot. Still, it was done, the seed had been planted and at least Tom was behind the idea. Good old, happy-go-lucky Tom. He saw things so simply. Imogen made him happy and that was enough for him. If only the rest of life's dilemmas could be resolved as easily. Why was it that we adults seemed to add such intricate layers of complexity? Somewhere in life's learnings it was being knocked out of us by a cynical and untrusting man-made and so called civilised world.

But somewhere in our conversation, something that one of us had said had struck a chord in my mind and for the life of me I could not recall what it was. But it had sparked an idea. Ludicrous, mad and impossible perhaps, but it nagged away and like a tick on a dog, it wouldn't let go. I too would need to take some long walks alone to fathom it out and just maybe turn it into our future.

I looked at my phone; there were still no messages from Imogen. I desperately wanted to speak to her, to see her smiling face, to run my hands through her luxurious hair, to reassure me that all was well. But it would have been unfair of me to call and so I resisted the temptation and turned my attention to preparing lunch.

The boys returned hot and panting and I waited until they had drunk their fill before asking what they had been up to.

"We saw a kestrel," Freddie announced, happily tucking into the cheese and tomato sandwiches I had freshly prepared. "At first we thought it was a Buzzard, but it was too small for one of them and its wings weren't so pointed."

"I couldn't tell the difference. How did you know that?" I asked in quiet admiration.

"Don't you remember the other day, when we were coming back from seeing the General? I saw one and Imogen told us what it was and told us how we could spot the difference between the two."

"And there are lots more Buzzards in this country than Kestrels. And you can sometimes see Kestrels sitting on posts by motorways watching the cars going by," Tom added his own slant to the imparted knowledge.

"They're not watching the cars go by, Tom." Freddie rolled his eyes before continuing: "They're looking for their prey."

"And did this one catch anything to eat?" I asked, pleased with the interest they were showing.

"Well dad, it was really cool because when we first saw it, it was really high up in the sky, like a little black speck. Then it started to go around and around in a wide circle and it was…what do you call it Freddie?" Tom asked his brother eagerly.

"Gliding," Freddie replied, happy to be consulted.

"That's it, it was gliding. And then it dived right down, like it just fell out of the sky, so we think it must have seen something to eat and jumped on it." Tom sat back proudly at his description, his hands tearing his sandwich into bite sized pieces and feeding them one after the other into his mouth.

"Birds don't jump, they dive," Freddie corrected his brother, but without rancour or smug pleasure.

"Tom, don't stuff all of that into your mouth in one go, or you're going to choke," I warned, but too late. Tom's little Adam's apple started to bob up and down rapidly, his chin jutting out as his throat started to wretch. A moment later a large ball of congealed bread, cheese and tomato landed back in his plate.

"Oops, sorry," he apologised, wiping away the tears from his eyes. Then without a thought, Tom tore a smaller lump from the half-chewed mass in front of him and stuffed it back into his mouth.

"Gross!" Freddie hooted with amusement.

"That has to be one of the most disgusting things I have ever seen, Tom Meredith," I reprimanded him, though with a smile upon my lips.

The boys made no mention of our earlier conversation and after spending a quiet hour around the camp, letting our food digest, the boys took off once more to explore and seek fresh adventure.

I retrieved my new songbook from inside the Yurt and flicked through the various tunes until I found one to my liking. Creasing back the pages so it would lie flat, I picked up my guitar, pulled a plectrum from the back pocket of my shorts and settled down to some good old-fashioned rock and roll.

Sweating profusely with my shirt sticking uncomfortably to my back, I found the lack of sleep from the night before catching up. No doubt the heavy-handed shot of whisky I had also poured into the coffee immediately after lunch also adding to my drowsy state. So promising myself that it would be just a quick nap, I sought the cool protection of the canvas and lay down upon my bed.

The next thing I knew was that there was pressure upon my lips and I had trouble breathing. My eyes flicked open in shock and my head jumped from the pillow.

"I've always wanted to do that." Imogen was smiling mischievously, her face inches away from my own.

"God, you gave me a shock." I let my head fall back into the pillows.

"I wonder if that's how Snow White felt when she was kissed by Prince Charming?" Imogen giggled.

"How was your day?" I asked once we had kissed again, but this time properly.

"To be honest I was quite miserable, but once you start to get into the swing of it, the time goes by quickly enough. And there was plenty of cataloguing to do and new books to stack so it fairly flew by. What about you?" I could see the tentative look in her eyes as though not sure she really wanted to know the answer.

"Tell you what. I could murder a cup of tea and I expect you want to get changed. So if I get the kettle on and you slip into something cool and comfortable, then I'll tell you all about it."

"You just want to see me take my clothes off!" she laughed again. She had only been gone a few hours but I had missed that giggle and throaty laugh more than I thought possible.

"Absolutely. I just want to check that there's nothing missing."

I left the door open so we could see the children approaching as Imogen made the most of removing her clothes.

Running a cool flannel under her arms and around her neck, she gently patted herself dry, before slipping into a knee length, cream embroidered patchwork dress that showed off her figure to perfection.

With the sugary tea clearing the dulled mind, I had just finished giving Imogen a debrief on the events of the day when I spotted one of the boys running towards us. They were still too far away to make out their face, but from the head down and only one top gear haring pace it had to be Tom. He waved at us whilst he ran and we returned his wave with gusto.

It took him a good five minutes to reach us and when he did, he threw himself on the blanket, his chest heaving as he tried to suck in oxygen. He was pointing down the hill and though his words were completely unintelligible through his gasping breaths, it was evident that there was a serious problem.

"Slow down, Tom, that's it, nice slow deep breaths. Good lad, now what's the matter, where's Freddie?" I asked, trying to keep the sense of alarm and foreboding from my tone.

"He's...he's hurt. Hurt his...his arm." He stopped to concentrate on breathing for a moment, then continued in one explosive stream of noise. "Freddie's hurt his arm and he's got it stuck and we can't get it out."

Tears of panic now erupted, which, coupled with his laboured breathing, made it impossible to get any coherent sense from him for a further two minutes.

"Just concentrate on breathing, Tom, then you can tell us all about it." Imogen held him to her chest and soothed his sopping hair away from his eyes. Her calming, motherly touch worked and shortly we were able to discover what had happened.

"Okay Tom-Tom, Freddie's hurt his arm and it's stuck, is that what you're telling us?" Tom nodded frantically, his brown eyes wide and scared.

"Where is he Tom?" I demanded forcefully, no longer able to keep the impatience and churning worry at bay.

"We went to the Chalk mine and he fell and that's when he hurt his arm," Tom bawled.

"The Chalk mine? But you've been told not..." I broke off mid-sentence at a steely glare from Imogen, warning that now was not the time for chastisement.

"Do you know where it is?" she asked. I shook my head.

"Can you take us there, Tom? Can we get the Landrover down there?"

He nodded again.

"Right, Tom, in the passenger seat, let's go." I snatched up the car keys to see Imogen bundling the blanket into the back of the car, along with a couple of bottles of water and some towels.

I threw the Landrover into gear and we tore off down the hill following Tom's directions until we came to the edge of a copse preventing further progress by vehicle.

"This way!" Tom shouted, leaping over a rickety wooden stile, ignoring the nettle stings as they whipped about his bare legs.

"You go on with Tom, I'll follow," Imogen urged as I tried to help her over the stile, hampered by the bundle in her arms.

"Freddie, Freddie, we're coming!" Tom shouted as he ran through the copse, scarcely checking his speed as he ducked, swerved and sidestepped trees and low hanging branches.

Seeing a barbed wire fence up ahead I called out a warning to Tom. But using an old, sorely rusted sign with a hand painted skull and cross bones as a platform, he hurdled the barbed wire and shortly came to a stop.

"Freddie, Freddie, daddy's coming. Are you all right?" He appeared to be shouting into the ground.

I reached Tom moments later and a groan of dismay and horror escaped my lips.

Lying in a narrow man-made fissure some ten feet down, clearly outlined by the white chalk that surrounded him, lay Freddie. He was lying on top of a pile of rocks and turned his head towards the opening as he heard our approach.

"Daddy, my arm's stuck and it hurts," he whimpered faintly.

"All right darling. Don't you worry, we'll have you out of there in no time. Now, does it hurt anywhere else?" He was alive, breathing and conscious, sending a huge sense of relief through me like a tidal wave.

"I banged my head and it's bleeding, but my arm really hurts, daddy." Freddie started to cry.

"I just need you to be brave for a little bit longer," I tried to soothe him as I scoured the area for a means to get down and back out of the pit.

Imogen joined us and placed a comforting arm around Tom who had now started to shake with the onset of shock.

"Come and sit over here, Tom. We wouldn't want you to fall down there as well, would we?" She smiled calmly and placed the blanket about his shoulders.

In the meantime I had found several sizeable logs and dragged them to the lip. When placed on top of one another they would give me sufficient height to pull myself back out of the pit.

The pit was some fifteen feet long and gave me plenty of space to lower myself down, dropping the last two feet, without the risk of landing on Freddie.

The rocks were precariously balanced and would need to be removed carefully to avoid further rock fall.

"Here you go Freddie, wash some of that dust out first; then have a nice cool drink." He raised his head from the rocks and I could see congealed blood that had run down the side of his face, matted in his whitened hair. I held the bottle to his dusty lips until he had had his fill.

"Now then, brave lad, just a little longer whilst I move these rocks." I hid my fears, quickly scanning and breathing a deep sigh of relief when I could find no fresh blood.

Stepping carefully over loose rocks I studied the rockslide formation, quickly determining the safest order in which to unravel this chalk puzzle. Imogen's voice floated down from above, offering soothing and comforting words to Freddie, and though he continued to moan in pain, the stark fear in his eyes dissipated.

I used the no entry sign to create an overhang, thereby protecting Freddie from further minor rockfall and immediately went to work. It was hot work and within five minutes my shirt was stuck to my back and my face, arms and bare legs were coated in the fine white dust, which mixed with the sweat, stuck to my face in a ghoulish mask.

At last I had cleared away enough of the rocks to be able to see what was trapping his arm. His wrist had fallen between two rocks and a larger, heavier rock had fallen on top, in effect handcuffing him.

I tried to move the large rock that held his arm, but it stood fast and a trickle of smaller stones and rocks banged onto the sign above our heads, reminding us of the danger of an erratic move.

Giving myself time to think, I gave both Freddie and myself another drink from the water. The rock itself, some three feet long and four inches wide, had been roughly hewn from the rockface many years ago, long before even Freddie was born, and the coating of chalk dust prevented hands from establishing a decent grip.

"Leverage principles," I yelled out in jubilation and though quizzical, Imogen handed down the picnic blanket as asked.

Loosely coiling the blanket, I wrapped it around the end of the rock slab that stood proud of the slide. Using one of the rocks as a pivot point I heaved upon the rope blanket and to my immediate relief I felt the rock rise an inch before having to let it slip gently back to its resting position. With slippery hands feeling as though they were immersed in water, I needed to gain a secure grip; to drop the rock would not only fail to release Freddie but could cause a further and more significant slide, trapping us both.

I wrapped the blanket tightly once around my wrist and then around my fist before taking up the slack once more.

Manmade and natural fibres groaned in unison as they took the strain. With fibres stretching and distorting, the veins in my biceps like those at my temples throbbing and standing proud, I leaned back and felt the slab rise once more. Slowly it rose whilst sweat blinded me as it ran unchecked into my eyes and my back muscles screamed for relief.

"Freddie, can you get your hand out?" I asked through gritted teeth.

"No. It hurts so much when I try to move it!" he screamed as the effort went through him.

"What about now?" I hissed, feeling my muscles begin to shake with an effort that could not be maintained for much longer.

"I can't, it hurts too much to move it," he wailed pitifully.

"You can do it, Freddie," Imogen added her encouragement from above. "As soon as you've got your hand out, it'll all be over. Come on, nice and quickly."

"Come on Freddie, I can't hold it forever." I could feel the blanket slipping in my grasp and dug my feet in once more to repel the opposing force.

"I can't."

"Yes you can and you must, Freddie, come on, try!" I urged him, this time almost an order. Spittle flew from my clenched teeth as I tried to lever the slab still higher.

With a high-pitched scream Freddie, using his good hand, pulled his trapped hand free from its prison. At last I could lower the slab and relieve the muscle spasms jerking in my lower back. There was a sudden heart stopping moment as we looked up in fear as the vibrations set off a further small landslide, but was held back by the now sagging sign.

Creating a cradle from the blanket and the towels, I climbed back out of the pit before heaving Freddie back to the surface. A stabbing pain ripped at my lower back, but Freddie was safe and that was all that mattered.

Imogen gently washed his scalp to check for a more serious head injury, and was relieved to find no further sign of trauma.

"I suspect just a couple of stitches in his forehead, which will leave a very small, but extremely dashing and heroic scar, but I'm pretty sure he's broken his wrist. We need to get him to hospital as quickly as we can just to make sure he hasn't crushed any arteries preventing blood getting through to his hand." She expertly folded a towel into a makeshift sling and carefully placed it under his arm, trapping it close to his body and then tied it behind his neck.

With deceptively treacherous ground underfoot followed by bumpy, uneven ground for the landrover to navigate, it was a slow and painful journey just to reach the main road. But once we had tarmac and white lines beneath the wheels we could finally build up speed and within half an hour had reached the hospital.

With a dressing hiding the three stitches in his forehead and a garishly coloured cast from wrist to just below elbow, Freddie was sat up in bed bravely recounting his accident to Imogen as I returned from meeting the doctor. Whilst nothing further had been detected from the x-rays and he did not seem to be suffering from visible signs of concussion, as a precaution they felt it safest to keep him in overnight.

"Well, brave lad, they want to keep you in for tonight, just to make sure everything's all right." I smiled down at him. He looked up concerned. With his face and hair washed clean of the dust and grime, his healthy tan prevailed, though he still looked exhausted and a good night's rest in a proper bed would do him no harm.

"But I want to come home with all of you." With raw emotion still so close to the surface, his tears welled easily.

"But the doctors want you to stay and they do know best," I replied, reaching out to squeeze his foot through the bedcovers in reassurance.

"But I don't want to be left here all on my own." Fear rising in his voice.

"Freddie, we can't all stay here, we've got to go back to the camp. But I promise we'll be back to pick you up first thing in the morning. Okay?" I pleaded with him to try to understand, but his tired and frightened mind was past caring and comprehension. I understood his fears; more than that, I could feel and taste them. The last time I had been in hospital had been the day Laura had died. The combination of empty wheelchairs parked in dark corners, the smell of a sterile environment and the sight of hospital beds, people, tubes and monitors left a queasy sensation in my stomach as though I was suffering from food poisoning and was about to vomit.

"No, it's not okay. I want you to stay." And he burst into tears.

"If it was all right with the nurses, what if I stayed here with you, would that be okay?" Imogen asked him calmly. "That way daddy can take Tom back home and be back first thing in the morning with some clean clothes. And you and I can have a long talk about whatever you choose."

He thought about it for a moment then nodded and smiled shyly. "Then you can tell me about the Duke of Wellington again."

"Not again!" she moaned in mock exasperation, her eyes rolling in her head.

It was settled. The nurses were extremely apologetic that the best they could offer was a small armchair and a blanket for Imogen, but she assured them it was fine and thanked them for going out of their way to be helpful.

"I don't know what I'd have done without you." We parted at the main hospital front door and I kissed her on the lips, causing Tom to clamp his hand firmly over his mouth and point at us, all the while howling with inane laughter.

"You'd have been fine." She kissed me back, then stuck her tongue out at Tom and crossed her eyes. "And this will give Freddie and me some time to ourselves to talk about things that may be preying on his mind."

Words were poor substitutes for how I felt and what I needed Imogen to understand. About the fears that had rushed through my mind, how she had taken Tom under her wing whilst I was getting Freddie out of that damned pit and was now going to spend the night in an uncomfortable chair looking after my eldest child. I trusted that time would grant me the wisdom and adequacy to be able to articulate my love and admiration for her.

Imogen stood at the entrance for a while, watching our progress through the carpark to the Landrover, then turned on her heel and was swallowed up in the sea of people crowding the foyer of the hospital.

Chapter Twelve

The following morning as promised we returned to the hospital to pick up Freddie and Imogen. Stepping out of the lift into the corridor we heard their laughter long before we reached Freddie's room and it was a happy reunion for the family to be back together again.

Imogen had sent several text messages during the night to allay my fears, letting me know that things were fine and that they missed us. She mentioned that they had talked for a good many hours and had hinted that some deep and meaningful conversation had passed between them. Though it was not until we returned to the camp and were sitting in front of the fire that evening, with both boys tucked up safely in their beds, that she gave me the full account of their night together.

After we had left, Freddie had cried for a while until he fell asleep and had dozed for an hour, then awoken much refreshed and ready to hear once more about the Duke of Wellington. The evening meal arrived and though he did not feel hungry, Imogen encouraged him to eat a little, so he had tucked into the carrots and peas though left the mass in the middle which neither of them were sure of its content. "It's not as good as daddy's cooking and I bet they're not organic vegetables," Freddie had complained, but at least the ice cream had gone down without issue.

Freddie with a comfortable bed beneath him, warm food in his stomach and the adrenaline rush now behind him, slept again until midnight, when he woke with a start. Disorientated and though the subtle corridor lights filtered through the blinds into his room, he had called out for her in alarm. She had cradled him whilst the fear was blown from the recesses of his mind and after pouring him a glass of water from the bedside jug, they had talked some more.

Slowly and hesitantly at first he had told her of my conversation with them that morning. That he did not want another mummy. That he still missed her terribly, but that as he was a big boy now and looked after Tom, and felt that he couldn't show it. Shyly, he let Imogen know that he liked her a great deal and that she was clever and fun, but his mummy was his mummy and no-one could take her place.

Imogen in turn had reassured him, her soft voice calming and loving in the darkened room, that she wouldn't try to replace Laura, but loved me, loved him and Tom and wanted to be with us. To share our lives and would be proud just to be their special friend, who would help when needed, was a friend to talk to when troubled or uncertain, and someone to share the joy in their successes.

It was one of the happiest and most touching moments in her life as Freddie told her that he wanted her to stay with us. He had explained his rationale that he didn't want another mother, but as he didn't have a sister and he now liked Imogen more than his Aunt Jo, so Imogen could be somewhere in between and become his Sisunt. They had both laughed and she had held him close so he could not see her tears falling silently upon her cheeks.

Returning to camp, it had not taken much to persuade Imogen to call in sick and, after a quick cup of coffee, she spent most of the morning asleep on her bed. We propped Freddie up on my bed and surrounded him with books where he spent much of the day reading quietly or dozing fitfully. Tom and I picked up our guitars and the now misshapen picnic blanket and moved down the hill to be within calling distance, but far enough away that our racket was not a disturbance.

After lunch Freddie had called Tom into the tent to discuss "something important," leaving Imogen and myself to relax in the sunshine.

Throughout this summer holiday I had laughed, loved, cried, shouted and yelled. I had enjoyed the bonds that had been built with my children, the unsuspecting love that I now felt for Imogen and was openly returned, and the inordinate pleasure of time to think. Above all I had lived. But it had taken the distress, fears and pain of separation of the past twenty-four hours to realise just how complete we had become during our stay in the valley. Four parts made up the whole and with a part missing, we were incomplete, a part of ourselves lost. The sum of our individual parts was less than the whole.

Muttering my need for a walk I left Imogen content to lie in the sun and headed down the hill. There was no conscious decision in my mind about destination; it was the need to find time to think through, without distraction, a plan for our future, if we were to have one.

With the stabbing pain from torn muscles in my lower back I did not get far, keeping up all appearances of a stout pace until the camp was out of sight and I could collapse into the long grass, rubbing the muscles until the pain abated.

Lying in the long grass watching soft white clouds pass overhead, I picked up on the genesis of the idea that had come to mind days before. I thought it through, I added fanciful embellishments to it, dropped them and pondered some more. I laughed and shook my head in outrage at the madness of it all, silencing the crickets that had forgotten my presence.

Surfacing from my thoughts I checked my watch to find a pale band of skin around my wrist in its place. Looking at where the sun sat overhead in our valley I knew it must be about four o'clock and time to return to camp; tea and biscuits beckoned. It would need more time to think through, but, I thought to myself, once you had overcome the initial hurdle of the lunacy of the whole idea, it could and might just work.

"Are you all right?" Imogen sat up with concern at my arrival. The uphill walk had taken its toll and I was no longer able to keep up the pretence and my healthy confident pace had become something of an old man's shuffle by the time I crested the hill and reached the camp.

"I think I must have torn some bloody muscles yesterday." I swore at the pain.

"Do you need nurse Imogen to come to your rescue?" She gave me her shoulder to lean upon and helped me into a chair.

"Seeing you in uniform would probably send my back into a permanent spasm and I would wind up bent over like a hunchback," I replied with a deadpan expression, not daring to laugh because of the pain the convulsions sent through my body.

"What about a massage then? You probably need some of that muscle relaxer spray stuff. I can get some tomorrow when I get back from work."

"Let me get the kettle on for a cup of tea and then I would love you to give me a long relaxing massage." I started to rise from the chair.

"You stay put," she commanded and pushed me back into the seat.

The sound of the biscuit tin lid being prised off stirred the boys within the tent and even Freddie made his first foray of the day outside the confines of the canvas.

"They've been in there since you left," Imogen whispered in my ear. "Have you put them up to more shenanigans, Mr Meredith?"

"Promise I know nothing about it, though I am sure we will when they're good and ready." I winced as she playfully nipped my fleshy lobe.

Still squinting against the glare of the bright sunlight, Freddie matched Tom biscuit for biscuit until only crumbs rattled in the bottom of the tin. Then with a complete lack of subtlety they jerked their heads in the direction of the Yurt and after Tom had helped Freddie back to his feet they marched back into the Yurt to await my arrival.

"Seems like I am wanted. Won't be long." I hobbled after them, closing the door but not before I heard Imogen calling out after me in lighthearted horror: "Oh, these Meredith boys and their secrets!"

The boys were seated solemnly on my bed. Clearly a great deal of thought had gone into what they were about to say, so drawing up a chair and easing myself gingerly into it, I applied my serious face and sat as formally upright as my back muscles would permit.

Freddie spoke up, his voice grave and pensive. "We have decided that we want Imogen to be our special friend and we also want her to come and live with us."

I nodded stiffly in agreement whilst my heart somersaulted with delight and relief at their decision.

"We therefore think that we should have a ceremony so she can be in the family properly." Freddie looked to Tom for his agreement.

"Yeah," Tom endorsed the decision with his usual eloquence.

I gave this the impression of serious thought and after a few moments nodded soberly in agreement.

"Hooray!" the boys cheered simultaneously.

So the following evening, Imogen was inducted into the Fighting Meredith tribe. Despite her protestations that we had given her no clues as to what was going to happen, though I did give her some warning to make sure she was wearing some underwear, her eyes were burning with anticipation.

The boys demanded that no-one else except themselves were allowed into the Yurt and I was tasked with getting the fire lit and keeping Imogen amused until they were ready.

As darkness pulled back its blanket over the land, the fire roared and crackled brightly in the night and at last the boys emerged from the tent and the ceremony began.

Despite being slightly glassy eyed after half a bottle of white wine, Imogen recognised the importance and significance of the ceremony and played her part with a serious face and upon receipt of her pendant became quite wrapped up in the theatre of the occasion. She clapped her hands in delight at being renamed "Lady with sun in her hair, or Sunny" for short, and gravely accepted the title of tribal storyteller.

She stuck her chin out trustingly to receive her tribal paint and swore her oath of allegiance with truth in her voice and was it a tear in her eye that I noticed?

At the ritual cleansing I was relieved to find she had taken my advice to not just wear her underwear but had opted for a two-piece bikini as she stripped her dress nonchalantly over her head. Our ears were soon filled with the familiar screams as the cold water covered her warm body, but she gamely finished the ritual to applause and whooping from us, warm and dry on the bank.

Returning to camp, Imogen slipped into the Yurt to don some dry clothes, but had been inside for less than a minute when she poked her head back through the door and beckoned me inside.

Once she had physically averted my drooling gaze from the towel she had wrapped loosely about her, my eyes beheld a sight so wonderful I had not even dreamed of, for fear of offending the gods.

"The boys?" I whispered, placing an arm around her shoulders.

"The boys!" she confirmed with a giggle and wrapped her own arms around my waist, the movement causing the towel to fall in a puddle around her ankles, but my eyes could not be drawn from the even more magnificent sight that lay before us.

Tom, no doubt under Freddie's expert direction, had dragged Imogen's inflatable mattress next to mine, spread my double duvet over both mattresses and for *la pièce de résistance*, they had laid her unzipped sleeping bag on top.

Imogen had been accepted and we had their wholehearted blessing.

Today was more than a good day—it was simply the best.

Over the following few days, life slipped back into something of a chaotic routine. Imogen would get ready for work whilst I made the coffee and after a quick breakfast, would leave for the bookshop, and with the boys still asleep it gave me the perfect time to finalise my plan. The boys would get up and I would sit with them chatting about this and that, then we'd get ready for the day that lay ahead. In the evening Imogen would return to find a glass of wine waiting for her, supper on the go and the boys eager to tell her about what they had been up to. After eating, some music followed to help the digestion, then bed for the boys and a quiet half an hour for Imogen and myself watching the sun setting whilst we chatted about things that ranged from our hopes and fears of the future to the weather. And finally to bed, together.

That week I received three further messages from Jo. The first two were polite, but the frustration was evident in the tone of her voice, requesting that I call her at home. In her third message, understandably blunt and terse, yet also concerned, she explained that they had had no word from us and neither had Mrs Fry and was everyone all right. Lastly, she reminded me that the school term was due to start in a week's time.

Still shocked by her message I turned to Imogen, innocently asking what day it was.

"Friday of course," she replied casually. "The whole blissful weekend together with no bloody bookshop."

"No, what day of the month?" This time more tension in my voice as I interrupted her.

"It's the first of September tomorrow of course. We're off to visit Stonehenge, remember. Why?"

"That was the big, bad world knocking on the door," I pointed at the accursed invention of the modern world, "reminding me that the boys are due back at school on Tuesday. Damn it to hell and back." I swore in frustration.

Imogen tried to hide the shock but after pacing up and down on the same spot for five minutes, the skin on the top of her thumb receiving a merciless, sub-conscious chewing, her worry was more than apparent.

Time had finally caught up with us and was now banging on our door, threatening to bring down our shared dreams.

"What are you going to do?" she eventually plucked up the courage to ask.

"Like the eternal procrastinator I'm going to think about it. Just over the weekend," I added quickly as I saw lines of irritation flash in the corners of her eyes. This was not the time to be joking, or light-hearted about such a matter. "Even though school starts next week, we're not going to be going home just yet. I have part of a plan, but it's not ready to reveal just yet."

"Why can't you tell me now?" she demanded to know, suspicion and anger growing in her voice.

I knew she hated secrets and would perhaps feel she was being left out of decisions that would affect her, but it had to be done.

"It's not ready to share just yet. In fact, it's so off-the-wall that you'll probably think I've gone quite mad, so I need to make sure I've thought it all through before opening my mouth. So when you get back from work on Monday, I'll get Andrew to take the boys off on some pretext and I promise you we will then go through the plan from start to finish, irrespective of its condition, and you can let me know what you think. Okay?"

"Mmm." She was tight lipped and clearly not convinced.

"I beg you to trust me on this. I promise you that all I want for all of us is to be able to be happy and to be together," I pleaded with her, taking her limp hands in my own. "I never thought I could be this happy and I promise you that if you don't like the idea, we'll scrap it."

My words touched the right buttons and though not wholly convinced, Imogen smiled and agreed to let me have the weekend, but no more. Come hell or high water, I would be telling her something on Monday, no matter how well thought through it was.

The weekend flashed past quicker than the blink of an eye and though a sombre cloud hung over us, we did our best to keep it from impacting the boys. How time goes quicker when you want it to stop and allow a moment to last a lifetime, and conversely how it drags each minute out painfully slowly when you need it to go rapidly!

We spent Saturday morning at Stonehenge. I was fascinated from the more practical, architectural design perspective about how the Neolithic and Bronze Age megalithic monument had been constructed. Not forgetting all of its logistical nightmares in getting the stones to the site in the first instance, never mind their erection. Imogen on the other hand held the boys attention, giving them a running commentary on the more romantic folk tales and suppositions regarding its purpose and its development over thousands of years. The magic of Merlin, giants, the chivalry and bravery of Arthur's court, the morbid fascination with the devil, the mysticism of the ancient druids brought vividly to life in the imagination of the children. My own excitement with pulleys, laws of gravity and lever principles did not offer much competition and soon found my own enthusiasm waning. I tagged along just in time to hear Imogen wax lyrical about a further, more recently suggested link to Woodhenge and Durrington Walls and the association between wood and life, stone and the ancestral dead. The rites of passage between the living and the dead.

At the mention of these additional sites the boys' ears pricked up and after a quick lunch in a pub outside Amesbury, we were back out on the archaeological trail. Visiting Woodhenge, just to the north of Amesbury itself and then still further north to Durrington Walls. This in turn provoked a visit on our way back to the camp, to the even older and larger site of the stones at Avebury, outside Marlborough.

More was to follow on Sunday with a trip to the ancient city of Bath and for myself a trip down memory lane, where as a student the city's pubs had become a part of Philip and my stomping ground. The poetic beauty of this historic city is unforgettable and, amongst so many wonderful sites, is home to Britain's only hot springs at the Roman Baths. It was a frantic effort to cram as much into as short a space of time as possible—to fill the corners of the mind with as many memories of this special time as was possible. I had even found my digital camera that had lain forgotten, unwanted and unnoticed in my bags and we all took it in turn to snap away like the stereotyped Japanese tourist.

We returned to the camp that evening physically exhausted, our feet sore and aching, no longer used to walking for long periods of time on concrete. The boys fell asleep on the return journey and upon reaching the camp, only woke long enough to stagger from the car to their beds before falling back to sleep once more. With Monday looming and the threat of having to expose my mad capped scheme ever closer, I wanted to stay up and delay the irrepressible march of time, but Imogen was tired and wanted to go to bed and fall asleep in my arms. Needless to say Imogen fluttered her eyelashes and the battle was won.

By the time Imogen returned from work the following afternoon I was as ready for her as I ever would be. I had made a quick trip into Monkhampton to purchase a few props to help with the explanation of my plan. Andrew had arrived on cue and taken the boys off to check the state of the fencing on the far side of the estate and promised me two hours of uninterrupted peace and quiet. He had given me a knowing wink and sly grin as he jumped into his battered vehicle and took off up the track. I did not bother to correct him; at this moment in time I would have been far more embarrassed trying to explain the real reason why I wanted Imogen to myself for a couple of hours; so let him think what he likes, I thought dismissively.

She seemed apprehensive as she approached the camp and for once her kiss, from dry nervous lips, lacked passion that wouldn't have even caused a ripple upon a still pool. We traded brief courtesies, enquiring as to how each other's day had been, but with both our eyes drawn to the pad of paper on the table I had prepared in readiness. I was eager to get this over with, despite the butterflies fluttering in my stomach.

"If it's okay with you I'd like to spend a moment going back over what I want to achieve and why? I'll only take a moment and then we can get straight into the idea itself."

Imogen nodded her approval and took a hasty sip from the glass of wine cradled in her lap.

"I want to be able to do three main things. Three goals, ambitions, call them what you will. The first is to spend more time with the boys than I used to before our holiday. The second is I that I love you dearly and want to be with you, and lastly I want to be able to financially support all of us. So far so good?"

"Go on, I'm right with you so far." She smiled and some of the tension slid from her shoulders.

"Great." I smiled back briefly before returning to my notes. "The idea also needs to be able to ensure that the boys gain a broad education, not just classroom based, but also an education of life, filled with all sorts of different experiences and lessons. Secondly, that they enjoy their time as children and don't let the time slip through their fingers with computer games and mindless drivel on the T.V. I don't want a twenty-year old mind in a twelve-year old's body. Basically I want to ensure that they are given every opportunity to be confident, happy, socially responsible, creative and well adjusted children."

"You don't want much then?" Imogen chuckled but with the imperceptible nodding of her head, I knew I had said nothing that she would have disagreed with and could only approve of my desires.

"Only what most parents start out life wanting for their children, but wake up to find out it's all too late, or life never gives them the opportunity to find they have deviated from the path, or some who never even find the path in the first place," I added sadly before continuing with renewed confidence.

"So now the plan. That comes in three parts, the first of which is my job." I heard an intake of breath from Imogen, but no release. "When we started up Meredith and Pearce Architects I was young and had no children. My ambitions were to become the biggest and the best and along the way to make a heap of money. I was your archetypal Y.U.P.P.I.E (Young Upwardly Mobile Professional Person) designed and released upon the world in the nineteen eighties.

"The business is successful but if it is to remain that way it will demand more time and energy than I am prepared to give. Fifty to sixty hours a week at work, including weekends is not a fair balance to spend time with Freddie, Tom and you, my dearest Imogen. I am therefore going to sell my share in the business." I stated this calmly and rationally.

A further sharp intake of breath from Imogen, followed by a hasty gulp at her wine.

"That's a bit dramatic isn't it? I mean, what are you going to do for an income?" she spluttered, her hand quickly halting a trickle of wine that threatened to spill from her chin and stain her dress.

"Well, income comes in part two, but if, as and when I want to go back to work, I will start up another business, but this time a small, one-man band that is not trying to dominate the world. Perhaps a nice little country consultantcy that provides a steady income that allows me to balance my time more evenly."

"What do you mean *if* you want to go back to work?" Her sharp mind had not missed a word.

"All will become clear in part two," I promised and took a quick sip of my whisky before continuing.

"This next part all comes in a bit of a rush, so bear with me whilst I get it all out."

Imogen nodded again, her blue eyes encouraging, seemingly willing me on to deliver a plan for a future together that she could sign up to.

"Giving up my job was the hardest thing to reconcile my mind to. All my conditioning screamed out that this was what I had fought for, for years. Sweated and at times lived for. But accepting that a job is purely a means to securing money to provide shelter and sustenance for my family and myself was like a pressure tap being released inside me. By selling my share in the partnership I am not only freeing up my time to be with the family, but it will also provide a pretty substantial lump sum that I can use to support the family."

"Not that it matters much because I would love you even if you were a pauper, but how substantial is pretty substantial?" There was a complete lack of avarice in her voice, just a simple question requiring a simple answer.

"Well, I'm not too sure, but I think I can say with a certain amount of confidence that if I don't want to work again, I don't have to. However, though it would be great fun to spend the lot, I want to make sure that the boys are not having to sell their blood to make ends meet, so I plan to put a good portion into some sort of a trust fund for each of them."

My response met with her approval and, building my house on rock rather than sand, I felt it was safe to continue.

"I also have a good sized house in a not too shabby part of London, now with no mortgage," I started.

"You're not going to sell your house, are you?" she interrupted without thinking.

"No, no, not at all," I placated her with a reassuring laugh. "But this is where it all spills out at the same time, so bear with me."

"What I want to do is take the boys out of school and take them around the world. Not forever, but for a year at least, more perhaps. I want to pack this wonderful tent, that has been an instrumental part in bringing us so closely together, back on the roof of the Landrover and travel the world. I would draw up points on the map of places to go." I pulled out the Map of Europe that I had brought earlier in the day and opened it at the pages I had already selected and stabbed my finger at highlighted town and city names marked on the map. "History lessons in Normandy, Flanders, Waterloo, Talavera, Agincourt, Auschwitz and so on. Art in Paris, Rome, Vienna, Geography, the Loire, the Rhine, the Alps, and the Pyrennes. Languages— take your pick. And that's just Europe. Learning other people's customs and traditional beliefs. How about celebrating Christmas with Los Tres Reyes, in Spain, Bullfighting, French winemaking, Roman Catholicism in the Pope's backyard."

I stopped talking and realising that I had survived the last two minutes purely on passion rather than oxygen, I took a deep breath and looked at Imogen.

She hadn't moved and was simply staring at me.

"What?" I asked.

"My God, Meredith, you *said* it was mad!" she gasped at the madness and fantasy-like audacity of the idea. "I'm just trying to take it all in, so I can determine quite how mad."

Not wanting to leave things unfinished I took a further swig of my whisky and ran for home. "As I mentioned earlier, I have a house in London. A friend of mine who's an Estate Agent up in town mentioned to me some years ago that if I cared to let the place he could get me a positively indecent sum of rent for the place. For Embassy staff, global corporate company executives from overseas, that sort of thing. The rent alone would more than cover the costs of our monthly outgoings on our travels."

"And you really are serious about this?" She shook her head in wonder at what she had just heard.

"I have never been more serious about anything in my life before. Just thinking about how much the boys have learnt in the last month or so, whilst we've been here, is simply staggering. They would never have picked all of that up, never mind the confidence it's given them, how healthy they've become." The passion and conviction clear in my response, my heart pinned firmly to my sleeve.

"And when are you thinking about going on this mad adventure?"

"I want us to stick our Yurt back on the roof of the Landrover right now, go home, sort out the house, the paperwork, repack some bags, grab passports and then only be in the country long enough to get the Landrover down to the docks and onto a ferry. Realistically though certainly before the end of September. Strike whilst the iron is hot and all that. So, what do you think, will you come with me, with us and share our lives?" I dared to ask the question.

Imogen looked at me for a moment, then giggled. "If your plan had been any less barking mad I would have doubted your sincerity in wanting to change the way you lived, to spend more time with the boys and therefore I would have said no. But..."

"But?" I asked eagerly.

"But I think it's so utterly hair brained, that it's simply wonderful, and if they don't lock you up in the lunatic asylum first, the boys will get the most unbelievable education."

"But will you come with us, with me?" I desperately sought her answer.

"Oh Meredith, of course I will come with you. You don't think I'm going to let you go just yet, do you? It has taken me so long to find you, a little madness is not going to put me off wanting to spend the rest of my life with you." She held my face and tenderly kissed me on the lips.

Then we both started shouting and whooping, dancing madly around the campfire. We had a plan; just maybe we now had the chance of a future.

Chapter Thirteen

That evening, aware that I was delaying a potentially confrontational issue, rather than call Jo, I sent her a text message to let her know all was well but that we would be back a week later than anticipated.

Imogen and I then sat around the table and agreed upon the timetable that would see us in France before the month was out. The boys and I would return home the following Monday and start our preparations for departure; Imogen would resign on the same day and give her boss a week's notice. I felt it was more than he deserved given the way he had treated her over the years, but it was important for Imogen to do things her way. Unfortunately, but unavoidably, she would have to spend that week back home with her mother. It was not a prospect she relished with any great appetite, but with gold at the end of the rainbow, it was a trial worth enduring. She would eventually join us in London after the weekend and a week later we would be sailing for France.

The exhilaration coursing through both our bodies as we added more detail to the plans made one feel quite heady, almost drunk though without the unpleasant side affects of double vision and heave and pitch of ground swell.

By the time Andrew dropped the boys off at the campsite we had tidied the papers away, deciding it would be like giving a child e-numbers just before bedtime and give them the news the following morning. They could then expend their hyperactive enthusiasm throughout the day rather than explode just before bedtime.

"Why was Andrew grinning like an idiot and then winked at you when you thanked him for looking after the boys?" Imogen was puzzled by the strange behaviour.

I told her with a lecherous grin of my own, "Andrew thought that I wanted the boys out of the way so you and I could have some time to ourselves to indulge in a little hanky-panky, a little slap and tickle, and I rather forgot to straighten him out on that point."

"Oh, how funny," she giggled. "Though I'm sure that if I wasn't in such a happy mood, I'd be quite mortified. Perhaps we ought to put the record straight a little later?"

"I'm not going to chase after Andrew and tell him that I haven't been having my wicked way with you but just wanted to have a chat. I'd never live it down." I was horrified at the suggestion.

She reached over to caress my outstretched leg. "No silly," she purred seductively, "I meant that if Andrew thought that you were having your wicked way with me, then it would be a shame for him to be proven incorrect after he's done us such a big favour, don't you think?"

"I think a little evening stroll after the boys have gone to bed would be very much in order." I smiled in return, finally getting the unsubtle hint.

Strangely enough, both boys woke early the following morning so Imogen was able to share in their delight and excitement at our news. The thought of being able to visit the sites where his hero The Duke of Wellington fought and won some of his famous battles was almost too much for Freddie to cope with. And with his broken arm restricting him from the same demonstrative delight that his young brother was showing with cartwheels and pirouettes in and out of the tent, he had to content himself with sudden, unprompted screams, hollers and the occasional American Indian war dance around the wood burning stove.

Once the camp had calmed down and Imogen had reluctantly left for work, I settled myself down to the more serious business of organising what needed to be undertaken. By mid-morning an impressive amount of paper, covered with scribbles and notes lay on the table, an ever-growing "To Do" list sitting at the top of the pile.

The remainder of the morning was spent on my recently neglected mobile phone. Amongst the numerous calls, I warned Mrs Fry of our arrival date and asked if she could stock the fridge and followed this up with a rewarding conversation with my old friend Dan Holland who worked for Hutchinson Estate Agents. Dan booked us into his diary for a visit the day after our return home, and also informed me rather jovially, though much to my delight, that I was an ignorant architect and way behind the times on London house rental prices. He would also bring along contact numbers for a highly reputable removal firm and a storage company.

The wheels were now well and truly in motion. The idea was still mad, no matter how you looked at it, but perhaps only because it sat outside what convention would deem the norm, not because it was impossible.

And from that moment on our last week fairly flew by. The weather had also begun to turn and though the days were still bright and clear, the evening campfires were a welcome source of warmth surrounded by the chilly night air. As ever, we had a thoroughly enjoyable and amusing evening with the General, and his dry wit and endless supply of anecdotes from a bygone age mixed with grumpy insights of this insufferable new modern era had our sides aching long after we had left his company.

"Tell that rascal Philip it's about time he settled down and started a family of his own," the old man asked of me as we shook hands on the steps where we had first met only six weeks before. I assured him I would encourage him to do so at the gallop, but deep down, ruefully, we both knew Philip's character and subsequent attention had other priorities in mind. We arrived as strangers and parted as family friends, saddened to be parting from a lonely man whose company we had come so much to enjoy in such a short space of time. Freddie and Imogen promised they would keep up a running bombardment of postcards from all the major battlefields of Europe. Our lives were so much the richer for having come to get to know the General and of course we would forever be in his debt that he should have permitted a family of strangers to come and stay upon his estate. His kindness could never be repaid, though perhaps our ongoing friendship would count for something.

We said farewell to the deer that looked at us without affection or loathing, just curious and wishing to be left in peace; just as indifferent to our reasons for being there in the first place as to our leaving. We waved good-bye to them none-the-less, grateful to have been surrounded by their gentle nature and unassuming beauty.

And on our last night at the camp, we paid our respects to the valley. Once Imogen had returned from work, we all slowly made our way down the hill to visit our favourite spots, occasionally stooping to let the long grass run through our hands, or simply halting to smell the warm early evening air; to admire the swallows' graceful flight as they fed on the wing, or simply to stop and admire the breathtaking view we had come to know as home. A last dip in the pool, the magical silence of the old folly where Imogen and I had first declared our love, seemingly so very long ago. Such memories would indeed last a lifetime.

We dropped by the gatekeeper's cottage and though the evening was still light, the outside light was turned on and we were warmly invited inside. Andrew and his wife Trish demanded, without much resistance, that we have a farewell drink with them and the stars were in the heavens by the time we staggered back down the track to the Yurt for the last time. It gave me a warm feeling to know that when we returned to this part of the world, and for some inexplicable reason I knew, simply and confidently that one day we would indeed return, that we had people here that we could call good friends.

Physically tired and with exciting thoughts of what lay before us, the boys quickly slipped off to sleep, though for Imogen and myself we lay side by side restless and unable to find the peace in our dreams. An exciting yet uncertain door was opening and yet, another door to a part of our lives was closing. The door to the cherished room that had brought us together, to find love, to find peace and a joy to life that both of us had thought would forever remain elusive would be closed for all time. We had ridden the euphoric crest of the wave of young love. The future was now giving us a chance to have a fresh start at life, no guarantees, no definite happy ever after ending, but a chance to find the next wave of life, and as delicate as butterfly wings we were nervous of touching for fear of crushing it.

By late morning following Imogen's own sad departure for work, bags, cooker, tables and chairs filled the back of the Landrover and I was checking the straps for the second time that held the tent firmly in place on the roof.

With Paul Young's nineteen-eighties chart success playing in my mind I kept repeating the line "Wherever I lay my Yurt that's my home", over and over again until even the boys told me to shut up because it was getting on their nerves.

"Ready boys?" I clasped them both on the shoulder and took one last, lingering look about us. "It's been fun, hasn't it?"

"It's been brilliant, dad, and though going to France and places like that is really exciting, a part of me doesn't want to go, but stay here." Freddie could feel the shallow roots we had put down in our short time in the valley.

"I know what you mean," I ruffled his hair fondly.

"I want to come back here again!" Tom shouted out, his words carried away on the wind to every corner of the valley.

I nodded my head, that strange confidence that we would indeed return one day, clear and certain in my mind. "The Fighting Meredith tribe was created here, so it's a very special place. I'm sure we'll be back. Besides, the General would never forgive us if we didn't come back to tell him about our adventures."

I turned the key and the powerful turbo diesel engine kicked into life and we made our way slowly up the uneven track to the main road and then home.

"Are we there yet?" Freddie's snigger came from the back.

Chapter Fourteen

The sense of sadness was quickly replaced by one of claustrophobia as the grey, foreboding high rise flats and offices of London came into view. Already my sprit felt hemmed in as the countryside petered away to be replaced by narrow roads, concrete and brickwork, preventing me from feeling the sun upon my skin.

Mrs Fry rushed to the door to greet us, effusive and bustling as ever, a handkerchief appearing like a magician's flowers from a sleeve of her bright orange summer dress, to dab at her joyful tears at the reunion.

"Ooh, you do look so brown and healthy! I bet you've been eatin' all your greens," she gushed at the boys appearance, her eyes skittering wildly trying to take everything in at once, such a difference from the pallid and apathetic children she had last seen less than two months previously.

"And I've been eating all my carrots as well," Tom shouted out, as he endeavoured to extricate himself from the depths of her all-consuming bosom. "Because I can see in the dark as well now."

"Ooh Master Freddie, what's happened to you?" she said in dismay, finally noticing the green, dirty cast on his arm.

"I was attacked by Zulus, but it's all right because me and the General made short shrift of them, what!" Freddie laughed carelessly, copying the General's brusque manner and one of his favourite expressions.

"Well I never, you'd better come in and tell me all about it while I get the kettle on for your father," she laughed, and leaving a heavy presence of violet scent in the hallway, disappeared downstairs into the kitchen with two hollering American Indians demanding her scalp.

By the time I had dragged the last of the bags into the hallway, leaving them there to disembowel later, Joan Fry's offer of coffee was a welcome respite. The house was of course immaculate, and no less than I expected as I peered into rooms along the hallway before descending the stairs to the kitchen. Woodwork gleamed, mirrors sparkled and immaculate carpets proudly awaited our usage. But instead of feeling relief and pleasure at returning home, to be surrounded by the comfort of one's personal effects, I felt oddly self-conscious and uneasy. Perhaps it was my deflated *joie de vivre*, but the house lacked something; it lacked the homeliness, it lacked the life and soul of the Yurt. Shoes weren't discarded carelessly on the stairs, clothes on the banisters, dirty shoeprints on the carpet. Even the sound of voices and laughter was deadened and muted by the thick walls, ceilings and expanse of the building. It also smelt impersonal, not the clinical detergent smell of hospital corridors, but when I lifted my nose into the still air, there was nothing. I hadn't realised how much I had come to enjoy the smell of canvas and natural wood, the surprise of scents brought on the breeze and hell, I even missed the whiff of Tom's smelly feet.

"I'm sorry, Mr Meredith. Look here, I am sat here, listenin' to the boys an' I 'aven't even put the kettle on." She made to rise as I entered, but I motioned her to stay where she was.

"Don't you worry, Joan, I'll do it, you'd better sit and listen to each and every one of their adventures or I fear they may both explode. And don't worry if you don't catch it all first time, because I guarantee you'll hear it again." I laughed easily and made drinks for all of us.

For once Joan was reduced to singular exclamations of admiration and amusement at the boys' barrage of stories of our holiday, openly horrified that a rifle and deadly sword were now lurking in the house. Her eyebrows were raised in interest at the regular mention of Imogen, our special friend, but she tactfully refrained from probing the matter.

"And you'll never guess, but we're not going back to school, we're running away to France!" Tom cheered.

"All right you two, time to let me have a chat with Mrs Fry. You take your bags upstairs and unpack." Like obedient whirlwinds they swept themselves from the room, raising eyebrows once more on Joan's bemused face. "Put all your clothes in the dirty washing pile," I added, shouting after their retreating forms.

"Well I never did!" she exclaimed, the surprise evident in her voice. "It sounds like you had a lovely time, Mr Meredith."

"That we did, Joan, that we did. Did us all the power of good I think." I sat back in the chair and looked about the spotless kitchen.

"You've got milk and bread and there's a Shepherd's pie in the fridge for tonight."

I thanked her most sincerely for a wonderful welcome home, then turned matters to the future. Her eyes lit up with interest and using her folded arms to rearrange her mighty bosom, she sat forward and rested them on the table.

"Firstly we will be having a friend to stay from next Monday," I started with a smile on my face, knowing how much this gossip would be worth to Joan, amongst her friends and social circle.

"I'll get the spare bed made up and put some fresh towels out on Friday," she confirmed.

"No, Joan, that won't be necessary." I didn't expand further.

"Oh, oh, ooh." The bulging, wide-eyed stare and slack, open mouth told me that the message had been interpreted and the implications had sunk in. "Well I never," she managed to squawk.

I then went on to explain my plans for the future. The handkerchief appeared and disappeared a number of times, until the cotton had become a sodden mass and she kept it clenched in her large hand and resorted to the tissue box on the windowsill. She put on a stoical front, but clearly the thought of us not only going away again, but also of complete and utter strangers coming to live in her house, was almost more than she could bear.

With various people still to tell I asked for her discretion in the matter until I had told others in my own good time. God did not grant Joan Fry with discretion as one of her natural virtues in life, far from it, but her loyalty was beyond question and playing upon this, I knew I could depend upon her silence, albeit for the moment.

Around eleven o'clock my mobile phone rang. It was Imogen.

"Did I wake you?" She sounded so far away and lonely.

"No, I've been lying here in this bed, that's far too comfortable, all on my own and feeling very sorry for myself," I answered sleepily.

"Me too."

"In fact, I'm thinking of inflating my inflatable mattress to sleep on. I may even go so far as to drag it outside."

She laughed, then said, "I wish I could be with you now. To be in your bed, beside you."

It sounded as though she were about to cry.

"How's your day been? I hope your mother has been behaving herself?"

"Pretty shitty, to be honest. Brian had a complete fit when I told him I was resigning. Demanded that I give him a month's notice and when I told him no, he told me I was ungrateful for all that he had done for me, that I was a complete wreck, that no-one else would have taken me on, but he did. And then I do this to him. Even when I told him that I'd met you and that at last I had a chance of happiness and that I hoped he would have understood, he just laughed and told me it would never work out because I was one of life's great losers. Then he threw me out of the shop and slammed the door shut in my face." She started to cry and just when she needed me I was a hundred miles away.

Yet another man had let her down, had scorned her belief in trying to do the right thing by them and it had been hurled spitefully back in her face.

"Darling, I'm so sorry and I wish so much that we could be together right now so I could kiss away your pain." I felt so helpless and so angry with that bloody arrogant and thoroughly unpleasant man. For a moment I even wondered whether it was too late to call Joan Fry and ask her to look after the boys whilst I went to Imogen and then sought out her former boss and give him a damned good thrashing. But instead I tried to calm her down, to reassure her she had done the right thing and that in under a week's time we would be together until the very sands of time ran out.

"And dare I ask about your mother?" I repeated, not wishing to ask, but also knowing that she would not thank me for walking on eggshells around her.

A moment of silence before she replied almost guiltily, "Actually she's been quite decent so far. Even made me a cup of tea when I came back in such a pathetic state."

"And you've told her that you're leaving?"

"Yes. Surprisingly she took it very well. I think our last argument made her sit up and think about our relationship and I think she's worried that she may lose me forever, so she's now making a bit more of an effort."

I found it hard to believe that the evil bitch that had chased her own daughter out of her house and then spat after her could have such a change of heart. Mainly because you needed to have a heart in the first place and this scabby witch most certainly did not have one. Though the alarm bells were ringing I said nothing; if it was a comfort to Imogen, then that was good enough for me.

"How are the boys?" she asked quietly.

"Fine, and they send their love. It was highly amusing this morning though. They mentioned your name about a dozen times in two minutes to our housekeeper and I thought she would just explode for wanting to ask about you. But she couldn't. Then when I told her that a very special woman was coming to stay and not to worry about putting sheets on the spare bed, she almost screamed eureka. I expect she will be the toast of the town gossips by this time tomorrow." I propped myself up against my pillow whilst Imogen laughed.

"Oh, I love you, Meredith, you always know the right things to say and you do make me laugh. Do you think I should wear a flaming red dress, like some scarlet woman, to meet your housekeeper?"

I laughed down the phone. "I suspect it would either go right over her head, or she would love your dress sense and want one just like it. Seriously though, you'll love her, she's an absolute saint and we all love her to bits."

We spoke for over an hour. I suggested that as she now had nothing delaying her, she could come up straight away, but she wanted to spend the time with her mother, to attempt reconciliation, to rebuild what had always been a rocky relationship. Nothing serious and nothing that half an hour later I could remember clearly either. Her voice sounding so small and hurt, I wanted to look after her, to call her mine and like the knights of old to challenge any who inflicted pain or caused sorrow to cross my lady's brow.

We said goodnight and with her voice getting quieter and quieter I felt certain she would cry again once she had put the phone down. With anger and helpless frustration in my heart, sleep was the last thing on my mind, so I rose and went downstairs to the family room. There I found my guitar resting up against the sofa. After quickly tuning the strings I played quietly, yet with such passion that before realising it, tears were running down my cheeks. Eventually the gentle hand of sleep closed my wet eyes and I slept.

The following days were filled with a head-spinning array of different activities. The boys threw themselves into even the most menial tasks with an enthusiasm that no longer surprised me, but quite took poor Joan's breath away.

Clothes were washed and repacked. New clothes were purchased and others discarded. A larger mattress was also purchased along with new duvet and bottom sheets. We filled our map with places we wanted to visit, things to do and places to see. These were relayed to Imogen each evening and cross-checked against the map she was also going through; I had never realised that Europe was such an interesting place for we had so many small red circles on our map, often so closely grouped that they overlapped. A year or two? Perhaps four or five, I thought to myself.

Tickets were bought, passports checked for expiry dates, euros ordered. The removal men were booked for the week after we had left and the storage company awaited with anticipation, delighted to be of service to their newest customer. Passports were checked again. The list had ticks and children's smiley faces against each of the main items, all except one that had been heavily underscored. I had one last major task upon my list to complete and it was one that I dreaded. I needed to go and see Jo.

The evening was already closing in on London when I turned into the familiar surroundings of Cavendish Walk. There was a certain damp quality in the air and a cold night beckoned with a clear view of stars overhead. Whilst my heart was clear about what I now had to do, to light the fuse that burns the bridges, it was not without a degree of trepidation that I hammered the cast iron knocker against the front door. I was rewarded shortly by the sound of heels on tiled floor drawing closer, a rattle of chain and a lock being turned.

An intoxicating suffusion of light, smell and sound assailed my senses as the door swung open. Bright light from the hallway, heat from radiators only recently turned on after a long period of inactivity reached out to caress my cold cheeks and a gentle breeze carrying the familiar scent that I remembered lingering on my pillows a lifetime ago, kissed my nose. And there before me, with her face in the shadows created by the light shining behind her, was Jo.

"Yes?" she asked the stranger who stood before her. Nervous, but confident, then a wrinkle of her brows as confusion took hold, followed a few seconds later by, "Ahhhh. Oh my God. Meredith darling, what has happened, you look like a tramp!" She screamed, then threw her arms tightly around my neck, kissing both whiskered cheeks.

She dragged me into the warmth, slamming the door behind us with a well practised back heel kick and continued to assault me with a verbal barrage.

"Where are the boys, are they alright? How long have you been back? Why haven't you been in contact sooner? Oh my God, darling, you've got an earring, how awful! No, you don't look like a tramp…a hippie. That's it, you look just like one of those terrible hippies."

"Hi Jo, I missed you too," I laughed as she steered me down the hallway and into the sitting room.

A minute or two later, a glass of very expensive red wine in my hand and we were sitting at opposite ends of one of a pair of sofas either side of the crackling fireplace. I was back in the lap of luxury, once more surrounded by comfort, understated elegance and expense.

"You've decorated Jo, very nice," I mused, surveying the room; its walls now covered in a warm, bright, welcoming yellow and a pattern I could not quite discern.

"What, oh yes. Glad you like it." Jo looked pleased, as though my opinion really mattered on such matters. "Richard's not so sure, but I told him that as he's hardly ever here, he should consider it like one of the many hotel rooms where he spends the majority of his life. But enough of us, tell me all, darling Meredith, I am all ears."

Ears and then some, I noticed, as she kicked off her shoes, drawing her slim stockinged legs beneath her, briefly revealing a glimpse of her shapely thighs, bringing back intoxicating memories now shrouded in the mists of time. Following my gaze she smiled then modestly pulled at the hem of her skirt and recaptured my attention. A statement that shrieked that door was forever closed and would never be mentioned again whilst there was breath in her lungs, even if it had ever happened at all.

"So how's it been?" she smiled over the top of her glass.

"Jo, it's been fantastic. No, more than that, it's been life changing, for all of us. Christ, you know what life was like for us at first after Laura's death." I noticed Jo wince at these words. Maybe not the words, but perhaps that I was able to bring Laura's name to the surface so easily, without pain, without embarrassment of emotion or sentiment. "But we worked through it. And the last few months certainly the best decision we could ever have made. And what about you guys? Where are Richard and the boys?"

"Richard? Still at work, of course. It is only half past seven, he won't be home for at least another half an hour and the boys are both upstairs doing their homework, I hope." She laughed and still with humour in her tone, she added, "You were very naughty not to have the boys back for the start of term. We were extremely worried and we didn't know what to do. All the tongues wagging on the school run and us not a clue as to whether you were alive, dead, or merely on the run. I don't mind saying it was all very embarrassing. But that's now all in the past, isn't it, so more importantly now that you're back, how are they?"

"Running Bear and Runs Like the Wind?" I laughed back, though immediately noticed Jo's frown of incomprehension at their family tribal names. "Sorry, Freddie and Tom are both fine. They're tanned, fit and healthier than they've probably ever been and enjoying life to the full." I continued with a chuckle, "Freddie even managed to keep his nose out of his books long enough to break his wrist on a rather exciting adventure a couple of weeks ago."

"Oh my God, the poor little mite, is he alright? Do you need me to do anything? I can be around as soon as Richard's back if you need me." Clearly the tone in my voice was a little too off-hand and unconcerned for Jo's liking and for one moment I thought she was about to jump off the sofa to go and pack a bag to ensure no more harm could come to her nephews.

"He's fine Jo, he's got a foot of plaster up his arm and he's loving every minute of the attention. He's getting out of his chores, spending plenty of time reading and has the most wonderful expression of a hurt puppy whenever you ask him to do something that he doesn't want to do."

At that moment we heard the front door slam and a minute later Richard stuck his head around the door.

"Good grief, are the natives friendly?" he chortled as we shook hands warmly.

"How's work, Richard?" I asked.

"Very busy at the moment you know. Something very big, very hush-hush and all that. Wouldn't want to bore you. But you, my dear boy, look disgustingly healthy." Richard boomed across the room in his clipped, quasi-amiable tones. One could never be quite sure whether Richard was a genuinely feeling person, or whether it was the way he expressed himself, largely due to the large silver spoon stuck in his mouth at birth that had never been surgically removed by a dose of the real world.

"Darling, do top us up and grab a glass for yourself. Meredith was just telling me all about their adventures and that Freddie has broken his wrist in the most horrific accident."

"Marvellous, straight out of the boys annuals I expect, carry on dear boy." Richard's liberal wine pouring made it necessary to take a large swig from the glass before it was safe to put down without spilling.

"He's absolutely fine, though found it extremely frustrating that I wouldn't let him go charging around the woods with Tom and even more so when we had to wrap his arm up in a plastic bag whenever we went down to the river for a swim." I laughed again at the memory.

"Swimming in a *river*? My God, Meredith, I'm surprised you haven't caught some awful disease, you really need to be more responsible. And the boys—I should think they're only too pleased to get back to a proper bed, a warm bath and a degree of civilisation," Jo chastised.

The tone in her voice had changed albeit ever so perceptibly, though I was surprised that it hadn't come sooner. Just a quick confession, take the impending storm and then I am out of here, I thought, forcing myself to remain calm and unruffled by the changing tide.

"So, what's next, dear boy? When are you going to get Tom Sawyer and Huckleberry Finn back to that expensive prison and regain the controls of your business empire?" Richard steered the titanic past the first iceberg with his warm and innocent question.

So above it all, I smiled inwardly, that's why I love Richard. Does n't let anything get to him, just changes course and bumbles on. So with the rudder set firmly now on an unavoidable collision course with iceberg number two, I took a breath, set down my glass to give me a couple of seconds to compose my thoughts and started.

"Well, that's why I've come around this evening—to give you all a little bit of an update on the future of family Meredith." The light tone of harmless conversation had slipped and a more serious tone had subconsciously taken over. Jo was now leaning forward, alert, ready to pounce and Richard, like a vulture, had now perched himself on the arm of his wife's sofa.

I swallowed and pressed the plunger. "Actually, the boys aren't going back to school. Well, at least not for the time being..."

"What?" Jo exclaimed, her wineglass frozen half way to her lips as the bridge blew.

"Wait a second and just let me finish," I quickly interjected before she could sally forth.

"I think you'd better, old boy, gung ho and all that." Richard was also now leaning forward and at risk of slipping from his perch.

"You both know what life was like for us after Laura died." Both Jo and Richard winced again, but said nothing. "But these last few months I had planned to be a time for us to mourn, to come together, a healing process if you like. Well, we achieved that, but it also gave us so much more. It made me realise what is truly important to us as a family. It reminded me why Laura and I both wanted children in the first place. Can either of you tell me why you had the boys?" I moved my gaze from Jo to Richard and back again. There was pain and anguish in their eyes and I wondered how they had moved on after Laura's death. Did they still say her name out loud? I doubted it.

"Well, dear boy, we just wanted children, the done thing, carry on the family line and all that."

I smiled benevolently, non-judgmentally. " It took me a week to think the answer through for just that one question. Time away from all of this," I waved my hand at the trappings about us, "gave me a great deal of time to think these things through. For Laura and I it was because we loved each other and we wanted something special to come from that love. Something in turn that we could love, cherish, nurture. A continuation of our own love for one another, a bond that we would have for all time."

Both had gone silent, though the tears running openly down Jo's cheeks said enough and Richard was clearly out of his comfort zone and had fixed his attention firmly on his immaculate classic brogues.

"My house, my job no longer have the same importance that they did before; to some extent they have become meaningless to me. The most important thing I can do on this earth now is to look after my boys. To be there for them, protect them, give them a warm embrace of safety, security and above all to love them openly and unconditionally. Also to educate them in readiness for when it becomes their time to fly the nest."

I took a sip of wine in silence before continuing. "Our time camping in that tent brought us close together, closer than I thought possible. At times I thought I would suffocate and die from the guilt I felt for not having really known the boys before. This time closed the gaps in our lives; it made us whole again. And it made me realise that I can never go back to my old world without sacrificing what we now have. And that is not something I am prepared to let happen. Freddie and Tom are the most... no, the only things of any importance in my life. Pretty Zen huh?" I smiled lamely.

"Meredith, I am so glad that you and the boys have come together at last, happy for both you and them." Jo wiped the tears from her eyes before continuing, "But can't you see that now they need to get back into a routine, back to the world in which they belong? A great school, a privileged education, their friends, their home, and all the potential for a wonderful future. And you need to come back too."

I had run through this part of the conversation a hundred times in my head, but still needed a second or two to compose myself, and even when it did come out, I felt I had not done it justice. Missed out some part of the truth, failed to explain the deep yearning chasm between the old world and the new. And as Laura had said so many times and with such soulful deep regret, life's too damned short.

"I am taking the boys abroad. They're going to get that education, perhaps a different education, perhaps the same education but from a different perspective. Either way it will be a real education, not read in the books, in a sterile classroom, but out there in the real world, together. Call it an alternative education; call it what you will. I'm not sure how long we'll be gone, a year perhaps, however long it takes."

"You can't do it!" Jo shouted angrily from across the room. It was the spontaneous response I had anticipated. She was Laura's sister and I knew that she would try to imagine and then stand by whatever she thought Laura would have wanted. I could not be angry. Understanding, sad at the potential threat of breakdown in our relationship and sympathetic yes, but angry no.

"My dear boy, I do understand, but what's that got to do with not sending them back to school, about coming back home and getting on with your life?" Richard probed sensitively.

"I'm sorry, clearly I'm confusing, not explaining. Let me try again." I stared at the dancing flames, hoping to find a modicum of inspiration before allowing my gaze to return to the two attentive figures. "My children need the feeling of support, of protection, of love and devotion. The physical aspects of protection in the bricks and mortar are immaterial. And to travel, every day different to the previous one, as to the next, life's big school. I'm taking full responsibility for my children, not sub-letting that responsibility out to others. ." I threw my last effort into the ring, then sat back and waited for the response. I didn't have to wait long.

"You can't, it isn't normal, I simply won't let you!" Jo snapped quickly, the blood rising in her cheeks and a matching flush spreading across her chest.

"Steady on, old girl." Richard reached out a hand of support, but Jo visibly recoiled from his attempt.

"He can't do this. It's mad. Meredith, I know you loved my sister dearly, but you're still not over her loss, you're not thinking straight." Her dark hair fell wildly about her beautiful features as she shook her head in denial.

"Jo, Richard, I have been through a long and hard journey, but I have come through the other side and I have come through with a far clearer picture of who I was, not a very good father. But more importantly I know who I want to be, who I need to be and what I need to do. Teaching from home is unusual yes, perhaps a little whacky and not the norm, but it is not unheard of. And if it doesn't work, or the boys want to come back, then we'll do just that." I smiled in an attempt to placate. "I love my boys more than anything and I promise you that I will not turn them into freaks, losers or drug addicts. I promise to give them an education that will make you proud of them. Different, yes, and in this day and age given where the damned economy is going and the changing shift in marketplace requiring a very different range of employment skills, that's probably not a bad thing."

I reflected that my wineglass had been empty for almost five minutes, a sure sign that my warm welcome had been overstayed and that it was time to leave.

Richard saw me to the door. Jo had remained in the sitting room, weeping openly, refusing to meet my eye or return my farewell. "Don't worry old boy, she'll come around. All just a bit of a shock you know. Laura her sister, feels she is the next best thing they have to a mother now. Very protective, mother hen and all that."

"I know Richard, give her my love, and tell her I appreciate how difficult it must be for her. But do tell her that this is something I must do and I hope one day she'll understand." I shook his hand warmly as the cold night air once again wrapped around me.

"Must admit I never quite saw you as the teacher type though. Too good with children I expect." Richard returned the handshake with a friendly hand on my shoulder.

"I'm not," I faltered, well aware of the implications of what I was about to say. "I have a friend. A close friend and she's going to be coming with us. The boys have also become very attached to her and she's going to teach them. Very good at history," I added for no particular reason.

"If you don't mind, Meredith, I may just keep that bit of news between us. May be a little too much for Jo to take in at the moment." Richard's loyalty to his wife was evident in his curt humourless tone, so out of character, but perhaps not unexpected. Forgive and move on, I thought.

"Of course. Whatever you think is best, you're probably right." I hit the pavement and heard the door, with typical Richard decorum, close quietly behind me.

It was late and had started to rain, but as I turned my collar up and tucked my chin firmly into my chest, I felt a huge burden removed from my shoulders. And it was with a straight, erect back that I sauntered down the road, a smile lighting my wet face, ignoring the rain that soaked my clothes, not feeling the slap of my feet upon the hard pavement.

Chapter Fifteen

At last Monday was upon us, another majestic day was dawning, and Imogen was coming to stay—the next magical landmark in the creation of our new world, another part of our jigsaw slipping neatly into place. The boys and I ran around like headless chickens, desperate to impress; the house was tidied, hair and teeth were given extra special attention and by lunchtime it felt as though things were being put away even before they had been taken out. Worried that we were becoming noticeably anal in our nervous anticipation, I took the boys into town after lunch to buy our one luxury item, a laptop. Irrespective of whether we believed that this was an essential or luxury piece of modern day wizardry, we were all agreed it would be an ideal multi-purpose tool for all of us—somewhere to store pictures, to keep journals and where possible to send emails to friends. Even the octogenarian General professed to having a computer that Philip had bought him for Christmas and though the mild arthritis that frustrated his limbs, especially so in the depths of winter, prevented him from being the quickest typist, it was his portal to the world outside. He regularly spoke to friends all over the world and even Philip had been known to drop him a line whenever a nagging sense of guilt crept into mind.

"That'll be her." The boys' feet thundered from the top of the house. My mobile was ringing from somewhere downstairs. It was a little after eight in the evening and we had been eagerly awaiting Imogen's call to let us know she had reached Paddington and we would then go and pick her up. A dash down the stairs and a frantic search found the phone resting innocently on the arm of a sofa and I reached it just before it diverted to answer phone.

"Hello, it that you?" I panted, slightly out of breath.

There was no answer, but the line had not gone dead. "Hello, Imogen? Hello, is anybody there?" I asked once more.

"It's me." Her voice was quiet and the disturbing lack of background noise from one of the world's busiest train stations sent a chill down my spine.

"Hello me, are you there yet? Shall we come and pick you up?" I asked hopefully, though the sense of foreboding and naked fear was heavy in my voice.

"Meredith." An agonising cry from a woman whose heart was being subjected to unimaginable torture. "I'm still at home."

Then more silence, though I thought I heard an intake of breath, uncontrollable and painfully drawn down past a constricted throat and into starving lungs.

"When can we expect you? The boys are so excited and I can't wait to see you either," I pushed more forcibly, twisting the knife knowingly and cruelly with reference to the boys.

"I'm not coming, I just can't. I…" She trailed off into silence.

"Imogen, what's the matter, why can't you come, what's going on?" I demanded to know, desperation shrieking in my ears and numbing my senses.

"It's my mother, she needs me. This last week she's made me realise how good she's been to me. She looked after me after…" She paused to find the right words. "After my episode with Bill. And she's given me a refuge for these last years and that if I go, then I'll be opening myself up to all that pain all over again and I just don't think I could cope to have to go through it all again. And if I go there'll be no one to look after her and I can't do that to her. It's my...my duty." She was openly crying.

"Your duty is to yourself, Imogen. Darling, listen to me." I fought for breath and the wallowing sense of despair that churned in my stomach. "Bill was a mean selfish bastard who didn't deserve you. Think how happy you've been since we met. You know me, you know I could never do anything like that to you, or to anyone. I want a family, I want you. After all we talked about, our hopes and dreams."

"Yes, my dearest Meredith, just hopes and dreams. Just wisps of smoke that simply disappear in the air. It could never have worked. It was just a holiday romance and we've been foolish to think it could be anything more." Her words sounded hollow. She didn't believe them, but they still cut me to the bone.

"No!" I roared down the phone, refusing to accept the barbed words and self-created delusional barriers that were catching in Imogen's throat and choking her. "That's not true. Imogen, darling, I love you so very deeply and completely that I do not want a day to go past that I am not sharing every minute, every second of it with you. I am half a person without you. I want you to be a part of my life, the boys want you to be a part of their lives, they love you too, Imogen. Surely you realise that?"

"Stop, please stop," she begged, confusion all around her like carrion around a carcass.

"No, I won't stop, Imogen. I'm going to fight, because if anything is worth having, like the future we've promised ourselves, then it's worth fighting for. Of course there are no guarantees in life, only that sooner or later we will go to face our maker and then we can reflect upon whether we lived a life worth living. Gratefully living every miraculous, magical moment to the full, or whether we chose to hide away in fear of living, in fear of getting hurt. Share your life and your love with us, live your life, please, I beg you," I pleaded with her, hoarse with passion and burning anguish.

"I love you too, Meredith, so much that my heart breaks every time we say goodbye. But I'm so scared of what lies outside my safe, little world. It's not very exciting and it's far from rewarding, but at least it's safe and also it's my mother, she really does need me..." The raging fear tore at her heaving, panting chest.

"I never had the chance to ask you whether you felt that two children was enough for a family like ours, or whether you wanted more. I've been thinking we should have at least another two. With your blonde hair and bluest eyes, or maybe one with my green eyes. Would you want girls, boys, or both? I wouldn't care, I would love them just because they were a part of us, a reflection of our love for one another. Something good and miraculous that had come from our love." It was a low blow and I knew it would hurt deeply, but there again someone once said that all was fair in love and war.

"Don't, Meredith, that's not fair. We had a holiday romance. We're both adults and we should have known better than to get carried away with dreaming that anything could come of it." She sobbed down the line, each cry stabbing and ripping like barbed arrows into my flesh.

"Dreams come true, darling Imogen, if only you're prepared to believe in them and reach out with all your strength and passion and take them with both hands." My hands were clenched, reaching out, beseeching her to change her mind, to come to us so we could wrap her in the comfort and security of our loving embrace.

There was silence from the other end of the phone. No, not silence, but the harsh sound of a heart breaking.

"The boys and myself have that dream and you are there standing right beside us, smiling, happy and completely satiated with life, surrounded by those who love you and who you in turn adore. We think that dream is worth living, fighting for and yes perhaps getting hurt for, but we're going to go for it all the same. We're going to catch that boat and we're going to go to France and Italy and Spain and we're going to chase our rainbow, because if we don't then our lives will have no meaning and will forever be empty, passionless and our souls will be damned for all eternity."

"I'm sorry Meredith, but I just can't do it." Her tears had run dry, but her voice was as one of the eternally damned.

"What do you want me to tell Freddie and Tom, or do you want to tell them yourself?" I asked savagely.

"Don't Meredith, please, I hate myself more than you will ever be able to. Tell them I love them and will always be thinking of them."

"Imogen, darling Imogen, I don't hate you. I love you. I love you with all my heart and I know you love me. We have a future together; if only you will trust in it, both of us can make it come true, if only you'll give it a chance." My mouth was dry; there was no more to be said.

I stayed on the phone long after she must have hung up. Numbed, disorientated and bitterly sad and angry with myself for allowing her to get into the affections of my children, who were now going to suffer crushing disappointment and excruciating, heart-wrenching pain.

I shook myself out of the stupor and threw the phone into the sofa and turned to go back upstairs to break the news to the boys, but they were sitting there, silently on the stairs, just looking at me, not accusing, but not understanding and utterly, utterly distraught.

"Why doesn't Imogen want to come and stay with us?" Freddie asked the question that only ten minutes earlier had been on my own lips.

"Yes, I want Imogen to come with us. Has she stopped liking us, daddy?" Tom asked with his brutal honesty.

I squeezed in between them on the step and explained as best I could, that no matter how I felt right now, deep down I still loved Imogen beyond mere words and I could not find it in myself to blame her for the pain we were now enduring. I extolled her kindness and her love for us, but she needed to look after her terribly ill mother, but that we would see her again when we returned from our trip abroad.

"So we're still going!" Freddie visibly brightened at the news, then perceptibly dipped once more.

"What's the matter?" I probed softly.

"It's just that Imogen knew so much about everything and well, you don't." He said it so simply and with such honesty that it made me burst out laughing, which infected the boys and they too began to laugh.

"I guess we'll have to rely on tour guide books in that case." I ruffled his hair fondly.

Lying in bed that night Imogen came to me in my dreams, surrounded by faceless thousands who reached out of a seething, writhing black, glutinous sea to grab at her ankles to pull her under; their minds void of thought, the sea of souls who had voluntarily given up their rights to live their own lives, their fate to be drowned forever in a lonely, apathetic hopelessness. I reached out to take her outstretched arms, but I was not strong enough and she was slowly pulled from my grasp. And before she was lost forever beneath the liquefied mass, she looked up into my eyes, tucking a blonde curl behind an ear and whispered soothingly, "Don't worry my love. It's all right, it's for the best." And then she was gone.

"No." I sat up in bed, sweat covered my body from head to toe, the duvet wrestled to the floor, the bottom sheet in disarray. "Damn it, I'm not going to let this happen. I'm going to fight her and if necessary I'll bloody well go down there and drag her back here kicking and screaming."

It was four o'clock in the morning, the sun no longer dominated the skies, darkness reigned now; and for the next six months would continue to encroach upon England's precious daylight hours. I took a long invigorating shower, then slipping on a dressing gown went downstairs and made some coffee.

I retreated back into the family room and noticed the flashing blue light of the mobile phone. I took a sip of coffee, the caffeine immediately kicking in, the mind crunching through the gears until it was capable of cohesive and rational thought.

"Right, Lady with sun in her hair, it's time you found out quite how serious the Meredith family are about you belonging to our tribe," I muttered firmly out loud to the four walls. Hitting the contact address book, I picked out her name and hit the dial button and put the phone to my ear.

I must have phoned half a dozen times that day and again the day after that. Not unsurprisingly the calls went to the messaging service each and every time. So I began a sort of personal journal, a verbal diary for Imogen, telling her my thoughts, my love, what we were doing or whatever else may have been in my head at the time of calling. I wasn't angry, it wasn't a rant against the injustice, the pain caused to my children, it was an open and honest reflection of our time together. A simple, straightforward consideration of a shared future, that some risks were worth taking and that the pain from getting hurt was not nearly so crippling as the pain of never having stretched out and tried in the first place.

Joan was a rock of compassion and though she was considerate and sympathetic to our feelings, I couldn't but help feel that the occasional look I received from her as she put a comforting arm about the boys said in so many words, "You silly bugger. At your age, you really should know better. Holiday romance, heard that before, always ends in tears."

She was right of course, but there again the heart bows to no-one and follows no laws, protocols or predicted direction. It simply is and does.

On the third evening, I phoned her number and to my surprise the call was quickly accepted after two or three rings.

"Hello darling," she answered, her voice soft, warm and enriched with love.

Flustered by both the fact that she had answered and that I was talking to the woman I had fallen in love with, not the sad and depressed stranger who had given up her future for the fears that tormented her very being, I said, "Hello you, how are you?" It was all that I could muster whilst my mind fought for control.

"Oh, I'm fine, feeling much better now," she giggled mischievously.

I was completely thrown into confusion and panic. Had I just had a lucky escape from being tied to a psychopath with schizophrenic tendencies? Had the last three days of mental hell really happened, or was it all one nightmare?

"That's good. What are you up to?" I enquired trying to inject some calm into my voice.

"Oh, a bit of this and that. Many thanks for your messages by the way. They were so touching and so very you, darling Meredith. If ever I needed to remember why I love you so much I'll only have to play them and it'll all come back."

Above me the doorbell rang. "Who the bloody hell can that be at this time of night and at this bloody moment?" I swore silently.

"Look, the doorbell's just rung. Promise me you won't hang up on me, I'll only be a minute." I took the stairs two at a time.

The doorbell rang again, demanding attention.

"I miss you, so very much," I told her simply as I walked down the hallway, turning lights on as I went.

"And I miss you too, my darling Meredith, and your two beautiful boys, more than I can ever say."

I turned on the porch light and preceded to open the door, the phone nestled uncomfortably into my shoulder.

There with a nervous smile, her phone to her ear and two large bags either side of her stood Imogen.

"I've got to go," I whispered huskily into the phone. "The woman I'm going to spend the rest of my life with has just arrived."

"Hello," she said simply. Standing there in a plain white dress she looked so small and vulnerable against the dark, shadow-strewn street behind her. I went forward slowly and gently wrapped my arms around her and hugged her to me.

Her soft hair smelt of roses after rain, comforting, reassuring and calming my pounding heart.

After a while, I could not say for how long, for time had lost all sense of relativity and dimension, she gently moved backwards so she could look directly into my eyes.

"I've been a total idiot and I wouldn't blame you for one moment if you were to slam the door in my face."

"*Ssh*, you don't need to say anything. You're here and that's all that matters." I brushed her hair away from her face.

"No, I need to explain, I need you to understand." Her jaw jutted out, determined and not prepared to be swayed by an easier option.

"When I got home, my mother was so different. Like she used to be, kind, funny, interested in what I'd been doing, not so totally immersed in her own selfish world. I told her all about you and the boys and our plans and she seemed so happy for me. And so stupidly I let my defences down, let my doubts creep back in and she so subtly drip-fed my fears, reminding me about Bill, bringing it all back so vividly, so painfully. Imperceptibly she weaved her own woes into the situation, playing on my guilt and my sense of duty to her, that she may not be around the next time I needed a place to run and hide, no safe refuge to lick my wounds.

"It all became so confusing and I was scared, so very scared. And then when Monday came I was so absolutely petrified that I couldn't move. I was shaking and crying; it was as though I was having a complete mental breakdown. I wanted to be with you, but my deep-rooted fears just wouldn't let me. I just couldn't come because I couldn't leave, no matter how much I wanted to." She paused to rub the tired muscles beneath her eyes before continuing.

"And then you kept calling and I would listen to your messages over and over again, so painful, yet so comforting, and I couldn't wait for your next call and kept looking at my phone hoping you'd call again. To hear your voice so tender, so loving and trusting, telling me what you and the boys had been doing, the life that I was missing. It knocked some bloody sense into me and made me realise how much I want to spend every waking and sleeping moment of my life with you. I want to live our dream. I have treated you and Freddie and Tom so very badly and for that I can never forgive myself."

"Yes, you will forgive yourself," I interrupted, smiling down at her as she nervously tucked a strand of hair behind her ear. "Because there's nothing to forgive. The boys, me, we understand, darling Imogen, and if there's any forgiving to be done around here, it's you forgiving me for not being more understanding, not being there to support you when you needed me most."

"No, I need to hear it from you." She pressed firmly, desperately, urgently, needing the heavy burden to be taken from her shoulders. "Can you forgive me?"

"Darling Imogen, I forgive you with all of my heart," I replied solemnly and kissed her on the lips and hugged her to me once more.

"So after you've had to change all your plans, have you still got room for a not so small, but extremely comfortably built person?" she joked lightly as her fears and sorrows of the past slipped away, banished forever, never to return.

"I have room for the most beautiful woman in the world, our lady with sun in her hair," I said earnestly, then added in a mock-serious tone, "Though we need to discuss how many children we're going to have, because I'm not too sure we'll have room for all those nappies, prams and the such like." And dragging her bags into the hallway I kicked the door shut behind us.

"Come on upstairs, there are some people I want you to see." I took her hand and led her upstairs.

With the light from the landing casting shadows before us, I silently pushed open the door to Freddie's room. His reading light still burned brightly and as ever his latest book was lying open in his lap and though he still wore his glasses perched precariously on his nose, he was fast asleep. The dreams of the innocent had removed all worries from his angelic face and his light, even breathing reached out and pulled at my heartstrings causing me to involuntarily squeeze Imogen's hand.

She smiled back at me and returned the meaningful gesture, sharing in the feelings that words could never do justice, finally at peace with the world. Then gently disengaging her hand from mine and softly tiptoeing to his bed, she gently removed his glasses and placed them on his bedside table.

"I missed you," she whispered to his sleeping form, and raising her hand to her lips, she kissed her fingers then placed her hand on his forehead. "Sleep tight."

Today was a good day.

Chapter Sixteen

The lights of Portsmouth twinkled like diamonds against a dark, velvet backcloth as we bade farewell to England, but not to home. Our home lay firmly strapped to the roof of the groaning Landrover in the stomach of the ferry beneath our feet. Home lay in the smiles that we wore on our faces and safely stored in every pore and fibre of our bodies.

Our imagination was captured by the romance of the sea air as it flooded our nostrils and somewhere a foghorn called out through the dark night air. In the distance small lights warned us of a ship's presence, bright and bold amidst the pitch black that surrounded them, yet so lonely in their isolation. The deck throbbed and grumbled beneath our feet, pitching ever so slightly as its bows carved through the chilly waters below. And somewhere out there lay the French coastline, Cherbourg and the beaches of Normandy.

Imogen was there at the railing, the wind running its cool fingers through her long blonde hair. The tired, dark rings around her eyes had already receded and in the sea breeze rosy cheeks had appeared and were offset beautifully against her honey coloured skin. She was leaning over the boys, already setting their imagination afire with the background to a famous date in World history. The sixth of June, nineteen forty-four, D-day. Hundreds of ships lying in wait in the Solent, the thoughts and very real fears of the thousands of soldiers who were to give up their lives in the name of freedom.

The names of Ohama, Juno, Gold and Utah and Sword would soon have meaning in their lives and hopefully an appreciation of the debt we owed the soldiers who fought and died on the beaches of Normandy. A pact shortly to be made between ourselves and those, in both wars and from many nations, who in their thousands, so far from home, now lie in the neatly tended cemeteries of Northern Europe. It was appropriate that this should be our first stop, where we would be able to pass on the stark and dignified words from the poignant epitaph etched on memorials across the globe, finally of significance and meaning to the next generation.

"When you go home, tell them of us and say, For your tomorrow we gave our today."

Our most heartfelt thanks for our today and after that, time would only tell what happened next and in which direction we went.

The dream had come alive. From the recesses of one's deepest imagination the picture so simply formed seated beside a tent beneath a warm summer's sun, now had form. It was a physical presence, it vibrated and throbbed beneath one's feet, diesel motors sang out across the darkened waters and lights from the shore winked and waved us on our way.

I ran my tongue over my lips, tasting the fresh and honest taste of sea salt, inducing sentiments of our new buccaneer lifestyle of freedom and adventure and slowly walked back to where my family stood patiently awaiting my return.

"Are we there yet?" I called out to them.

"Very funny dad," the boys called back.

Printed in the United Kingdom by
Lightning Source UK Ltd., Milton Keynes
142356UK00001B/3/P